ALSO BY ANNE ENRIGHT

FICTION

The Portable Virgin

The Wig My Father Wore

What Are You Like?

The Pleasure of Eliza Lynch

The Gathering

Taking Pictures

Yesterday's Weather

The Forgotten Waltz

The Green Road

Actress

NON-FICTION

Making Babies: Stumbling into Motherhood

ANNE ENRIGHT

Anne Enright was born in Dublin, where she now lives and works. She has written two collections of stories, published together as *Yesterday's Weather*, one book of non-fiction, *Making Babies*, and eight novels, including *The Gathering*, which won the 2007 Man Booker Prize, *The Forgotten Waltz*, which was awarded the Andrew Carnegie Medal for Excellence in Fiction, and *The Green Road*, which was the Bord Gáis Energy Novel of the Year and won the Kerry Group Irish Fiction Award. In 2015 she was appointed as the first Laureate for Irish Fiction, and in 2018 she received the Irish PEN Award for Outstanding Contribution to Irish Literature. She is also the recipient of the 2022 Irish Book Awards Lifetime Achievement Award.

ANNE ENRIGHT

The Wren, The Wren

VINTAGE

1 3 5 7 9 10 8 6 4 2

Vintage is part of the Penguin Random House group of companies
whose addresses can be found at global.penguinrandomhouse.com

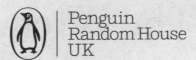

Penguin
Random House
UK

First published in Vintage in 2024
First published in hardback by Jonathan Cape in 2023

Copyright © Anne Enright 2023

Anne Enright has asserted her right to be identified as the author of this
Work in accordance with the Copyright, Designs and Patents Act 1988

penguin.co.uk/vintage

Printed and bound in Great Britain by Clays Ltd, Elcograf S.p.A.

The authorised representative in the EEA is Penguin Random House Ireland,
Morrison Chambers, 32 Nassau Street, Dublin D02 YH68

A CIP catalogue record for this book is available from the British Library

ISBN 9781529922905

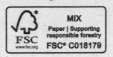

For Claire Bracken

NELL

THERE IS A psychologist in Nevada called Russell T. Hurl-burt who is interested in the different ways people think. In 2009, he fitted a young woman called Melanie with a beeper that went off randomly during the day, prompting her to record everything in her awareness at that moment, and she later reconstructed these mental events for his research.

On the third day of Melanie's experiment, as her boy-friend was asking her a question about insurance, she was trying to remember the word 'periodontist'. On the fourth day, she was having a strong urge to go scuba diving. On the sixth day, she was picking flower petals from the sink while hearing echoes of the phrase 'nice long time'.

Dr Hurlburt says that there are great variations in the way our inner lives play themselves out in our heads. 'My research says that there are a lot of people who don't ever naturally form images, and then there are other people who form very florid, high-fidelity, Technicolor, moving images.' Some people have inner lives dominated by speech, body sensations or emotions, and yet others by 'unsymbolized thinking' that can take the form of wordless questions like, 'Should I have the ham sandwich or the roast beef?'

I find this experiment very useful and attractive. No explanations are sought or given. Melanie thinks this way because that is the way that Melanie thinks. There may be no reason for Melanie to have the mind of a poet, with her sink full of faded petals, and her inner ear enjoying the words 'nice long time', where other people would see used teabags and think 'my life is turning to shit'.

I wonder what was going through her boyfriend's mind at these moments.

Let's get insured!

or:

Why is she ignoring me?

or:

Oh my god her breasts.

or:

I need to insure this bitch before I murder her, goddammit.

or:

If we switched providers there could be significant reduction in costs. Perhaps if I made a spreadsheet she would see the potential risks and also the savings to be made.

or:

If I talk about insurance I don't have to think about my erection.

If I talk about insurance I don't have to think about my failure to earn enough money, in a system that screws you at every turn.

If I talk about insurance I don't have to think about death, except usefully.

I am usefully in love, and I love being useful.

I want nice, I want 'yes'.

I want to die now, all the time, and also in her arms.

*

Don't be silly, Melanie's boyfriend is, of course, thinking about the football. Because this is what men tell you they are thinking, if you ever ask them. And of course these men are telling the truth. Although, under the football ... something else stirring, some big old lizard with a flickering tongue. Somewhere under the football. The painful pad of his right thumb, a slight itch on the bony bit of his skull. And under the itch, or beyond the itch, an opening. A gap. A place. The bang of a blue sky on some far planet (he is a boy, remember) where three moons rise and set.

And he has the ball, he runs with the ball, he's there, he's done it! Touchdown! Yes! Under the football, he is thinking, Vindication! Thousands of men surging as one man from their plastic stadium chairs, Yes!

Melanie, meanwhile, is sucking at her dental implant, which feels a little loose, and this tiny sound is just terrible for her boyfriend who is very sensitive to anatomically internal noises, especially ones inside other people, especially inside their mouths. Melanie's boyfriend is very acutely aware of the tongues and the saliva of other human beings and sometimes also the dog, at night, when it is licking itself. Apples are the worst. It is as though the slurp and chomp of other people's mastication happens inside his brain – no respecting that line between his inner life and the outside world. It is a complete invasion, like torture almost – while he is trying to sort out the post. Trying to sort the goddamn insurance.

But you know.

Melanie and her boyfriend. I wish them well. I think she is a dreamer and he is a treasure, he keeps them both safe. And in time – in time – they will each learn exactly what the other one thinks.

He thinks:

soft

that smell
She thinks:
a nice long time

We don't walk down the same street as the person walking beside us. All we can do is tell the other person what we see. We can point at things and try to name them. If we do this well, our friend can look at the world in a new way. We can meet.

When I began thinking about all this I was interested in empathy, like it's the solution (and it is! it is!) to pretty much everything. I thought about gender and empathy, religion and empathy, the evolutionary benefits of empathy. I had a big beautiful cake in my head called 'Feeling the Pain of Others' and I sliced it this way and that because I thought that emotion is the bridge between people, sentiment crosses space, sympathy is a gas, exhaled by one, inhaled by the other. Empathy! It's just like melting.

We can merge, you know. We can connect. We can cry at the same movie. You and I.

But some people can't do this – really quite complicated – thing. There is a gap.

These days, I think there is a real gap between me and the next person, there is a space between every human being. And it is not a frightening space. The empty air which exists between people might be crossed by emotion, but it might not. You need something else, or you need something *first*. This is the thing Russell T. Hurlburt was talking about when he discussed different kinds of mental experience. People are different and they think differently. Now, I think the word we need is 'translation'.

It took me a long time to get to this point of happy separateness. When I was a child, I thought we were all the same. Like, I had telepathic powers and *you* had telepathic powers and that was so nice. We were all together. So it was hard – it was very lonely – to discover that this was not true.

But, listen:

That girl who gave birth in a toilet who did not even know she was pregnant? How could that happen? we say, and of course she was in denial. She was poor.

That is one girl.

Then there is the other girl – and she has pain, not just before and during childbirth, not just before and during her period, but when she ovulates. A girl who feels the actual egg flooping into the fallopian tube. *Mittelschmerz* – it has a name in German so it must be real. I knew one of those girls at school. She felt everything. She was distracted in class by the tenderness in her breasts the week before, by cramps in her stomach, four, three, two days before, and by the whole shebang when her period finally showed. Every month, it was a ten-day event. A third of her life. Tampons did not go in. Pads did not suffice. She fainted. She stained. She took iron tablets. She went to bed and her mother said, Oh dear. And really, she said, she dreamed of taking her pants off and sitting on the earth itself, because then she would know there was enough underneath her to take it all in. This was Maya, my friend, who was always in some kind of pain, and who was so often fobbed off and denied and made to feel she was wrong about herself, about her own sensations. And I think that is something pain does to you. The pain makes you feel accused of making the pain up.

Even the way you open your mouth to say, It hurts.

You say, It is inside me. This pain. Please try to imagine how it feels. Though I am not imagining how it feels. That is the difference between us.

Maya would really know if she was pregnant, that's all. I

don't think she would be shocked and surprised to see a baby coming out of her after nine months of it kicking her guts and sitting on her bladder. *I thought it was indigestion!* That is not what Maya would say. I think she would say *Gaaaahh!* For nine months straight.

Gaaaahh!

Some people have bodies that are a bit dumb. And other people have bodies that are loud, talky or slightly bonkers; bodies that are always declaring themselves and sharing their news. *Oh no, itchy!*

Gaaaahh!

Mine has always been alright. I have always had an alright body to live in, move about in. I mean, I look in the mirror and, whaa-aat? But walking around: sex, food, noises, those things? I have always been fine. I eat. I run. I love running. It feels like flying to me.

This is a roundabout way of saying that I fell in love when I was twenty-two years of age, and it was a complete surprise. As if this tender beast had been inside me all along, kicking and turning, and I had not known it was there.

Gaaaahh!

I say 'fell in love' because that is the technical term for what happened. There was no gap, no need for translation. I felt understood, merged. And this feeling was euphoric.

A year out of college, I was poking my snout and whiskers into the fresh adult air and I knew how to be, I want to remember that. My body was not on mute. I knew how to enjoy sex, eat, get drunk and recover, touch myself, touch someone else. I knew how to dance, get a little out of it and have big deep stupid discussions; a sweet overnight session with a girl I liked, or something more demanding and cha- otic with a guy, who was usually someone I did not like so much – a kind of antagonism there, truth be told. Sex with a guy always felt a bit like fighting, you could get hurt, or realise that you *had* been hurt when the hangover hit. Hard to say what you felt at the time. (Am I a masochist? Oh, I can't remember.) But actually, emotionally, it was the girls who could break me, especially if they did that chilly, disdainful thing, which was exactly what attracted me in the first place. But there you go.

I had a great gang from Trinity, we found each other on, like, day five. A guy cycled across this beautiful grass you are not supposed to even walk on, in his long coat and Byronic (his word) hair and we were three girls watching him, me, Lily and Shona and he was Malachy, clearly gay, clearly a laugh, and he sat down almost beside us, and we all knew what we had to do, now.

Malachy's father was in property, so he had a boxy flat in the city centre that we slowly trashed over the course of that first year, though it was not the drinking and late nights I liked, it was waking up to a long stupid day of breakfast followed by nothing much, hanging around, rolling thin little joints. And just before we got too drifty, it all made a massive amount of sense. We knew how to fix it – the great theft of our future by the planet-fuckers of the past – or we knew we were finished before we had even begun. It kind of alternated. What held us tight was some dream we had of mankind getting *ahead* of its stupid self, of us in particular getting ahead of the too-lateness of our times.

Chiddik. Chiddik.

I also spent time, when I was very stoned, going deep into the birdsong coming from the evergreens outside Mal's window. Six huge pines with red trunks and spreading branches – they had to construct the complex around them. The price of three residential units, each one. Nature as museum. The trees were a reproach to us, as we lolled about in a concrete box, honeycombed with other glass-fronted boxes, watching the freedom of the birds in their branches, listening to the wind comb through.

I began to think I could talk to them.

Fink fink
Pink pink
Qwer-wer
Skrawww

When I got sad, I wasn't worried about the end of the world so much as about very small things – which may just be my anxiety style. All through college, I was unfashionably fretful about the nightjar, which is a bird we used to have in Ireland and don't have much anymore. It's just this drab little thing. The nightjar looks like a pine cone with big night eyes. The mottled plumage matches the bark of a particular tree, and this is one reason you don't see the nightjar, the other reason is that, when you go looking, it is already getting dark. And the third reason you don't see the nightjar is because it isn't there – not anymore. There are almost none left. The most recent Irish sighting was at Inchy Bridge, Timoleague, 'when a male was observed hawking for insects over typical breeding habitat on three nights between 1st and 8th June 2012'. Anyway, it is a little migrant that feeds on insects at dusk, and now the insects are gone or the habitat is gone, and its call is a distant sewing machine, shifting down a gear and then up.

Churrrr. Chirr.
Thick cloth. Thin.
Thick cloth. ThinThin.

Of course, because I am online – as opposed to shivering in a bird-hide in the foothills of the Knockmealdown mountains – my sadness about the nightjar segues very quickly to an interest in the raven's cronk which is a

8

location call and its rasp which signals anger, apparently. I would like to make a dictionary of bird sounds. I could start with the word 'syrinx', which is the anatomical box below the larynx and this is the mechanism throwing those huge noises out of that teeny-tiny bird.

The nightjar, by the way, can ventriloquise. Its song sounds as though it is coming from the other tree. This must be confusing, when mating with a nightjar – you'd have to land on a lot of other trees first.

So, this is me. I look at a video clip of a talking raven while my friend Lily worries about fascism, and while my friends are breaking the back of the patriarchy I start to cry about the unbearable fate of the bees. Later, when we are very stoned, I play clips of snail sex with the sound turned up really high. I tell my friends they are fixated on *The Man* and that I am not fixated on *The Man*. My friends were all about authority. And I was all about roots and tendrils. They did surveillance culture, I did the weather.

I was interested in the nightjar, in that tiny little heart-break bird, and for a very long time that amount of dread was enough dread for me.

So.

His name is Felim. He lives in Dublin but he grew up in the country. His mother says the rosary every night, a fact I found amazing and also hilarious until he told me it wasn't.

But that was later. (All the things Felim accused me of were true, by the way. I suppose I should say that first.)

So Felim's mother is religious, his father works the farm. He was reared on soda bread and rashers and is six feet three in his socks, very fit from hauling bags of feed, and his party trick is to pick people up by the head. This was, in fact, how we met. It was in a nightclub – he lifted my friend

Lily up by the head and put her down again, and I tapped him on the shoulder to do me next. He assessed the job, turned me round and cupped both hands under my chin, from the back. His thumbs pushed into the curve at the base of my skull and I felt my spine stretch as he pulled me clean off the floor. A feeling of ritual in there, some initiation. Quite a rush. When I landed again I was shrieky and coy. Like one of those girls – the shrieky, coy kind of girl.

I shouted up at him, over the music: Are you trying to pick me up or what?

What?

Are you trying to pick me up or what?

I was making my way out in the big bad world, and for some reason this involved a lot of staying in. Mornings were spent in bed, surfing and typing, meeting deadlines for agency work, which I got through a friend of Lily's in London. I was producing content non-stop and also trying to work up a Twitter following, just when everyone I knew had moved over to Instagram. The pay was terrible. Mostly I wrote travel pieces about places I had never been. I looked out at the grey Dublin sky and they poured out of me: *Nusa Lembongan is the Goldilocks island between tourist Bali and the hipster heaven of Gili Trawangan.* The agency also threw me the occasional bone, which is how I started doing stories about yoga breaks and spa experiences for an actress/eco-influencer called Meg. She liked the tone so much she wanted other stuff: a piece on suncream and the planet, the difference between sisal and paper panama hats, palm oil in your moisturiser, silica in your eye cream. I started a running dialogue – a mini soap opera – for her Maltipoos. This should have been fun, but it was surprisingly hard to do.

– *Don't judge me.*

– *Mood.*

I was also trying to write my own stuff and living away from home, though back and forwards still to the fantastic, well-stocked fridge and to my Dear Old Mum. Because, much as I love her, we were both sadly agreed that there comes a time when a girl needs a place to call her own.

My mother is a very practical person and – I don't know how to describe it – for Carmel, there is either a problem or no problem. Anything else is, You're making it up.

She could never get my friend Maya, for example. When we were little. I mean she was friendly, she was nice, she provided ice cream (which Maya refused) but as soon as her mother took her home, as soon as the front door closed, Carm rolled her eyes all the way into the back of her head.

That *child*, she said.

And I'd say, What?

She won't eat *ice cream*?

It hurts her teeth.

What?!

My mother is strongly of the opinion that, if you don't think about yourself then you won't have any problems. For Carmel, having a pain means you are self-obsessed, because being self-obsessed comes first and having a pain comes second – or an allergy, an intolerance, a sensitivity even. She *might* allow someone to have an allergy, if they are, for example, in anaphylaxis and groping for the EpiPen, but when I was little, she did not 'believe in' food intolerances – as though her belief was the deciding factor there. People who have these problems deserve to have them, according to Carmel, because these people invented them: they have 'too much imagination'.

She is quite an infuriating person.

You cannot shout at my mother. The way Maya used to shout at her mother Bronagh? That seemed to me like taking a shit in the middle of the floor. (Not right of course. But tempting.)

No. If you shout at Carmel, all the lights go out, one by one. It's like watching Manhattan die.

Not that I haven't brought Gotham down, in my day.

I have shouted, she has shouted. We have wandered around in that big-city blackout, as a lady calls for her little dog and the distant sirens go, Whoop whoop.

No.

Much as I love my mother, much as I love that fabulous fridge, the free heating, the coffee grinder with whole, organic beans, much as I love reading on the sofa while she shifts and grunts over her Sudoku, I really did need to get away.

Meanwhile, some oozing, inner self knew what I was doing when I loaded up the boot of her car and broke her heart. When I made my mother drive me across town to a damp room in a run-down street, whose only attraction was the fact that she was not in it. I was going to fall apart. I had been so good, I had done all the things. Now, I wanted to sleep under a hedge and wake to the rain.

I also wanted to move out of this crap, overpriced town but I had not figured out where to go yet, so I was in a house in Ballybough that belonged to someone's dead granny, first of all with Lily and, when she left for London, with her friend Stuart and one other randomer in the box room. Every time I went online, I found light-flooded interiors with potted plants the size of our kitchen. Outside, the red-brick streets were starting to look curated and I was just flicking through a life that wasn't mine. Just flicking through.

There was a gap of some weeks between the head-lift and the next time I saw Felim, in a shop on the quays. I was queuing for the till. He was looking at the magazine rack, and this physical act of browsing seemed completely normal and then weird – who looks at real-life magazines? Until that moment I had not known you could buy such a thing. Felim finished thumbing through one and put it back on the shelf, a picture of a red convertible on the front. The glossy paper made it look handled and sad.

It was summer, and it was a Saturday. I don't know what I had been doing before I arrived to queue for my bottle of water. There was no indication I can remember, that I had been walking up to a cliff edge with my arms outstretched. I was twenty-two. Being unattractive, being alone, these were the disasters that plagued me. The disaster was never standing there, checking through *Classic Car*.

'Corvette Goes Topless'.

Felim looked real. Or he looked like being real was his thing. And real was what I wanted. It was my thing too.

Recently, I went back to see what had been going through my mind in the weeks and months I spent falling apart in that horrible, mouldy house, while going out clubbing and getting lifted up by the head. Mal was disappearing onto Instagram, posting photo after photo of his long shadow on the grass, his bent shadow on a building, his shadow on the water. I was trying to write poetry on pieces of paper, because I thought that using real paper meant they were real poems. Meanwhile, I supplied a list of 'things overheard on the bus' to a woman who had not been on a bus in many years. I went through her Maltipoo pics thinking, If only one of them was a Jack Russell, there would be so many jokes here.

For inspiration, I watched animal-reunion videos. A kitten bounds over to play with an eagerly trotting hen. A huge rabbit nuzzles a small dog. A swan is released from a sack and it dashes across the pond to join another swan: they twist neck to neck, making hearts, making curves. Humans did not interest me so much, unless one of them was in uniform – Mom's been in Iraq, Daddy's back from Kandahar. I was also supremely held by the spiritual precision of coffins received home from war.

What I was addicted to, I think, in my little bubble of sorrow in Ballybough, was the prick of tears. That tiny painful surge in the eyeball rind. It did not produce much liquid. I usually took the tear back into me, down some tiny, inner drain.

If I wanted a proper cry, an achieved cry, if I wanted tears that rolled all the way down and went cold on the underside of my chin, I watched cochlear-implant videos. This is such a terrific subgenre. A deaf little boy (nearly always a boy) is given a hearing aid that goes through his skull into his brain and he hears his mother's voice for the first time.

The tears fell for this one. I wept freely and on repeat. Each time I viewed the clip, the gland spiked at the same millisecond, precisely.

Boy looks up
Tear initiation
Something happens in his face
Tear confirmation
He turns
Liquid formation
He points
Full, swelling droplet
She responds
Tear release. Copious

Before they get the implants stuck through the side of their skulls, some of these children are completely deaf, so when the machine is switched on, their brains experience sound – whatever that is – for the first time. Their eyes widen as they hear the silence of the room, which is a different kind of noiselessness to the one they have lived in all their lives. It is the hush you can hear. Then, a voice. The doctor or their mother says, Hello, or, I love you, or, Hi Thomas. Hi Buddy. Some children recognise the source – already! – and turn. It is as though they had always known, always hoped it would be there.

And the look on their face is one of revelation. Of massive confirmation.

Yes!

Mother!

What is that? To hear a voice, before you know what a voice is? Or *who* a voice is? The thrum of sound waves through the wood of the table. The vibrations felt in the womb.

Which makes me write down, with an actual pen: A revelation is the way things make sense when we are wired for some kind of knowledge, but not yet switched on.

This was me, making notes in an apple green Moleskine I thought might look good on Insta, before getting back onscreen, lying on the stained sofa in the house-share in Ballybough, wrapped in an old sleeping bag, waiting for something to be revealed.

The face of one boy before he gets the implant is serenely self-enclosed. This little person cannot hear himself laugh, he cannot hear his footsteps on the floor. There is no echo. He lives in a world without mirrors of the audible kind and he looks oddly perfect, as a statue might be perfect. He is so completely unselfconscious, you might wish he never had to change.

That is what it was like when I saw Felim: a new order of silence opened up for me, like something had been switched on. It happened when I saw the wings of his broad back shift under pale blue cotton, in a newsagents on the quays.

And in the moment before his eyes landed on mine, the future reached towards me with a knife in its hand.

Here I come.

But also, *Car magazines? Really?*

I finished paying for my plastic bottle of water, and turned with my head tucked down, and bumped it right into his chest bone.

He said, Hey.

I said, Oh, hey.

So Lily's gone to London.

I said, Oh yeah she's been posting all kinds of like, stuff.

The next day, a request, quickly followed by a picture of Lily and me at an afterparty, a few months back.

– *Old times.*

Has he been stalking us? For a second, I am stunned by the thought that he was there in front of me, and I missed him. And why was he taking pictures? Maybe he was with Lily.

– *No!! NO!! He was with your one from Belfast.*

To him, typing fast, I say – *Thanx I miss her!*

Keeping everything sweet. He sends me Dietrich singing 'Lili Marlene'.

I send him Disaster Girl meme, that little girl who smiles at the camera while her house burns down, and the caption says Bad Things Happen When You Make Lily Sad.

He laughs – *Haha.*

After that silence. One day, another day.

Late one evening, a random track by Betty Davis, though he calls her *Miles Davis first wife*, and this would make me laugh except the music is stunning. All new to me, a true gift. The track is called 'Nasty Gal'.

– *Chewin it.*

– *Nasssty.*

This text was sent at half past ten on a Tuesday evening.

I remember wondering where he was and what made him think of me, just then. I pictured him at home, getting ready for bed, or on a long commute, with the rain hitting the window. Perhaps he was in a bar, alone.

I worried that I answered too fast.

No response.

A week later – *You going to this thing at Alice's?*

– Who?

– I thought you knew her.

We meet in someone's kitchen, where we talk about music mostly. It is late afternoon.

He says, You're really smart. Do people say that to you a lot?

And then back to his place to see (I know!) his collection of vinyl. Twenty minutes later, Betty Davis is on his turntable and I am in his bed, having a hearty and frolicsome interlude, in my otherwise less than eventful day.

Oh yes. This bit, that bit, muscle under skin, his feet a bit ugly (never mind), his fitness and his timing and the light, the light. The first time can be so decorous, so choreographed, so mutually helpful and polite.

We lay around for a while afterwards and he made toast with peanut butter, cracked a few cans of beer. We stood out of bed to brush the toast crumbs off the mattress, me hiding myself with the duvet, him shadow-cupping his crotch as he moved his powerful other hand over the cotton. We had sex again and I stayed over, waking in the morning to the sight of him asleep, his lips easy and full, the air slipping into his body and slipping out again. One fiery hair, sprung from a brown curl, intensely backlit.

I saw him pause in his sleep, and open his eyes to me.

Good morning, I said.

And I got my things together like a good girl, refused a cup of coffee, and left.

What did we talk about, that first long night?

Most of the time, I think, people aren't listening to each other, they are just waiting their turn to speak. But I listened to everything. He listened.

I asked him about his life at home, how many brothers and sisters he had, how the whole farm thing worked. He told me he had an older brother. He told me his mother said the rosary every evening, and he laughed at that and I laughed with him. I asked about cows. I was interested in cows, I read somewhere they are more dangerous than they used to be because they are overbred. Their udders drag on the ground and get infected because they are too big for their bodies and he said, It's all stock, these days.

You mean meat?

I suppose.

I said I read about an autistic woman who designed abattoirs, she wanted them to be less cruel, so she invented a spiral walkway which made the cows feel secure because they couldn't see what was waiting for them at the end of it.

You know a fierce amount about cattle, he said.

It's all about the methane, I said.

But actually I had this romantic thing in my head about haymaking, suckling, sunshine, all of which matched the smell of his skin. Felim was so healthy, it would heal you to touch him – that was one mad thing I felt. And I was, in truth, interested in farming. 'The cut worm forgives the plough', I told him the line from William Blake and he glowed up a little – quoting poetry was, you could tell, not his usual style.

A long time since I was ploughing anything, he said. Excepting women.

This was a joke about sex, and I laughed at it.

He told me about his job. He spoke up at the ceiling and then he stopped speaking. I saw his Adam's apple bob.

He said, I always thought I would be in Montana or someplace. Big country. Not living in a box. I grew up in the open air, he said. Makes it hard to fit in small. I always thought I would be my own man.

When he turned to me, there were tears in his eyes and we moved towards each other so simply, *My heart*, I thought. *Oh, my heart.* This second bout was sad and then a bit frantic. An emptiness in the middle stretch, like he was running the wrong race. Afterwards, I felt we had achieved something difficult. I lay there not touching him, except a little, where the top of my foot met his shinbone.

Sometime before he slept, he reached over and drew a spiral on the skin of my hip. He told me there was a stone found on the land – it was in the museum now, in some back room. His great-grandfather turned it out of the far field and it was carved like the tombs at Newgrange, though the ones in Newgrange were triple and this was a single spiral. He went to the schoolteacher with it and the stone was taken down to Dublin. They never saw it after.

The far field? I said.

Why?

That's what you call it?

That's what it is, he said, and I thought this was a lovely thing to say.

It's all go in County Meath.

Louth actually.

I echoed it back to him, smiling and stroking his face.

Louth actually.

In the morning, there was the usual, Don't mind me, we only had sex, about the way I refused the offer of coffee and got into my clothes at a reasonable pace while he started his morning on the other side of the bedroom door. When I emerged from the bathroom, he was busy in the kitchenette, cracking an egg into a frying pan. I checked in with a bright smile, Right! That's me. To hear him say, like a gentleman, That was a lot of fun, let's hang out, yeah?

Sure!

Always the same excruciation about the latch, an urge to lean back against the wood once the click happened and the door was solid behind me.

Closed.

Inside the flat, his life continued. He took toast from the toaster, poked a teabag around in a cup of boiling water, scooped the egg out on to a white plate. He sat at the small table, checked his phone screen, broke into the yolk with a fork. He ate a bit.

I was down the corridor and into the echoing stairwell, I was down the steps and out the glass front door before I fell in love.

It didn't happen below his window where I was slicked, briefly, by the possibility of his gaze. It happened as I turned the corner, out of view. Bam. I was in love. I stopped, stared at the path and then carried on, full of self-hugging, secret joy. Love! Bam. It kept happening on the bus, Bam! and getting off the bus, the after-scent released when I stood up to go, the pang, the hidden delight, the street becoming a meaningful street, BAM, it just kept happening and rising, the knowledge, the beauty, the hopefulness, my feet not touching the ground, my cheek not feeling the air, the love the swoop and swoon the blood mashing in my ears the any moment now the any second now he will call, the beauty of the day, the beauty of the sky, the jolt of missed time and had I missed it? Did he text? Is my battery dead? Did I pick up somebody else's phone, now? If I see five magpies, three yellow mini-coopers, if I read every horoscope, he will text me love me he will call. The curtains drawn the not calling the not messaging the not yet not yet the love the love the love.

I spent hours reconstructing his flat in my head, and him moving around in it; his white bedroom with a white laminate wardrobe and a white paper globe for a lampshade. I watched him, at two in the morning, dipping to pick up yesterday's jocks to cover himself on the way to the bathroom. Me lying there considering whether the big muscly size of him made his dick look small, or if it was actually small. Because, inside me, it was a different order of object. Inside me, it had been an event.

Outside, not so much.

The sarcasm continued. In the months that came after, I had this nagging, chirpy counter-voice going, about the many shortcomings of this man. And there was nothing between this godawful sarcasm and:

Gaah!

Prostration.

Silence.

We walked around town. He said, I like the way you do the sky, my mother never could figure out the weather, you'd see her half-mad, running around at the washing line, it was always a surprise. Like how long do you have to be looking up at it? But the rain, fuck it, the rain, it stops you thinking and that's not a bad thing.

He touched my face and said, You spend a long time looking.

He kissed me, and we were making out right there while

the pedestrians gathered at the lights, and walked across, and gathered again.

Red man. Green man. Red.

This is what happens to people when they are struck by lightning: *confusion, seizures, dizziness, muscle aches, deafness, headaches, memory deficits, distractibility, personality changes and chronic pain.*

Some people – usually Americans, usually from the Midwest – say that, after they were struck by lightning, they were able to do new things. One man said he felt the approach of snow in his bones, he knew the weather before it arrived. Or, sometimes, when he walked along a corridor, a light fixture blew over his head. He learned to play the piano for the first time. This man said that, after he was struck by lightning, he could talk to animals and he could hear what those animals said back to him.

This is not what happened to me when I fell in love.

Similar, but no.

Chiddik chiddik

Qwer-wer

Terue

At the weekend, I went home for Sunday dinner with Carmel and he went back up to the farm in Louth. I could almost see it: his pious mother ducking her head before picking up the cutlery, the cattle's slow rip of grass in the front field while he chewed through his supermarket beef. I, meanwhile, sat in companionable silence with Carmel and ate a curried cauliflower cheese followed by a sticky-toffee pudding. This is what my mother thinks I eat. And she is right, I do eat such things when I am with her. When I am not with her I eat coleslaw and crisps. Because I am a vegetarian.

How are you?

Good, yeah.

You look a bit pale.

Most of the time we have a quiet relationship, Me 'n' Maw. In here is a magic circle – and we have the scented candles to prove it – out there is attrition.

Do I?

Are you alright?

Me? Grand.

(I never tell my mother anything. I am not that stupid.)

You sure?

You can't tell Carmel you have a problem or she'll go out and beat someone up for you. My mother is the woman who goes over to jetski-guy on the beach, when you are five years old, shouting, How dare you frighten my child with that stupid, horrible machine. She is the woman who phones the government when your Irish exam is too hard (no really), she is, bless her, a crusader and a fighter – if you get a grope from some old perv on the bus she will get that damn CCTV footage, she will sue the buses, ring the cops, put you into therapy and then go and burn his house down.

So really, no, I do not tell Carmel about the perv on the bus – or anything else – I just get up and find another seat.

This is delicious. God, Mum. What's the green thing? Scallion?

Guess.

Just tell me.

Hah.

Is it leek?

When we sit around on a Sunday waiting for the oven timer to ping on the sticky-toffee pudding, I do not mention that, some days, in my house-share in Ballybough, I don't tidy up or wash myself or water the plants. I don't tell her that my job is not a real job (oh my god the number of

23

plants I have killed) or that I am writing scraggy-drunk poetry that ends with the pen going through the page.

I certainly do not tell her about Felim.

That's so lovely.

In the middle of the table, there is a shallow, overspilling mess of wild-looking flowers.

Smell it, go on.

Oh wow.

That's the sweet pea.

So what's with you, Mum? How's work?

Carmel likes to be asked about herself. She doesn't really answer – her life is just a life, it's a kind of annoyance to her. But in the bad old days, when I was a teenager and we were hammer and tongs, she would sit and stare for about an hour and then she might say, very quietly: *I exist too, you know.*

(Fair point.)

Oh, God, work. Oh I don't know. Do you want to go to Heidelberg?

Heidelberg?

I have fifty-six medical students coming in from Heidelberg.

Yo-del-ay-ee-hoo.

We talk about her students and we talk some more about the food, and everything in the room is lovely. She has thrown out the old cotton napkins and got linen ones from a shop in Wicklow where she went to see some rose garden in bloom. Her old friend Brian has bladder cancer.

You remember Brian?

Of course.

I haven't seen him in years, actually, and now this.

We just chat. And I feel good. That should go without saying – she's my mother.

I'm thinking of going to London, I say.

24

What for?

Lily's there. Just for a few weeks.

And the oven timer goes *ping*.

Carmel gets up to bang about on the kitchen counter and serve the pudding. She brings over two bowls and slides back on to her chair.

So, tell me, she says.

What?

What's in London?

You mean, apart from London?

Sometimes I think Carmel has a kind of object permanence thing going, because you have to explain everything to her. You have to construct full sentences and be specific.

Just to see Lily, I say.

Lily?

She's a bit sad.

What's she sad about?

Dunno. Yeah. Hard to explain.

Just tell me.

She has a lot of anxiety, I say.

Right.

My mother waits for two whole seconds.

I never know what that means. She – like, what? – she looks at her big toe and thinks she has cancer? Sorry, I know. I know it's a thing, only I don't exactly understand what it means. Like what?

What do you mean, *like, what*?

Carmel is blowing on the toffee pudding. She pokes her tongue out to tip it, and pulls back.

Hot!

Dear Lord, my mother's tongue, veined red at the sides, very compacted and oddly triangular. A kind of shaft.

Just *tell* me, she says.

So she nearly had a panic attack on the plane because the

guy beside her kept using his electronic device during take-off and she wanted to call the steward but she couldn't, even though she thought they were all going to die.

The air hostess, says Carmel.

Whatever.

But they weren't going to die.

She knew that! She *also* knew that they weren't going to die.

That's not anxiety, that's just stupid. Why is everyone so delighted about being stupid? Oh no. Oh dear. I'm sorry I have this problem you see – everyone has to do what I say now because the thing is, I'm really thick.

I mean, yeah, I think it's partly a control thing. She needs people to. You know.

Oh, control, says Carmel.

A swallow of toffee pudding later, she wipes the sticky crumbs from her mouth with a linen napkin of white and ecru stripes.

Good luck with that, she says.

Downstairs, when I sit on the loo, I see the black dots of his thumb-marks on my inner thighs and the sight looses in me a jagged run of pleasure. It is the same feeling I got from self-harming – for the thirty seconds or so I self-harmed at school. A skitter of something that settles into a single word:

Mine.

Same bathroom as back then. Tongue and groove panelling painted sea-blue, a wooden mirrored cabinet above the basin containing Carmel's L'Oréal shampoo, Aveeno body lotion, Clinique moisturiser, Ren radiance scrub, Euthymol toothpaste, Lancôme cleanser, cotton circles, Neutrogena hand cream. Down below, a wicker bin with a compostable liner that billows under one yellowed cotton bud, shiny at the tip. On the wall over the bath, three framed botanical prints, the interior paper spotted by damp. On the floor, the same rag rug, hard to wash, braided blue and green with a coral thread. I used to stare at it as I shat. I used to wash my hands and open the cabinet and wonder was there a woman on the planet more boring than my mother; she has made boredom her first love and occupation.

I go down to my old bedroom at the front of the house and open the door: A shelf of books, many boxes of dead eyeshadow, a heap of fluffy toys.

Every year, when I was little, Carmel asked me what I wanted from Santa and on Christmas morning there it was. Some toy from the telly. I just had to pick one and yearn for it, loudly. *Oh, I hope, I hope I get a blue plastic horse with a pink mane* and pull off the wrapping paper on the day. Five minutes later, the stupid horse was thrown in a corner because what I really wanted was something I had not asked for, something I could not imagine. I wanted a present that Santa had chosen, just for me.

Oh wow! (There was always a camera trained on you, at this point.) It's just what I wanted!

One year when I was eight or nine and had my suspicions, I wrote on my Christmas list: And a surprise please.

I got a new coat.

I go back upstairs and hug my mother who gives me anything I want, but only if I can tell her what it is. Carmel is shorter than me. She wraps her arms around my waist. I tilt and place my cheek on the crown of her head. Her dyed black hair is hot from sitting in the sun. She says, Oh my baby-baby. Come out and look at the garden, before you go.

※

27

Felim brought a shoulder of gin and a net of lemons. He swung the bag at me at the front door of Ballybough and he said, Get in there, get in! You hoo-er.

He said I had all the smarts.

He sat at the end of the bed and looked at his phone for a long time.

He fucked fast and then really slowly. He said, How does that feel? How does that feel now?

Felim said he would miss me at the weekend and he pulled the V of my jumper to kiss me at the collarbone.

Later, a text – *Hey gorgeous.*

Why is it, you look at the news and there's a small plane crashing on a highway, or into a building or into a lake. The headline says, 'Three people dead in light air crash' and this is a big story because these three people were up in the air until they weren't. People die on airplanes all the time, the stewards lay them out along the back row and give the other passengers a free drink. People also die in car crashes, which happen, boringly, on the ground. People die and die. Every day, in any square mile of city streets, someone dies from homelessness or poverty or stupid blind fate. Journalists are so lazy – tragedy all around and they spend their time waiting for a few rich people to literally fall out of the sky.

Felim said he used to be on the apps, but it wasn't where he was at. He wanted something unexpected, he wanted life to favour him (that is the word he used). Or he wanted to have it already, to check his pocket and find the money was in there all along. He wanted to be lucky.

He pulled my chin around and looked at me.

Like you, he said.

I'm lucky?

You don't know you were born.

We were on the river boardwalk, junkies sitting on the wooden boards, tourists on the benches. The teal Liffey water slid past, braiding itself along the walls.

It was one of those phrases that got harder to understand, the more you said it.

You don't know you were born.

I send my air-crash piece over to the agency but Meg doesn't like it. It's not really her tone.

– *Can we do more climate?*

I am stalking Meg. And I am also making Meg up. I click on her stuff all the time, looking for ideas. I stare deep into her photos. Her wildflower garden, her silvered wooden deck, her modern kitchen knocked out from a Victorian terrace in Shepherd's Bush, with a huge plate-glass window, the chairs along the wooden table in six different colours.

– *Twine or plastic ties for potted plants?*

– *Yes! Twine twine twine!*

I will never have chairs in six different colours. Much as I would love that. It does not seem like it will ever happen to me.

But I have a beautiful man in my bed. And sometimes, walking beside me in the street. And maybe, once or twice, in a bar.

Felim is so tall. I see strangers look up at him, with a tilt of the head that makes them happy.

Ah, there you are.

Felim says he is never online. He does not mention a half-dead account I found in about two minutes which is all over his local football team. I have read every post since it went live in 2012 and before it trickled out last year. All 435 of them. Several times.

Incredible win. Great day. Best of luck. The man the legend. Can history be repeated. Quality performance. Slight shoulder goes down like a sack. Did you know, the numbers of both players marking each other should add up to 17, news to me too. Last gasp. Snatch it at the death. A brave kick under the circumstances. You have one job and that is to get better.

I rolled up on my knees behind him and said, Stand up a minute. I like being naked when you are half dressed, the feel of your buckle and buttons and the demin. And he said, You do?

He kissed me at the open hall door. He slipped a hand under my dressing gown, said, Amazing. And the street was right there.

He did not ring till Thursday.

    – Sorry fell asleep call you later alright?

We were having sex for maybe the eighth time in our lives and I thought, This man is huge, he is an enormous human being and he is on top of me, and if I did not want that there is nothing I could do to stop him.

But I did want it. So that was exciting.

Afterwards he checked his phone and set it on the bedside locker, where I have a fabulous-pathetic feathered lampshade, in a light shade of pink.

Jesus, that yoke, he said.

I look up 'love at first sight' in the movies but apart from *The Little Mermaid*, it only happens to guys.

    See
    Know
    Want

Get
Only her

Felim said he bumped into a friend and the guy told him their old teacher had hanged himself right there in the school. In the staff toilets. He went in on the weekend, he had a key.

Fuck, I said. What was he like, the teacher?

And he said, Yeah, he was a bit of a cunt alright. Can you imagine though? Jesus. The next morning, Felim thought he might have dreamt the whole thing. He was a bit pissed, to be honest.

I said, Where were you?

Town, he said.

This teacher, they called him Ballsy McKenna. He had a wife no one knew about and three kids, all boys. And the thing is, he brought the dog in with him. When the care-taker opened up on the Monday, the dog was going ballistic, shit on the floor, he'd been drinking from the toilet bowls. And the kids had spent all Sunday out looking for the dog, up and down, calling. I mean what did he do that for?

A warning? He wanted to warn people?

Yeah. Nah.

You think?

Not if you knew Ballsy.

Where in town? I said.

Pure fucking spite, if you ask me.

What were you doing in town?

Excuse me?

Later, I told him he looked sad and then felt I had said the wrong thing.

When we had sex, he had trouble finishing and put his hand on my neck to get himself off. He said, Say it, say it, though I couldn't say anything, I couldn't catch a breath.

My blood dropped cold and I came, very sudden and hard. It was the shock. I felt I had been swallowed by my own body. Overtaken, in a wave.

Afterwards I said, What did you say?

And he said, You heard me.

He always came over to my place, even though it was less convenient, even though I had housemates: Stuart scratching the small of his back as he checked the fridge for food, Beatriz occupying the bathroom for hours in total silence. I wanted to say, Let's go back to yours, but I just couldn't.

He picked the phone up and switched it on and got dug in, his thumbs flicking and jabbing.

I said, Who is it?

And he said, What?

He sent the message.

Just someone, he said.

Felim said he used to get his latte from the same place around the corner at work every day, and every day the woman behind the counter gave him this lovely, crinkly look, and she was pretty old, but still, every morning. You think, I am going to turn away now with my coffee in my hand, and at the very last second she does her just-for-you smile, it makes him literally itchy. It's will she, won't she, every time. And one day he's in there in the afternoon, meeting someone, which was not his usual thing, and he watches her, and she's the same to everyone, man woman and child, the same crinkle, the same eye-to-eye. And the first few times he was a bit, Hey! Over here bitch! and after a while he didn't know what to think, he admired her and sort of hated her exactly the same. Like two same notes in either ear.

He lifted one hand and then the other.

Dinnnggggg. Dinnnggggg.

Like, the fuck? he said.

I realise I am not listening to him, I am just watching him for clues.

Felim said Your One from Belfast was a nut-job. He had not seen her for some time.

He pulled a picture up on his phone of a tractor the size of a kitchen, there was a man standing beside one of the huge wheels.

He said, Yeah, that's my Da.

The man was wearing a cap and he was smiling. I reached to take the phone, but he pulled it away.

Let's see? I said, but he swiped through another couple of images and shut down the screen.

He told me about some neighbours who drowned in their slurry tank, they were trying to rescue the dog. It happened in four foot of shit.

You pass out first from the fumes. He said, Better to have it above ground. It's all about the hydrogen sulphide.

He said, All that happened in *Louth actually*.

Then we had sex, which I did not enjoy.

I realised that every stupid, small thing I said that first night we got together had landed somewhere wrong in him, and it rose up now as a taunt. He wasn't listening to me, he was storing it all up. Despite which, I kept talking, I kept offering him the things I loved: a joke, a meme, a dream I had. I told him which people could hurt me, and all my hopes. It was like a song:

Love me! Love me!
Chiddik! Chiddik!

*

33

On my very sporadic Instagram I put an upside-down pair of eyes:

Remember, it might be on a sleepover, you are on the bed, your friend is lying on the floor, you have a staring contest, and it gets really amazing, total spooky love. And then she blinks. *From the bottom?*

Nusa Lembongan is the Goldilocks island between tourist Bali and the hipster heaven of Gili Trawangan. Full of local colour and things to do, it is ideal for families with older children. The harbour beach is home to seaweed farms and small boats whose fishermen will bring you out snorkelling the reef for a small fee. Surfers enjoy the permanent break with its own pontoon cafe out in the bay. Pretty beachfront restaurants serve fresh-caught fish and the evening is filled by chanting from the local temple. In the morning, you can swim with the manta rays.

By the end of August, I was stalking not just Meg my influencer, but also the supposed ex from Belfast. I clicked and checked, who knows how many hundred times a day. I knew the rent on the house where she lived in Drumcondra, I had seen, from above, its garden furniture, splayed about a round white table that might have been a parasol. I knew her name, and her father's name, her brother's application for planning permission for a side extension in Cypress Downs, the street near Stormont where she grew up. I knew she could get into the lotus position, that she once stood in tree pose at the edge of the Grand Canyon, that she had a cat, an astonishing yoga arse, that she liked taking photographs of the sea.

(Who doesn't?)

Are you seeing someone? I said.

And he said, Are we exclusive, then?

*

Lily texts:

– that is such a dikish thing to say this guy is not going to change GET OUT OF THE HOUSE HE IS ON THE EXTENSION

Nungwi beach, famed for its sugary sand and still, aquamarine sea, lies at the very northernmost tip of tropical Zanzibar. Fringed by palm trees and luxury villas and small thatched hotels, it is the closest you will come to paradise. Take a ride on a working dhow to snorkel in shallow waters, eat your fisherman's catch in a beachfront restaurant while the sun goes down. Wander in the cool of the evening from one nightspot to the next in bare feet while the moon rises over the sands.

Because Carmel believes in backups, I still have my lovely therapist from school. I could always go back to check in with Paschal, in his button-down shirts and corduroy bags, who picks a piece of lint from off his knee and says, Not cool, no? because Paschal talks like a teenager from twenty years ago. Carmel got me Paschal, like you might get a child a pet for mental health reasons, and also because she thought I needed a male figure in my life. That is how careful, how abiding, my mother is for me. Paschal loved my growing up and he was always on my side, and sometimes the thought of his smile gets me up to walk, close to dawn, which is the only time I leave the house now, and I come back with the daylight an expanding pain in my chest, like I am trying to open without cracking. I feel the attempt inside me to begin a new day.

There is no way I could tell Paschal what I am doing, my little adventure in abjection. What could I say?

Sorry, Paschal, I have failed at everything. Everything we talked about.

He makes me

He makes me

He

He

This guy, he is permanently aggrieved. You know?

He takes

He

This guy, he is built like a mock-up of a man, a plastic model of what-goes-where, his pecs look like you could click them off, he is his own armour and exoskeleton, and he moves like a landscape shifting under snow.

You know what?

He has never let me into his flat. After that first time. Not once.

He said, You

YOU

There!

And when I say the sex is not great, not anymore, not in the technical sense, when I say the arc of my arousal does not match the optimum human arc whatever that may be, I mean it's not even bad in a good way, or painful in a way that is also exciting. But you know, we started well. We began, as lovers do, by staying in bed for a long time. I lay there touching him, I saw the hairs on his skin rise.

I read somewhere there is some chemical floods your brain after too much sex, that is why you weep.

I could tell Paschal how I spent Thursday night kneeling on the floor of my bedroom, while Felim sat in front of me, stroking himself. He walked around, pushed my face on to the bed and tried to fuck me from behind. He said my legs were too short, hauled me further on to the bed, and tried again. I could say that the airlessness, the pointless jangle of my arms, the fear of exploding from the inside, all this felt like the completion of some thought that I had been trying to catch, all my life.

It made sense.

If ever I went back to Paschal I would ask him if that is what sex really is. Is that what women really are, what men really are? Are men sadistic by design (are you, Paschal, sadistic by design?) and he would say:

What do you think?

Actually, he would say something much nicer than that. I just don't know what.

After he is gone, I lie in my room and my body knows the horizon. My blood and lymph, the fluid in my inner ear; all tilt true to gravity, and are still.

He complains there is no television set in my bedroom and I say, Who has a TV? What am I, a family unit?

He puts his phone on the pillow and turns me round so he can watch porn, and fluffs himself up and pushes around a while, getting nowhere much, then he pulls my head back, to make me see it too, a little bright oblong of This in here that in there and Bigger one Oooh Aaah! jouncing and slipping on its nest of down. And even as I feel an unwelcome pang of arousal, I think, That's not what I want, either. That's just stupid.

That's not the thing to brush the wound
I had forgotten,
to wake
my livid
self
I want it in a turn of his head,
as seen from a cafe window
a thread of blood dropping
from a fat sky
my hands curled
on the tabletop

*

Felim, that fucker, does not know my secret. My secret is I want something more incidental, unperformed. I want worse.

Online, I fall into a rabbit-hole of people who died while trying to rescue their dogs. I think it might be worth a post, but hard to strike a tone. Some people leave their baby in a pushchair to jump in after their dog and the dog swims to safety while the baby is orphaned, right there in the buggy.

These impulsive dog-rescuing types usually die in rivers, but the sea is also a thing and there is a fair crop every year when the ice on lakes begins to thin. At least three dogs, followed by people, have jumped into hot springs – perhaps they were chasing a stick. In Yellowstone National Park, onlookers shouted at a man not to do it, and he said, Like hell I won't! before diving in, head first. This dog was called Moosie, and it wasn't even his. When the man was hauled out of the hot spring, he discovered he was blind. As he was led away, he said, That was stupid. How bad am I? That was a stupid thing I did. He died the next day.

Moosie must have died too, though this detail is not reported. His death would have solved the problem of what to do with such a dog. Do you just wait for them to dry off and bring them back home? And if they are sent to a rescue shelter, for example, is there a sign on the cage saying, This golden retriever is looking for his forever home. He loves getting his tummy rubbed and playing fetch on the beach (he doesn't always bring the stick back!). And also this dog is cursed.

My mother used to tell me not to dive head first into any stretch of water, until I knew what was down there. That is what happens to mothers, they lose their sense of adventure. Carmel had me on her own, and that can't have been easy.

She gave me her whole life, she told me once, *her whole life*, and I said, Fuck you, fuck you, fuck you, fuck you, fuck you.

Then again. There was always that empty half on the other side of her big bed, where I could crawl in on weekend mornings and chat away.

Then again.

We always had our spiralling love – that doomed, glorious, ever-closer closeness – Carmel pushing the hair behind my ear and saying, No, I am listening to you. I am. I just don't know what to say yet.

Water the colour of peppermint mouthwash, icing sugar sand, hammocks strung between the palm trees, a peaceful inner freshwater lagoon that is home to many species of exotic birds. This secret beach was in a military zone until five years ago and though it is now completely safe you can still find the occasional bullet casing in the dunes. A haven for turtles, which are protected here, you can also spot migrating humpbacks break offshore. A virgin utopia within most budgets, you will not see a beach umbrella for miles. Factor up!

Felim did not call for three weeks and then, in late September, a text.

– *Sunday morning? Dress nice.*

He looked at me at the door and said, Heels?

I went back up to find a pair and he seemed happy. He said, You scrub up nice, you know that? You've good teeth.

He told me to get in the car we were going on a trip and I said, Where to?

He did not reply.

The drive took more than an hour and he was normal the whole way, extravagantly normal, laid-back, at ease, pushing tracks on the music system, making comments back at the radio, telling me about his boss, asking me about work, about Mal. He was wearing a navy blue suit and a pinkish shirt, with a striped silver and light blue tie, and it was a different decade we were in, it might have been the last century. There was gel in his hair, the smell of aftershave. He reached over and put his hand on my knee. He looked through the windscreen at autumn skies and gathering, wheeling rooks. I wondered when the mood would shift, when he would leave me on the hard shoulder, crying. But he kept the patter going, indicating left off the motorway, indicating right, stopping smoothly at the pedestrian lights. He turned into a church car park, checked his watch and cut the engine. He said, My brother's had a baby.

Nothing happened for the next while, we just sat.

A few people came out, and then a crowd. Mass had finished and we went against the flow to get into the porch. Inside, the dark church echoed to the roof with a rageful screeching from a baby up by the altar, in a queue to be baptised.

Felim crossed himself, bobbed and eased sideways into pew. I made a vague movement in front of my face and slid in beside him, stood, knelt, sat back, while one baby after another was anointed and splashed, and their adult companions renounced Satan and all his works. The grown-ups did this in print dresses and good jackets, in strappy sandals and pastel ties. I don't go into churches very often, so it was like a public secret, this dragging of evil from out of swaddled infants on a Sunday at noon. There was no smoke, no sulphur, just that one screeching demon which the holy water failed to exorcise. In fact, it made the shrieking baby shriek even louder. His face went so red you felt like checking around for medical attention. I looked at the shushing, jigging mother and wondered how all that would work out, in the long run.

A few splashings down the line, one of the fathers took

off his jacket and rolled up his sleeves before stretching his baby out over the font. This man had a broad, likeable face with a gingered beard and his wife wore a wrap-over dress of blue. She stood behind her husband, one hand on his waist, another on the small daughter tucked between them, and she smiled around his shoulder at the babe in arms. It was an oil painting: the grouping was so sweetly monumental, and the parents were so happy. I took out my phone to take a photo, and then didn't.

Felim muttered, The fuck?

Just, I said.

This cheerful man was Felim's older brother Cathal. We were introduced in the church car park, also to Felim's parents. His mother was a round woman in a deep pink blazer, his father unrolled a cap in his hands, and put it back on a whitish, bald head. I don't know what I had been expecting.

You'll come back for something, the mother said, like a normal person.

Thanks, I said. I will.

And Felim also looked completely normal, if a little brightly lit, talking to his parents in the car-park sunshine.

The little convoy turned in through a gateway towards a neat house, painted white and overshadowed by two cavernous barns, one of which contained the blue tractor, which was so huge you'd need a ladder to get up into it. Three JCB buckets lay rusting on a pile of gravel. There was a little lake. I did not see any cattle.

I went back later on Google Earth and found the ghost JCB parked by the wall in the front field, and an entire, third barn I had not noticed at the time, distracted as I had been by a pyramid of silage bales, a sudden stink.

We did not pull into the yard in front of the neat white house, but drove past it, up over a rise, to a more substantial place, with two peaked roofs joined by a balustraded balcony over the main front door.

I thought of Carmel looking at all that good land and no garden to speak of – just a monkey-puzzle tree out front, in a bit of field pretending to be lawn. Inside, the decor was plain. A tiled floor went all through the downstairs and the furniture was worn and widely scattered like it had come from an older, smaller place. There was a squishy leather suite mushrooming in the living room. The kitchen was yellow pine.

I caught all this in glimpses. I did not look at anything for too long, though Felim seemed not to care what I did. He ambled away from me as soon as we were in the door, hands in pockets. After which, he spent the afternoon leaning against the kitchen counter, the table, the arm of the sofa, never sitting down. He was in ultra-casual mode.

But sure lookit
I will not
Are you telling me?
Ah now
Sure that fella
Right, right
Come here to me
A middle-aged woman introduced herself as Felim's sister, Maeve. I did not look surprised, or say that he had never mentioned a sister.

Yes, I said. Hello.

There were balloons tied to the chair-backs in the kitchen, where small children ran around. Two of these, at least, belonged to Maeve who threw reprimands at them with no sense that she might be obeyed. She introduced me to another brother who was nabbing sausages from a batch cooling on the counter.

You know Fiachra, sure. He's down in Dublin.

I did not know Fiachra. We nodded. He gave me a good looking over: the dress, the shoes.

So. How long do you know Felim? Maeve said.

A few months. Not long.

Their father was putting on a pair of boots by the back door.

I'll be on the land, he said.

Right so, where's Mam?

She's sitting down.

After that. I just kept smiling with my good teeth. I stuck close to Maeve, poured tea, cleared dishes, clicked about in my high heels. We talked about the fine weather, the colour of a dress, my location in Dublin, my remarkable lack of siblings (she did not ask if I had a father – no one ever does).

I asked which children were hers, how many years between herself and Felim, was he spoilt when he was little.

Oh! she said, That one!

and I said, Hilarious.

I don't think I spoke to any of the men, except to the father of the recently baptised baby, now back in his cheery shirtsleeves – Cathal, who came up to me and said, You're very welcome, thanks for coming, let me introduce you, tell me have you met my grandmother? as he led me into the living room and over to an ancient woman sitting in one of the vast, squishy chairs.

Her feet on the extendable footrest were encased in white ankle socks and beige sensible sandals. She was wearing an apron – though I had not seen her walking around – also a brown cardigan over a pink floral blouse, greenish trousers. Nothing matched or didn't match. It just was.

McDaragh, she said. Tell me, are you anything to the poet? You are. You are. Felim said as much.

I said, Yes.

43

You're the daughter.

No.

Oh he was a rare one.

Ah, no. I am the granddaughter.

Yes. That is right. That is what you are. Did you know him at all?

He died before I was born, I said.

He did. God rest him.

She lifted her face, which was, I saw, Felim's long, narrow face and, through shifting dentures, said:

> Lay your head on my dark heart,
> your honey mouth with scent of thyme
> give me your hand before we part,
> oh love, sweet love of mine.

The brother stood for this ghastly rendition with his head slightly bowed, and I said, Yes. That was him, yes.

You have the look of him, alright.

You think?

You are very welcome here, she said. And I thought I would run screaming out of the house tearing my hair and ripping off my clothes. I would streak naked through the near field and the long field and the fucking far field and there I would live, crouched and mad in the ditch. I also felt as though I had come home.

Thank you, I said.

Felim signalled to me around four o'clock, and we made a move. We waved and sat into the car in synch, pulled down the seat belts and drove in silence down the boreen, past the massive barns and the neat white house, through the sharp stink that came from the brown pond, which was – he did not have to tell me this now – a pool of slurry. He stopped the car, and leaned out the window to work the keypad on the oversized gates.

They seem nice, I said once we were through, and Felim said, Nice.

As we met the motorway, he said, Are you happy now?

Sorry?

You're happy now, are you?

After that – I don't know. I can't remember what the fight was or how we got into the fight, because nothing made sense. There is a lot of it I can't figure out.

But I remember thinking they had not rescued me from him, after all. Even though they knew his nature. Mammy and Daddy, Maeve, Cathal, Fiachra, Old Granny Poem. These people, who knew him better than anyone, looked at the girl Felim brought home and wondered how long I would last.

The interloper.

I had a fantasy they set me washing dishes in the granny's apron, that Fiachra pushed me over the sink and raped me in my high heels while their father was out on the land, their mother was in the other room, that Cathal looked regretful and said, But sure lookit, and Maeve said, Oh, take this plate of buns and put them out, would you? I love your dress. Which is pretty much what she did say. I had a fantasy where it was the same day, only much more explicit.

And the granny quoted poetry, throughout.

your honey mouth with scent of thyme

After that, Felim might text and drop in, sometimes two days in a row, then not for ages. When he did, I found it hard to tell the difference between sex and getting hurt in other ways. The thing that did not change, that never changed, was the waiting. That surge of expectation. Endlessly. And again.

Is that him

Is that him

Does he love me

Is that him

Waiting for this man was better than being with him, it was certainly more intense, the way longing kept eating itself and giving birth to more longing. And nothing, but nothing was better than that first flash of arrival.

He loves me

There he is

I have started a book of wonders, starling murmurations, a mountain hovering over the sea. People find a cellar under their floor, an extra, derelict room behind a mirror on the bathroom wall. A man discovers a dishwasher in his flat, that he thought was a fake cupboard. In Holland, researchers grow human tear glands – little balloons that swell and rupture, to dribble out salt water that also contains antibodies, stress hormones, pheromones, natural painkillers. They are so good for us, these little drops of water – science make our tears sound better than the milk of human kindness. I want us to build a crying farm; miles and miles of glass Petri dishes in which lonely tears cry themselves out, so mankind does not have to bother with that, anymore.

He said, I am going to sleep now. He said, I can't sleep here.

Felim said his father killed a sick dog by tying one end of a rope to the wall and the other end to the tractor, with the dog looped in the middle. He drove off, and did not turn to look until the rope snapped. He said his father said it was a quick death and, given the price of the vet, worth the loss of the bit of rope.

My influencer Meg wants a post about dildos, she wants one of her Maltipoos to fetch one like a found stick, because this will be hilarious. This dildo talk is just girl-bragging – which is absolutely fine by me, but I want to ask (how do I ask her this?) what style are we talking here? Is it big and gnarly, is it a knobby, veiny bit of plastic in prosthetic pink, or is it, like, slim and discreet and pale blue? I send a message to the agency: *Does she have the doggy dildo pic?*

The Maltipoo is tiny and white and fluffy. The dildo in its little mouth is black with a bend in it. Massive.

And I want to ask her, Why black, Meg?

Now the thing is out there, so to speak, now the thing is in her little dog's mouth, and ready to be viewed by her many, many thousands of followers, I want to ask, What is the point of fucking something that cannot feel?

(Of course that is the *whole point* – this fact becomes true as soon as I think about typing the question. I am such a fool.)

But, you know, if that is the case, if this thing is not human, if it is just a bit of landfill plastic you're shoving up your whoopsie then . . . Why black, Meg?

He sends a text,
– *Sup?*
– *Yeah, good* I say, and there is nothing for many hours. The next morning I try,
– *You?* and he says,
– *Ng* which could mean anything. Then later
– *Stuff!!!*
He sends a picture of his desk. I look at it, enlarge it. The desk has a curved front and fits into a corner space. There are two screens, a black and bulky keyboard on a long cable, a striped cup, a nearly empty Pot Noodle carton, corded headphones, corded mouse, a curly corded landline, two speakers also on cables, a neon-green plastic frog whose upturned, open mouth holds pens, scissors, highlighters; a

pile of paper with a stapler on top, a glass mug of some unfinished, dark liquid; a collapsing accordion file in beige cardboard, an orange plastic tumbler, a green file shedding sheets of paper.

I am taken by the amount of active, suspended, or abandoned eating and drinking on display. Everything is started and left unfinished by the same proportion – mostly gone, a bit to go. Felim does the same thing around my room, in the morning there are always leftovers for me to clear.

What is that? Is it a power play, a hoarding impulse? ADHD? Is it male entitlement?

I have seen him try to finish something, decide against finishing it, set it down and walk away.

Two yellow Post-its are stuck to one computer screen, which is dark, the other screen has a screensaver of two foxes. It seems likely that he took this photograph himself. The foxes are in dark undergrowth, one is staring straight to camera, the other is nibbling below its companion's ear.

– *Foxy!* I write.

There is no reply.

I look at the photograph many, many times. I think, I am his leavings. I am the thing he can not finish or throw away.

It's a Thursday night in Dublin town. I go out and fuck someone, a not very confident guy with super sweaty palms, I say, Oh yes yes do whatever you want, do whatever you want, though he is too drunk to do anything much, and I grind down on him a bit and slap the poor fucker, biff bash, left, right, and one more time for luck. I say, That's one from all the girls. In the bathroom I scrabble through his cabinet and make a double slice along my forearm with his disposable razor. The cuts are shallow and unsatisfying, but they sting like bejaysus. The guy stands in the door frame, in a striped dressing gown, which I

48

suddenly despise. He works in tech, so he is white as a maggot and rich as they come. I barge past him, pulling a photo off the wall on my way out. The taxi men won't stop for me: there is blood on my bare arm and I am too drunk.

Every few days, I send Mal a picture of the sky and he sends me a picture of his shadow on a wall, or on a roadway. He is in Berlin or Leipzig, he is in Budapest. I remember reading Rilke out in his flat in the care of those stately, red-barked museum trees. I remember a book about angels that he liked. I throw the I Ching, it says, You cannot argue your way into love. I work on my Maltipoo dialogue. I watch cochlear-implant videos while eating oatcakes from the box, thinking there is another consciousness waiting for us all. Some day in the future, we will shift up some unthinkable gear.

Carmel says, How are you, you look very pale. And I say, I am not, I am really fine, Mum. When we hug, she is wearing some perfume of my childhood. I hold her by the upper arms and she says, I've taken up boxing.

Of course you have.

I recommend it.

She has made chilli sin carne, white basmati, a yoghurty thing on the side. I spoon it into myself, waiting to feel something – the way, when I came home from school, it all came pouring out of me: the girl said, the boy said, my scraped knee, the teacher, my horrible friend. But there is nothing to say. There is nothing to pour.

Downstairs I go into her bedroom and find the perfume on her bedside locker, and I steal an amount to take away with me. It seems a bit floral for Carmel, who has not worn a skirt, not even for work, since I was about nine years old.

No, she is not gay, she told me. And, no she is not secretly trans. And just no, alright?

On the shelf in the corridor, I pick out a collection of my grandfather's poetry. I haven't opened this book for more than a decade and it feels stolen from me now. By experience, by time. By Old Granny Poem. I flick through, trying to find a way back in.

The book is full of birds.

> peacock and heron, dunnock and wren,
> the bullfinch with his lipstick breast
> of orange chiffon

I used to read these every night, almost. The poems were so gentle and clear, I could hear his voice speaking, just to me. Other girls had fathers, uncles, I had good old Phil, who made things lovely with words.

Sometimes, I look at my mother and wonder where all that went, how the family declined, father to daughter – from subtle to stupid in a single generation. Phil's work is, above all, tactful. A girl needs tact – this was not, from Carmel, what a girl was ever going to get. When things were bad, I would curl up with Phil and sweeten the hurt.

I close my eyes tight, close the book and open it at a random page.

A poem called 'Persephone'.

Thanks Phil.

After she is dragged down to hell by Hades, Persephone's mother plunges the world into its first winter. Before that, the seasons all happened at the same time – so this poem, bizarrely, could be about the weather these days.

> rose and crocus blooming together
> snowdrop and aster, lily and larkspur –
> every season in season: berry, leaf

and bud crowding the branch, before
he made winter from her mother's grief.

I take a pic and post it.
– *Climate change as seen by my grandfather Phil
McDaragh in . . . 1978.*
I remember the image of escape so well, Persephone as a
white egret, bashing her way out of a dark cave:

like a bird in the mouth, hell yawns her free

I want the line as a tattoo, running from armpit to hip, a
bird flying alongside it. Or from my pubis (my hell!!) all
the way up to that dent at the base of your neck called
(I look it up)
the suprasternal notch
(I am disappointed)

I want to write a book about foxes, but from the fox point
of view. This book would have a few laughs in it, but not
much by way of words.

Online, your one from Belfast is doing yoga in leggings
that are a blinding white. I click on everything. She is older
than me, but she looks a lot better. She lives in many
rooms, not one room. She has a statue of the Buddha on a
shelf. She has wooden candlesticks designed by Anders
Nørgaard in lavender and warm rose. She is replacing her
chrome taps with ones that look like copper – it is possible
she owns this place. All the rooms are painted different
shades of gunk: ointment-pink, putty, marsh. I can't look
away. In one picture, I am sure I see Felim's reflection in
a sheen of glass, on the door of her kitchen dresser.
The photo is of a flower arrangement on the counter;

shop-bought, but tousled and tasteful, dark purple, and acid green. The caption says:
– *Lucky me*

In the long days moving into winter, when Felim doesn't call, I write a story about a man eating a fried egg while, outside in the sunshine, a woman falls in love. And after the egg is eaten and the plate dumped in the sink, the man showers and gets dressed, he stuffs the laundry basket a little fuller, he brushes his teeth, and exits the flat, which is painted white. The abandoned cup cools. The unfinished egg slides a micro distance down the porcelain and, an hour or so later, darkens, stops and begins to crack. In the folds of the duvet, feathers settle. Bed springs slowly complete their rise and the exposed sheet yields its dampness to the surrounding air. A forgotten condom sits on the toilet cistern, wrapped in paper that becomes more stiff and brittle. The flat is silent. In a cupboard, some hidden meter clicks and briefly whirrs. A cloud comes between the earth and the sun.

In another part of the city, the woman feels a shift into sunshine as proof and vindication. In a different part of the city, a man feels unlucky and looks up to check for rain.

Felim rocks up in a Santa hat. He is really pissed. He says, The way you look at me it's like fucking a retard, I want you to say it, go on say it. Say, Give it to me. Do you like that? Say you like it, say, Thank you, Felim. You ungrateful bitch. Go on, say it. Give it to me, Felim. You want me to hurt you? I can't hear you, Nell. Say, Hurt me, Felim, please hurt me.
So I do.
What's my name?
Felim.
My name is Sir, you piece of shit.
I say, Sir.

It's a syllable. Felim does not need my sincerity. He needs chaos. His dick is softened by alcohol and this makes him frightening, the idea that he will try to hurt me in some other way.

So I do a bit of flailing, say Sir again. I give him some theatre, a surface fiction that he can penetrate. The Santa hat is fallen on the floor, I can see it in the corner of my eye. I am frightened. My body is stone cold. And somewhere in the middle of it I wonder:

If I believed all this was working, would it work?

Another time, he loves me. He controls the thing he loves. He is precise, I am the chaos. I feel the room carve in two in front of my jostled eyes and space remake itself. That is what the gristle of his soul-splitting prick can do to me. And when he has pulled me apart, I remain whole. When it stops, I am, magically, still here.

It seems a bit silly, in the circumstances, to call him Sir. I should call him Death I should call him Here It Comes and also The End of the World.

and you read
there's going to be a million people on waiting lists
and you read
about the drones
and you read about
the unimaginable lives of others
in their places, in their rooms

Online, I look at his reflection in the window of the kitchen dresser of Your One from Belfast, this is now my favourite picture of Felim, and when I think about him talking, all he says is: Bloke, bloke bloke bloke. Blokey bloking bloke, bloke-bloke bloking. And when I think of me talking back to him, all I say is: Please. Please.

A Scent of Thyme
(translated from 'Ceann Dubh Dílis',
anonymous, eighteenth century)

Lay your dark head upon my breast,
your honey mouth with scent of thyme
what man could not love you – so blest
and sweet, oh love, sweet love of mine.

The girls are on the march; they free
their hair and mourn their laddio,
the best in five parishes, but I deny
them all my love, sweet love, for you.

Lay your head on my dark heart,
your honey mouth with scent of thyme
give me your hand before we part,
oh love, sweet love of mine.

CARMEL

IT WAS NOT that he left when she was sick, it was the way he came back and ransacked the place looking, he said, for his watch which was lost or mislaid, or perhaps their mother had hidden it to annoy him; she had held on to it as some kind of keepsake. He went through the living room, he opened doors on the sideboard and scrabbled along the mantelpiece, rooted along the sofa, upending the cushions entirely, so they were tumbled about and gaping, and you could not think how to sit down again.

'Did you see it?'

The watch had a creamy face and a brown leather strap. Carmel knew it from her father's broad wrist, was familiar with the warmth of it, a small, heavy thing; it was slender and solid, like a ticking coin. He unbuttoned his cuffs and unlatched the clasp, and he was always leaving the watch somewhere – beside the ashtray, or on the shelf in the bathroom, or in the bedroom, where their mother was now listening as he went around the place, dragging stuff out from under the sink in the kitchen, where no watch was ever stored.

'Did you take it?'

And the thing was, her father could never find anything – he could be looking right at it. They used to laugh about how silly Daddo was in this regard. Her mother used to say, 'If it was a dog it would bite him,' a phrase that would take Carmel many years to understand.

When something was lost in that house, she would sing out a location, 'It's on the landing, it's on the bookshelf,' because their mother was the keeper of objects. She held everything in mind.

But she did not say where the watch was, and this annoyed their father. He banged about until her silence became a kind of wall he could not break through to go upstairs.

At least, that was Carmel's sense of the events on this particular afternoon. She was twelve years old: there were gaps in her memory, that seemed to open up even at the time. Mostly, they were about her own movements. Did she help look for the watch? More likely, she just stood there. Or she might have listened with her sister Imelda from the doorway of the front room. Even so, she could see her father, wherever he went in the house: it was like a story she knew from every angle, except her own. She watched him arrive at the foot of the stairs, put his hand to the banister and look up. And Carmel did not remember going after him, but that is what she must have done, because she really did remember him in the bedroom, where her mother lay. She saw him as you might see a stranger – from a distance. Though she also saw him in every detail.

Her father was then forty-seven years old. He wore a tweed jacket of greenish brown, the pockets dragged out of shape by little books and cigarette packs, cotton hankies and keys. His hair was shiny on his pink scalp. The chewed plastic of his glasses stuck out over one ear and the back of his neck was a deep, fat red.

This was the summer her mother had her breast cut off for a reason that could never be named. Their father ruffled through the clothes that were hanging in the wardrobe and he was crying. He pulled the little drawer of her bedside locker so hard it came all the way out and the contents emptied on to the floor. He looked down at them: her beads and bits, her appointment book, a tube of pink salve for the scar healing on her chest.

Their mother was in bed reclining against some pillows. She was propped up to facilitate drainage. Carmel had not seen the scar, whether it went up in a slit, or was horizontal with the blind skin tucked into it. Most likely, it was slant-wise up under her armpit, because the bandages went all around like a shoulder holster, and she could not lift her arm to get her nightie on; they had to rip the neck open along that side.

Her father noticed the uselessness of the empty wooden drawer in his hand and he let it drop behind him as he leaned forward and took her by the shoulders.

'Where is it?' he said.

She looked at him. Their father was hunched low, he was begging, but when she spoke her voice was very unyielding and cold.

'How would I know?' she said.

According to her sister Imelda, their father rifled through the bedding while she was lying in it. He frisked her down, saying 'Where did you put it? Where?' But as Carmel remembered it, their father made the bed. That was all. He plumped and patted the pillows and slipped his hands under the covers to smooth the sheet. He wanted to make their sick mother more comfortable. And of course, he might also have been looking for the watch, his intentions may have been mixed.

He stood at the end of the bed and lifted the comforter, a

soft thing of faded pink, that made a muffled sound as it fell to the floor. He did the same with a beige blanket which was twisted away. You could see her mother's knee and hip outlined under the thin cotton underneath, and her father groaned as he whipped this sheet high. It floated there; a rising cloth roof under which her mother's body was open to view. Carmel could not see her mother's obscured face, but the nightdress was ruched up and there was a little bare leg coming out of it, that twitched in the unexpected light. Her father let the sheet drop in a puddle and Imelda darted forwards, in order to pull the nightdress down.

Imelda was seventeen that summer, five years older than Carmel; she was entirely grown up. Later, she would say their father had drink taken, but at the time she nodded to him, and she did it in such a simple way that he bent to tuck the sheet back in, after she had flung it forward to drift over their mother's body. He pushed the edges in along the bottom of the mattress, before finding himself, abruptly, incompetent in the business of making beds.

'You do that,' he said, and turned away out of the room.

They heard him go down the stairs, and clatter through the hall. The front door opened and it did not close. A breeze from the garden found its way up to them, and they knew he was gone. This was the last time they saw their father in the bedroom, or in that mood. The next time he arrived at the house, everything had already changed.

It came back to Carmel in later years, watching ads for laundry, or when she worked for a summer as a chambermaid, or when she dressed her own single bed. The joy of cotton lifting, the difficulty beneath. At the age of twelve, Carmel felt something rise in her when the sheet rose up: there was a mixture of air and airlessness in her chest, and she did not know, for a moment, how to pick a side. The drifting cloth was beautiful, and the bare leg so pathetic. There was a snap of pain in there too – in the snap of the sheet. Her father stood with his arms wide and Carmel knew, of course, that he was in the wrong, that his anger about the watch was misplaced. But the insult to her mother's breast was very confusing. Carmel felt its tenderness as though in her own breast, which was still budding and sore. Sometimes it was not the flatness on her mother's ribcage that bothered her, nor even the secret slant of the cut, sometimes it was the bulge on the other side of her mother's torso – the way it slopped over to one side. And there was nothing to be done about that, now that it was on its own.

Her mother seemed distracted by her loss, as though her illness had come to remind her of something. That was the look it put in her eye: *Oh, I forgot. How could I have forgotten this one thing?* She was such a gentle person.

Their mother, Terry, read books all day, even when she was well. She lay in bed in the morning, she came down and propped the book against the teapot, she moved to a deckchair in the garden with her feet akimbo, and one arm flung high. If you spoke to her while she was reading she would look at you from a lovely distance.

And though you might imagine she was busy with two daughters and a husband to manage, she really wasn't that busy. She was never interested in cooking, for example, and often didn't. The Hoover sat gathering its own dust at the top of the stairs.

There was, under her smile, a kind of dryness which might have been reserve, or it might have been Terry forgiving people whatever it was that made them sad. 'Blessed are the Peacemakers' said the prayer on a decorative plate that she hung on her kitchen wall. Her daughters, when she was bed-bound, fought over the right to brush her hair.

Carmel's sister Imelda knew what the scar looked like because she dressed the wound in the evening, the nurse showed her how. Imelda went in to the bedroom with a white enamel basin and a folded cloth, and she turned to close the door with a holy look on her face. Afterwards, the only thing she said to Carmel was that she was to keep her trap shut.

'You hear me?'

Carmel was not sure her mouth was a 'trap'. Also, Imelda had slapped her cheek, before she spoke the words: You hear me?

And the slap made her voice hard to hear.

'Do you?'

'Do I what?'

'Don't give me that, alright?'

'What?'

'Just don't.'

Imelda slapped her again. And Carmel was in an utter sulk then, because who would she tell? And what would she say? She did not even know how to speak the word 'breast'. She tried it a few times in the bathroom: *breast*, *breast*, and it came out of her mouth all wrong.

The house was very quiet. The girls fought in whispers. Sometimes they heard their mother shift and sigh on the mattress, with its unpredictable interior twang. Or she might call for Imelda, and then again. Each time, she said the name neither louder nor softer than the time before.

'Imelda.'

'Imelda.'

'Imelda.'

'Imelda.'

Until Imelda was right there.

They sat her up on the pillows against a headboard of walnut veneer, with two carved gilt knobs on either side.

When the mattress dipped, a perilous gap opened below the board where you might put your arm down to retrieve lost books or other objects – which Carmel was sometimes asked to do. Or she fixed the window and settled the heavy, dark green curtain to keep the sunlight out of her mother's eyes. Then she sat in the button-back chair beside the wardrobe, if she was allowed to stay. She was as quiet as she could be, nested in her mother's discarded dressing gown and forgotten clothes.

After their father left that day, Imelda went downstairs to shut the front door and she came back up with tea. She bent over their mother, and held out a china cup through which the light shone. Carmel would always remember the inside line of golden tea, and the white circle of the china rim. There was a vagueness of space above the cup and, above that again, a curling haze of steam.

'Thank you darling. Thank you Imelda.'

The sun was on that part of the house all afternoon. It set, with great pageantry, in the bottom left-hand pane.

They must have set the place to rights, though Carmel did not remember this part of the day. Perhaps they left it as it was for a while; the sofa cushions scattered and every cupboard door wide open. Their father had broken a chair on his way out the door. He gave it a big kick. This chair had belonged to their mother's dead aunt, whose house it used to be. A decorative little thing, the aunt had stitched a needlepoint seat for it, in a design of flowers on a crimson ground. Phil had often scorned its delicacy. 'Who could sit on that?' he used to say.

Later he would confess there was trouble in his marriage. Later again he would say – as though he could not hear his own words – that his wife got sick and the marriage did not survive. He said this as though everyone listening would

know that, when a woman gets sick, the marriage deterio-
rates, clearly, the relationship cannot be sustained. Carmel
saw him say as much on television, in a recorded interview
some years later, but all she could think, when she watched
it was, *There he is. There he is. There he is.*

Carmel was in a pub on Suffolk Street at the time. The
clip was aired when she was in her last year at Trinity College, and she caught it by accident one evening, out drinking
with friends. So far as she knew, Phil was teaching in America. He was a poet of some reputation, and Carmel had
never really understood what that meant. Of course her
father was a man of consequence, that went without saying.
Her mother had married a poet. That is what she used to
call him, at those evening parties where people sorted
through the drinks tray, contemplating Campari now that
all the gin was gone. She called him 'my poet'.

'How's the poet?' the butcher might say, or even the
priest, and Terry loved all that.

'How's the poet?' she would repeat, at home, when she
told the girls of the most recent encounter.

'Oh, you know!' she would say back, as though life with
such a man could keep your eyeballs on a constant roll.

Their mother knew so little of the world. Terry went to a
boarding school in Dublin, spent a year minding young
children in Spain. In her first year at college, the rowing
team carried her down Grafton Street in a real boat. A poet
invited her for a walk, after which, a poem appeared in a
literary journal, with her name right there.

On Killiney Hill
for Terry

Through angelica and furze,
twice-scented meadow sweet,

releasing cocoanut, almond,
cardamon, some note beyond
my heart's circumference,
she peals her aromatic carillon,
my bluebell Protestant girl,
in the skirt she wore for Sundays

He courted her for three months straight. Terry came from the merchant classes of South County Dublin and Phil, who hadn't tuppence to his name, followed her declaiming, down one street and then down the next. The whole town was enthralled. One night she found a poem laid on her own pillow and, when she looked out, Phil was standing under the lamp post. She came out to kiss him in her nightie and never went back in, she said.

He had won her with verse.

They lived like teenagers, both of them. Terry had family money, but not enough of it, and when it ran out she just became confused. They had pork chops, they had no pork chops. There was nothing she could do.

When she turned twenty-five, Terry came into an inheritance and they moved their young family into a house in Dun Laoghaire, a harbour town on Dublin Bay. Here they began a suburban life, which was, for Phil, increasingly unproductive. He spent his Saturday morning digging vegetables in the long back garden, and this was how Carmel liked to remember him, heaping potato drills, a robin for company, his jacket slung on the handle of a fork close by.

Mostly, he was on his way out the door, patting his pockets and turning back for something left behind. He liked to walk out when the weather was good. He paused on the threshold to squint up at the sky, and he plucked a stolen buttonhole on his way to the bus stop, to drive the neighbours mad.

You never saw him write. Carmel thought of his poetry as entirely private. She opened her father's slim books with the same furtive, blanked-out pleasure as she might pull open his sock drawer.

This was the magic that made women kiss you, in their nighties, in the street.

Phil, the poet, had sleepy, straight eyelashes over bulbous brown eyes and a slim mouth always playing with the possibility of some small joke. He liked to tease a stalk of grass along his bottom lip. He liked to watch people and be amused. 'If you spend time around animals,' he used to say, 'there isn't much that will surprise you,' and something about his tone made cows sound really mysterious and rude.

And in the evenings, if he was home, he'd lift her on to his stocky thigh and dangle his watch into her hand.

'How are you, my old segocia?' he liked to say, and someone – she could not remember who – said, 'She's your spit, Phil. It's like looking at you twice.'

Carmel was twenty years old when she glanced up in a Dublin pub and saw an oddly familiar face on the wall-mounted TV; a man with her cow-lashed eyes who was talking, regretfully, about the end of his marriage to the woman who had inspired his most lyrical work. It is possible she was a little drunk already, though she felt just fine.

'Shush, everyone. *Shush.*'

Hours later, she was flat out on a friend's floor in a kip on Capel Street; the next morning, she would wake with vomit in her hair. But at the moment in the pub, when she looked up and saw her Daddo up there on screen, she had a rampaging sense of vindication. She lifted her fat pint glass high, and there was in the gesture, a glorious feeling, as though all the sheets in all the world had been lifted at once.

'Everyone. Shut UP!' she said. 'That's my fucking father up there.'

They glanced up at the TV.

'Which one?'

'That one,' she said.

It might have been his accent. Or maybe it was the rumpled old jacket he had on. But Carmel knew, by the discreet widening of their eyes, that a poet from Tullamore was, for her Trinity friends, a slightly comical figure.

'Oh, right.'

At one in the morning, Carmel was messy with drink, and there was a kind of hypocrisy to her sadness. She enjoyed it too much; the wailing and the tears, as she slopped about in the arms of the friend who was trying to lift her back on to the sofa from which she had slid, saying, 'My Daddo. My Dad.' It was a very great betrayal – her mouth making noises that her mind did not condone – and the next morning she knew she would not speak of her father again. The world was full of people who did not know him, except in a public kind of way. And the people who did know him – herself and her sister, especially – could not agree.

They fought about everything. Sometimes it was Imelda who said he only wanted to make the bed, and Carmel who claimed he was frisking their mother down, convinced she had stolen a stupid, cheap watch, because – as is well known – that is the kind of thing that bedridden women like to do.

There was sex also, that night in Capel Street. Not that Carmel had sex, but the friend who pulled her up off the floor, Aedemar Grant, got tired of her suddenly, delayed as she had been from her boyfriend in the bedroom next door. Carmel stretched out on the sofa in the living room, feeling very solid. The light from the street turned the wall beside her into a block of dull orange, the sky she saw through the window was a fathomless, electric ink. A passing car flicked a fan of white light across the ceiling, and after a while, another car did the same, surprising thing.

When the bedsprings started creaking on the other side of the wall, she experienced the sound as a repeated, sharp pain in her pubis that stayed in synch with the lovers for the first while and then was mercifully outpaced. It dropped away, as though her body had lost interest. It is possible that she slept. Sometime before morning, she left for the bathroom and puked herself a gush of acid, fluorescent beer.

The next time their father came to the house, it was no longer summer. Her mother's bandages, with their dreadful, stiffening stains, were gone. Hard to say how many weeks had passed – possibly only two or three. They put the bandages into the bin until the bin got too full and they had to remember the day and pull it out to the kerb. In the morning, they woke to a cry from their mother – they had not fixed the lid! So the girls ran around in their dressing gowns in the grey dawn, picking dirtied gauze and cotton wool from out of the neighbours' hedges. A few hours later, the bin was swung high by a man who walked at a slow swagger behind the lorry, and set down some yards further on. This man had tanned forearms and thick, dirty, workman's gloves.

Carmel brought the bin back up the path, empty. The inside of it was still crusted with stuff and Imelda hit her then. Imelda hit her all the time and Carmel could not cry out, for the sake of their mother. Imelda hit her silently around teatime. Or she hit her silently when they had to tidy up for Deirdre, their uncle's wife, who came to check up on them, knocking briskly at the front door, through which she stepped, turning to shake out an umbrella, before sailing through the hall. Auntie Deirdre specialised in comments about the plasterwork, which was surely falling down, and the colour schemes, such as they were, and the kitchen which was facing the wrong way, whatever that meant. Later, Carmel knew that she resented the size of the house. Also, she had five children of her own to tend. But, at the time, they hated Aunt Deirdre completely. It was one of the few things the two sisters agreed upon. They laughed for a week after she hugged Carmel's head.

Carmel was sitting at the kitchen table when Deirdre grabbed her whole skull and pulled it to her stomach. She pressed it there, so Carmel could practically smell her, under the skirt, and all she could hear was the creak of her girdle and the watery boom of her:

'There, there.'

'There, there.'

'There, there.'

'There, there.'

It was some time before Aunt Deirdre noticed that their father was gone – if she ever did notice he was gone – it was not a subject she ever discussed. Their mother was too sick for such talk. Besides, in those days, men were not expected to be around: the difference between married and deserted could be the seven hours your husband spent asleep in the bed. At least that is what Carmel thought later, when she wondered when the penny dropped for each of them.

And give us a pinny to bury the wran.

As for food, the girls lived on biscuits, rashers, sugar sandwiches. One day, when her mother was sitting up and pretending to be hungry, she sent Carmel to the butcher's for a 'side-line' chop. Carmel stood on the sawdusted floor as he pulled the rind away from the fat of the chop and she looked up at the poster of a cow, sectioned placidly for dismemberment.

'Where is the line?' she said. The butcher, who had dark eyebrows and dramatic, coarse white hair, pushed some of it away from his eyes, with the back of a hand that was raw from the cold, or darkened by blood.

He gave her a very blue-eyed look.

'Where do you think?' he said, and she did not know why he was laughing or what the joke was.

If Imelda slapped her too hard Carmel lit out the front door and went down to the seafront, where she idled along the road, waiting for a train to pass. She looked across the stretch of Dublin Bay, and down at the railway line with the grey stones that would cut you if you fell by accident over the wall. The weather slanted over the shining water and she said to herself that, if the train came before the rain, then her mother would get better. If the rain came first, her mother would die.

After the noise and relief of the train's passing, she would go to Orla Hughes' house and they would hang around in her bedroom. Orla Hughes was a bit fed up with Carmel, but her mother gave her buns to take back with her, that were, by the time she got to eat them, dense and moist from the Tupperware box. One time, when no one else was home, Orla's little brother let Carmel in, and they fried bananas in butter to see what would happen. They ate the whole bunch.

Carmel trailed home on these days knowing that she had been out too long and would soon be hit again. Usually about the shoulders but also on the side of her head. Sometimes so hard, the room took its time coming right again. And though she resented the unfairness, she did not blame Imelda for slipping into a temper, because somebody had to do it. The temper was always there, waiting for either one of them. When Imelda hit Carmel, it reorganised the pain.

And it was a kind of revelation, too. Afterwards, the world was very bright.

Of course Imelda refused to remember any 'hitting'. All she could say about that time was that Carmel was *such* a pain. That was the word she used. A 'pain'.

It passed. That also had to be said. The girls did so well. They did amazingly well. They were amazing girls. Their mother came home from hospital at the end of June, by the middle of August she was up and about, dressed to her shoes every day. She lay on the sofa, or sat in the armchair downstairs, where Imelda put a cushion on her lap, so she could hold her book high. She was pushing her own way up out of the chair.

Imelda got nine points in her Leaving Cert when she had been trying for twenty-three, and she wept for the first time that Carmel could remember. She shut her bedroom door and howled.

A few days later, she brought Carmel to a shop in Dun Laoghaire for her schoolbooks. They had to queue all the way up the stairs and hand the list over a counter at the top. In a room behind the counter, assistants ran from shelf to shelf to bring the books and tick the list, until there was a stack of them, each a different size, with a different smell and colour. Before they could claim them, Imelda had to write the amount on a cheque that she took from a secret place under her clothes, and this caused more running over and back, while they held up the whole queue.

A man came over and pointed to the signature on the cheque.

'Who is this?'

'It's my mother.'

'Is that her signature? I mean, is that her maiden name?'

'Sorry?'

Carmel was mortified as she walked back down the stairs and she was not sure, afterwards, whether to hate the new books or to love them anyway. Then her father was in the house, he just put his key in the door. This was days later. He had come 'about a cheque' or so they heard him say after he had shooed them out of the room to speak to their mother alone. Carmel had the sudden idea she would lose her new schoolbooks to her mother's stupidity. Of course she would. He had come to take the books back to the shop.

The other feeling she had was more painful. It was the hope that her father would put his arm around their mother to bring her upstairs, the way Imelda was now obliged to do. Carmel saw it so clearly, she almost thought it had taken place. Her mother with one good hand on the banister, her father with his arm about her slender waist. Slowly they went, her damaged side sheltered by his body as he supported her, one dragging step followed by the next.

People used to tell Carmel she had no imagination (*God, Carmel, you have no imagination*) but when she saw all this – and she saw it very vividly – she knew that he had left them. Or she knew that such a departure was possible. Your father, who opened the door and found you on the doorstep as the stork flew away, your father, to whom you had been *given* as a baby, could walk down to the bus stop and put his hand out for a number 46a, and never be seen again. And where did that leave you?

No one else lost their father. It was not a thing that happened to the girls at school.

After some low, moaning talk from the living room, he came out again, still wearing his overcoat. He turned to close the door behind him in humble, practical way – like a man coming out of the doctor's. And indeed, he walked towards the hall door slowly, with a slight limp.

Carmel and Imelda were on the first landing, and though Imelda tried to hold her back, Carmel ran down the stairs after him.

'Daddo. Daddo!'

The sky was doing its sunset thing over the houses across the way.

'Where are you?' she said, which was a strange thing to ask. What did she mean?

He looked down at her.

'There's my birdy. Will you take a peck?'

Carmel was a bit old for a peck, which was Daddo's word for a kiss, or the attempt at a kiss. It was your job, as a child, to wriggle away from a peck, a manoeuvre that started with a wrestle and ended up with you losing, squealing, to Daddo's planted lips. But for this peck, Carmel only managed to curve at the hip. Her feet were stuck to the floor as she leaned away from him, and when he caught the side of the face, the kiss ran through her in an arc, all down that side.

'Be good now,' he said.

After that, Carmel covered her schoolbooks with brown paper. And it wasn't long before she was tired of her mother and Imelda, the way they spent all their days mooning about. It also went without saying that, when Carmel had her own baby, many years later, she did not give it to any man. That would be like holding it out at arm's length and dropping it right there, on to the concrete. When Carmel had her baby, it came out of her silently, and it looked at her silently, and when they took it over to the other side of the room, she said, 'Bring it back.' She may have said this quite loudly. Because this baby was hers, and hers alone.

The Wren, The Wren
for Carmel

berry
glance
leaf
twisting
into bird
high-tailed
from hedge
to hand
she was mine

the wren
poked out
from the cup
of my fist
and was still

her eye, honour bright
to my vast eye
the whirr
of her pulse
ecstatic

the wren the wren
was a panic
of feathered air
in my opening hand
so fierce and light
I did not feel
the push

of her ascent
away from me

in a blur of love, to love
indistinguishable
my palm pin-pricked,
my earthbound heart
of her love's weight
relieved. And, oh,
my life, my daughter,
the far away sky is cold
and very blue.

IN THE EARLY spring of 1985, some months before Carmel's final exams, a man walked up the path one Saturday morning and knocked on the door. The women inside were all fully clothed – no one, in those days, went around in their dressing gown. So this person was let into the hall by Imelda who was wearing shoes with a medium heel, as might be expected on a Saturday morning at eleven, in Ireland in 1985. The caller was a small poet, in a large overcoat. His pupils were so huge they consumed the iris. This poet had been delegated by other poets, in Ireland and in America; they had dispatched him to the house because he was the right poet for the job. Harvey, he was called – which did not seem a poetic kind of name, but then neither was 'Phil' when you thought about it. Carmel joined Imelda in the hall while Harvey introduced himself as a friend of their father's and said, in a compelling soft voice, that he had come to speak to their mother, he had the saddest possible news. And indeed, there she was, standing in the kitchen doorway. Harvey moved swiftly towards her and although Carmel could not hear what words he used, she heard her mother's sharp little cry of response.

Many weeks later, after endless fuss and expensive phone calls, they drove to the mortuary chapel at Dublin airport to load up the coffin and follow it down to Tullamore. The hearse went slowly for a while and then, at some secret moment, started belting along the road. It took the bends so fast, Carmel became a little fixated on the square end of the box disappearing up ahead. This chase went on for three hours, then the hearse slammed on the brakes and they were right on top of it again. People turned to stare. A man took off his hat and nodded right at her, through the glass. A woman stood at a garden wall with her children lined up in a row, and they each made the sign of the cross as the cars crawled past. In the centre of Tullamore, shopkeepers stood in front of half-shuttered windows, pedestrians blessed themselves and, when she looked behind, Carmel saw these people step down off the kerb to follow the cortège, like zombies. That is what she said later to Aedemar Grant, it was Night of the Living Dead Culchie. These people, in their anoraks and tweed caps, were the residents of a place that Phil McDaragh had scorned in verse – excoriated – a town he refused to visit after his mother died. And still the local people came, as the priest later intoned, to welcome their poet home.

When they took their place at the top of the church, there was a man in military uniform in the other front pew; absurdly handsome and looped at the shoulder with fancy braid. The president of Ireland had sent him, apparently. He came over to shake their hands and to give a smart, heart-turning salute, and Carmel wanted to ask him if he thought Phil was any good, as a poet. Because no one her age thought he was any good, he was just an example of something. Also, this whole scene was an example of something. There were a few women in headscarves and about 400 middle-aged men, many of whom had started enjoying themselves right there in the church.

Her mother and Imelda were draped in matching black mantillas under which they plied little handkerchiefs with embroidered corners, while Carmel stuck to a packet of Kleenex and the truth. She was surrounded by hypocrites; her mother and sister especially, but also the liar talking up there on the altar and the various liars who came along to shake their hands before heading to the pub to get lubricated for the funeral the next day. They formed a slow shuffling queue, one man after another man, clasping and letting go her small hand. Carmel felt the silk of skin as they withdrew; shopkeepers and solicitors; the palm of a farmer cool and thick-skinned as the soles of her own feet.

Her father, Phil, also had calloused hands. He spent hours in the back garden working his long shovel, and she felt a sense of this toil touch her briefly in the sympathy of some man who moved along the line from Carmel to Imelda to Terry, murmuring and patting as he went. A woman in a coat of shushing, jade-coloured nylon paused in front of their mother, obliging her to look up. Terry rose from the pew to greet and embrace this person and the whole church noticed the gesture. Some old dear, her ankles gone crook over lace-up shoes.

The woman was – Carmel discovered this over hotel sandwiches – Phil's first girlfriend, the subject of one of his earliest poems, 'The Twining'. She turned up again for the funeral the next morning in the same old raincoat. An ordinary country woman with her grey hair firmly set under a Mass-going scarf. This was Phil's 'virgin ploughing'. Half the county could read as much in the local library, on a page that fell open at a single touch. And they could also read, if they had imagination enough to see it there, that her nipples were the colour of honeysuckle tips. Carmel could not forget the line. She remembered it every time she looked at a hedge. And the problem was – honeysuckle was all different shades, it was take your pick. Carmel looked at the bulbs of the woman's awful chest, pushed tight against her thin coat. She might have been fifty-six or seven, though she looked half dead to Carmel. She looked unfuckably old.

And she was not the only one. Carmel spotted others in the crowded church as the business of death proceeded; a large and sophisticated black hat, a pretty woman, her eyes red from weeping; flashes of glamour or grief that were out of place in this dismal congregation. These women caused a sharp little twist in her chest, which might have been pride. Her father was a charming man. Dumpy old Phil with the wet cough, the cigarette breath; the beautiful straight eyelashes, now completely still.

He had cut a swathe.

He threw a girl into the street, once, in her nightie, or he 'turned her out' into the street. A man told her this, back at the hotel. The man had a whiskey in one hand and a triangular sandwich in the other, and he did not know who he was talking to.

'Desperate stuff,' he said.

This must be the story about her mother coming out to kiss Phil in her nightie, Carmel thought. It had become corrupted by gossip, distorted over time.

'Why would he do that?' she said, and the man gave a short, plosive sound like a laugh.

'Pwuh!'

A woman had knocked at their own hall door, some years before. It happened on a winter evening, at the time when the milkman came to collect his money. But it wasn't the milkman. Terry opened the door to a woman's voice in the darkness outside. There was a low murmuring, that shifted into an altercation. The woman wanted to come inside, into the hall.

'We don't want your kind,' Terry said. 'We have no interest in your kind around here.' And she had pressed the door back against this person, whoever she was, until it clicked fully shut.

'Who was that?'

'Just someone,' Terry said, meaning the exact opposite.

The girls were very impressed by the way their gentle mother had turned fierce at the right moment. She had protected them all.

They peeked out from behind the curtains and saw the woman at the gate, looking back at the house. She held on to the bars with red woollen gloves.

Now, Carmel thought, she might be in the congregation behind them. *Just Someone* might walk after Phil's hearse along with everyone else. There was nothing to stop her. She could follow his dead body through the town to the cemetery, all the way to the lip of his grave.

What was she going to do then? Throw herself down on top of it, as they lowered him in? Turn skywards and let the earth fall?

There had been a couple of years, in which Phil's absence went oddly unremarked by the women in Dun Laoghaire. His post continued to drop through the letter box. There was a pile of envelopes built up for months on the hall table, until Terry lost patience and swept them all into the bin.

Carmel came home from school one day to find a postcard with her name on the back. On the front was an abstract nude made of blue segments. A message in Phil's open scrawl said, 'Just been to see this. Matisse so joyful and the best kind of [unreadable word], the dancing colour!!!! Love, Daddo.' She looked at it for a long time. Her eye interrogated the long curve of thigh and the slender torso. The breasts were tucked up under the nude's armpits and Carmel did not think it would be natural to have breasts that high up, or even practical. But the shape was very fluid and elegant. The postmark said 'Cannes'. Her mother – perhaps spitefully – suggested she might go to stay with him in France, if he ever sent an address, and this made Carmel more confused. How would she get there?

Another card arrived later the same year. It showed a white windmill with a skeleton sail and 'Mykonos' written in cursive underneath. This was addressed to the McDaragh Family and it answered a question none of them had asked: 'I am improving every day here, the bells come over the water, and the little cafe has a vine roof with bits of leaf drifting down. Grapes! Hic!' This was illustrated by a cheery cartoon of a tilted martini glass with a cocktail olive. 'Eternally yours, Daddo.'

None of them got excited about that one.

Out of the blue, two years later, a birthday letter.

'Dear Carmel, You are sixteen. I find that hard to believe and too lovely to believe. You are sixteen, and even though you take after me in looks, I know you must be beautiful because you are. Send a photograph to your old Daddo, the last I have, you are my birdy still.'

Carmel shifted on the wooden pew. She was wearing black tights borrowed from Imelda, whose wardrobe was always funeral-ready, but they were too small and this made her body feel tight and full of blood, like a tick.

'Weep no more, woeful shepherds, weep no more, /For Lycidas, your sorrow, is not dead'. A poet from Cork was up in the pulpit, delivering a eulogy. He clasped the wooden rail, leaned back and closed his eyes.

'He was born, the last of five children, in a stone cabin in the townland of Killiskea. He was born in one room, as the poem tells it, while in the other, the family day proceeded.

The thatch of that place is now rotted away, the walls fallen in, but his words are with us still.'

He opened his eyes and leaned towards them smiling, like he did not mean a word of it. He might break out a wink any minute.

'Phil McDaragh was the finest love poet of his generation. His first collection, *The Twining*, was a lyric flower plucked from a ditch, the next, *Sleeping With the Enemy*, was an argument with the English language itself. *Migrations*, his third, was an ode to the wandering human soul.'

He made it sound as though Phil had not left his family, so much as gone travelling for his work. Phil was off arguing with Dante or with Ovid because someone had to do all that. If her father stopped writing poetry, then something awful would happen. The veil of reality would be ripped away.

The last of his work was the sweetest. Written in exile, his *Versions* was a chapbook of poems translated from the Irish. These held a modest mirror up to the foolish hearts of lovers everywhere. They would be remembered for their fondness, their rich simplicities, and humble generosity.

> Lay your dark head upon my breast,
> your honey mouth with scent of thyme

'Every town needs a poet,' said the poet from Cork. 'In order to make them feel like someone. To make them feel eternalised.'

At which point, she could hold out no longer. Carmel turned to look at the American wife, who was three rows behind them, fumbling through the specially printed missalette. Because, as everyone in the church knew and no one knew how to say, Phil's foreign divorce had been followed within weeks by a foreign marriage in New York's City Hall.

This fact was not mentioned by anyone on the altar, certainly not by the poet from Cork, though the priest shifted to a 'special' voice to say, 'and all those Phil loved, including his dear friends across the pond'.

The American wife wore a black bouclé skirt and jacket – much nicer than Terry's – she dressed like Jackie Kennedy. She had arrived with a couple of tall male Americans in buff-coloured CIA trench coats (though they were, in fact, also poets). She was very pale and she did not cry. This woman existed and did not exist. Phil's second wife – his current and proper widow – was keeping her head down, because her instinct was keen and this was Ireland, a country where divorce was not legal, it was too unpoetical. The wonder was, they had let her get off the plane.

Inheritance

I am of Tullamore, the son
Of a gombeen man, so I know
The use of a good solicitor,
The value of nothing said,
The price of love lost
Or gained. To which we add
The cost of modern marriage,
The daily tally for the bag man
And the priest; ten Hail Marys
Twenty-two Glory Bees.
I know the gavel knock
On altar stone, wind at the door,
Ash in the grate,
A foreign body in the bed,
The bank of her belly,
The locked safe of her heart.

Dear Carmel,

You are sixteen. I find that hard to believe and too lovely to believe. You are sixteen, and even though you take after me in looks, I know you must be beautiful because you are. Send a photograph to your old Daddo; the last I have, you are my birdy still. There isn't a day passes that I do not miss you and miss your sister, and the things I gather in to me here are picked for you, the joy of Matisse, that crimson wallpaper, the wedges of blue. In Italy I wandered one gallery and watched two little girls as they looked at the beauty all arrayed, that soakage in their small faces, a pinched anxiety in one (but that would be more your sister) you were always a sensible child, dear Carmel, and I think you would very sensibly know what you were looking at when you saw it. Such was the infinity of my failure in your eyes (truthfully yes) I would like you to turn that infinite gaze to the masters of the Uffizi where I was that day, the Bronzinos especially. I am a wandering soul who is tethered still in you. Live beautifully. Live well. You are sixteen now, and you do not feel it, but the world is yours this day as it never will be again. You own your youth and everything that comes with that. It is all yours. All of it. Look after your mother, she knows my heart. Don't be good, she will tell you to be good, but there is no need. Dear child, dearest child. It is late now and I am looking over a glittering dark sea, westward to you.
    love eternal
    Daddo

AFTER HER FINAL exams, Carmel took a six-week TEFL course in the centre of Dublin, then she got on a plane and went to Italy. She started in Pisa at the beginning of September and moved to Milan a few months later, when Pisa went wrong for her in various ways. But Milan was corporate and dull and, after three months of it, she took another job in Florence, realising, as she saw a flock of pigeons rise over the statue of David in Piazza della Signoria, that the Italians drove her nuts. They looked at her as though she did not quite make sense. Why was she so uncouth? Why was she so assertive and so awkward at the same time? Please, they seemed to say. Please. Just.

She hung out with other English teachers, from Nottingham and Waterford and London: a roving band of young people who partied up and down the Via Fiesolana, falling in love and out of love. At weekends, they wound up in a place called the Bluebird that never seemed to close, and they drank sour red wine out of thick little tumblers until the noise of shutters going up for a new day scattered them to bed. Once or twice, she told someone the few bearable details of her childhood's end and was surprised to find, when they met her in daylight, that their eyes had not changed – despite the hugeness of her story. Perhaps they did not care.

But one girl put her arm around her at two in the morning in the Italian night air and wept. This person was called Vittoria. The next day, she dabbed a sprig of blossom on the edge of Carmel's lunch plate and Carmel's heart spilled out like a kicked bucket. The two of them sat long over espressos and harsh cigarettes and, no matter how often the Italian put the tiny, fat-rimmed cup to her lips, there always seemed to be some coffee left.

Vittoria knew how to eat, she knew how to dress, she knew how to live. She was so graceful in all her gestures, Carmel found it hard to know what she really felt about her new friend. This is what she blurted, in any case, late one night on Elba, where the gang went for the Easter break.

'I don't trust you,' she said.

'*Cosa?*'

They were staying in a large house on the north side of the island which belonged to Vittoria's family. No one lived there through the winter now: there were old linens in the cupboards, leather sandals gone stiff in a corner, the pictures on the walls were of flowers arranged in baskets, and the floors were of cool, worn stone. Something was mating in the rafters and no one could sleep. In the afternoons, four of them walked down to the village, which had no beach, and they ate custard tartlets sprinkled with pine nuts, before buying provisions and wine to haul back up the hill. On the last evening, Vittoria made a big stew filled with white beans and the wrong bits of pork. They drank brandy and danced to a cassette of Johnny Hallyday, because that was all they could find. At one point, Vittoria flopped down beside Carmel on the cane sofa and turned to her with a smile. She reached a hand over to her friend's hair and Carmel flinched back.

'*Cosa c'è?*'

It took a moment before Carmel found the large thing she needed to say.

'I just don't know if I can trust you,' she said. 'I just don't *trust* you, you know?'

Vittoria gave a puzzled look.

'Oh Carmel,' she said, giving each syllable of the Irish girl's name its own serious weight. And then she smiled.

Back in Florence, the espressos became less frequent. Vittoria went every day after class to the public swimming pool, a place where Carmel could not possibly follow.

'Come to the pool!' she said, as if she did not know that Carmel was Irish and would rather die than conduct a conversation while wet. She was capable of partying late into the night, however, and in early June there was a blundering series of events with Vittoria's boyfriend – though he was not, technically speaking, her boyfriend at the time. And though the sex was, technically speaking, sex, it was oddly empty – Vittoria was not 'there', as she had been 'there' in the sorrowful and lovely flirtation that preceded the physical act. This took place in Carmel's attic room, that was hot and stagnant with the smell of pizza and non-specific rot, and some white flower that had seeded in the gulley outside.

'You don't move so much,' he said afterwards, conjuring Vittoria – who thrashed about, presumably, like a dying swan – and Carmel listened to his footsteps, after he left, rising from the narrow street below.

Sex was not as interesting as the people who did it, she decided. It was almost the opposite of a relationship. It was certainly, often, the end of one.

Then Vittoria found out.

'It is you,' she hissed. 'It is you who cannot be trusted.'

Her anger was so theatrical and large, it made Carmel

feel a bit giddy. Vittoria had dumped the guy before the trip to Elba. Now she was crying because somebody else wanted him. Real tears. She turned her face up to the light, so you could see them.

'Oh fuck off, Vittoria,' Carmel said. 'He wasn't even any good.'

But the loneliness was baked into her as she walked the beautiful oven that was Florence in June. The eyes of her friends seemed changed because of the non-crime she had committed; stealing something from Vittoria, even though Vittoria had already thrown it away.

On the afternoon before she left for good, Carmel went to the Uffizi for the first time. Her packing was nearly completed, she would, later that evening, drop by the Blue-bird and say her loud and fake goodbyes. Meanwhile, she was lost in the beautiful havoc of the quattrocento. So many colours: coral and cobalt, ochre and ultramarine. She had arrived in Italy – properly, finally – on her very last day.

It took her some time to notice the statues, because they were white. She walked a long corridor lined with ancient busts of important middle-aged men, who looked just like modern middle-aged men. A small gallery was filled with ghostly, solid figures, some serene and forbidding, others reaching out in dread or supplication. There were frantic dramas of pursuit and capture, nymphs on eternal pause before the kiss. In the middle of its own room was a block of marble from which the peachy, never-moving bottom of a sleeping woman curved and fell. A lone male tourist was checking the front of this piece and when Carmel took her turn to look, furtively, on the figure's underside, she saw a simple breast on show, and also an equally simple cock and balls.

Outside, she tried to breathe, but the still hot air gave no respite. She sat under the awning of an expensive cafe, thought it was the shade she would miss here and not the sun. She would miss the hallways and courtyards and squares, the carefully guarded half-light where people lived their lives. Italy was a funny mix of beautiful spaces and gaudy *stuff*. The work on the walls of the Uffizi was not ugly, but it had inspired an enormous amount of ugliness, and she would not miss that.

Later, in her attic room, she tried to write a last note to Vittoria. The rip of the first sheet of paper was a tiny anguish to her, but when she tore the second draft up, over and back, it was the sound of her own indifference. She found it hard to care.

The whole episode was not a love affair so much as a falling-out with a woman who made her feel wanted or unwanted – and it would be many years and some dust-ups later before she could state it as a truth about herself: Carmel liked men – you might even say she preferred them – but she seemed to have trouble sleeping with them, and her emotional life was filled with women with whom she did not get along.

She arrived home after a year away; her backpack jammed with stale-smelling cotton sundresses, clapped-out flip-flops and badly chosen scarves. If she heard one more word of Italian, she said, she would explode.

The house in Dun Laoghaire was eerily itself. They all had tea in the kitchen, then Carmel headed upstairs to a bath. She pulled a towel she had forgotten out of the hot press and when she came down to the sitting room, clean and warm, she found them in the same chairs as when she had left an hour before – and also a year before that. Her mother and her sister: a woman and a similar woman sitting together, close enough to hold hands. The TV was on. The big rug was a Chinese maze of taupe and pastel pink, the armchairs were a floral chintz, the curtains a polyester velvet in Gainsborough blue. They sat in the middle of this madness: green cardigan and brown cardigan, skirt and skirt, brown shoes, black shoes.

Why are you not holding hands?

It was evident to Carmel they had not moved, in a year when she had moved so much: there had been so many fallings-in and fallings-out, so many people and farewells. These two seemed, to each other, to be sufficient. Imelda was finishing her doctorate out in UCD. She cycled in and was home by five, when she made a light tea. Neither of them ate very much, and the food they did eat was mysteriously bad – processed ham, sliced pan, tubs of coleslaw. All this was served by Imelda on white tablecloths, using china plates, as though it were something special. They sat together in one room and then another. They ate and rose, washed and dried, switched on the TV, complained about the TV, switched off the TV and moved, from one light switch to the next, upstairs to bed. They slept well – so far as anyone knew – and woke to do it all over again.

Imelda tended to her mother as though she were already a memory, or some kind of work in preparation. When the cancer returned it became clear what they had been waiting for. It took their mother eighteen months to die, much of which was indescribable to Carmel, even as it happened.

She had, by then, a job in a language school in the centre of Dublin. Class finished at four thirty, after which Carmel took the train out to Dun Laoghaire, waiting for the moment they would shoot clear of houses and back gardens, out along the edge of Dublin Bay. Some days, the waves surged against the wall by the railway track. Other times, the sand stretched to the horizon which was marked by a thin, brilliant thread of sea.

Carmel walked the half-mile up from the station and let

herself into the house to take over from the carer. She sorted what needed to be sorted, sat with her mother, first downstairs and some months later, up in her bedroom. She helped her out of the chair, and then out of the bed, hauling her up under the arms, moving her over to the commode, lifting her off the pot in a staggering embrace, trying not to let the groaning woman fall, as they lurched towards the bed.

When Imelda got in, Carmel went downstairs and did a round of laundry, washing or folding or taking in of her mother's towels and sheets, then she caught the train to town, looking out again at the tide, which was up close or fabulously distant; the water racing towards her over flat sands, or slipping away.

One afternoon in the hospice, Terry sat up – impossibly. She looked from one to the other daughter as though surprised to find them so grown, and she asked questions which they answered in a rush of wonder. She was herself again. Even her voice was strong.

Terry said that, 'Oh!' she had been dreaming of Spain; the time she spent as an au pair in Palma de Mallorca, when she was fresh out of school.

'It was nothing like tourist Spain it was like – you have no idea – all those rules and manners and you were never told what they were. Everyone, the old contessa and the cook, or whatever you called her, living in the highest state of disapproval, even the children looking at me like I hadn't a clue, and of course I didn't. I went out one afternoon when the whole place was asleep, I wanted to get to the sea and I got so lost of course I did. All those narrow streets. But I went down and down again. I thought I would die if I did not get to the water and then, there it was.'

This was an old story. It involved a bad man who clucked at her and made some obscene gesture as he moved to block her path. But in this – surely final – version the man did not make his customary appearance in the dark alleyway. Instead, Terry looked intently ahead of her, as though seeing again the gap between the old houses that gave on to the sparkling sea.

'Your father understood all that,' she said.

'Yes,' said Imelda.

Carmel said nothing. It was too painful, this foolishness of her mother's. Especially now.

'Of course there were repercussions,' she said, as though allowing for the fact of them, her children, in the room.

'No,' Imelda reassured her. 'No.'

At which, her mother brightened and glanced at the door.

'Any chance of a cup of tea?' she said. And though it had been weeks since her digestion had failed, days since she had taken anything by mouth, it felt to them all as though tea would be exactly right. It would be just the thing.

Imelda made as if to go, but she could not leave this vision, this miracle: the gift of their mother back in the room with them. Terry looked from one to the other of her daughters.

'What?' she said, fondly.

She lay back on the large hospice pillows and when Imelda said, 'Will I get you that tea?' it was like asking someone who was no longer there.

A bare four weeks later, the sisters sat in a solicitor's room on Georges Street and discovered that their father had left his deserted wife exposed to the debts he incurred after he had left her. According to the impeccable Mr Ledwidge, Terry's liability ended with the American divorce. Sadly, however, under Irish law, she was considered domiciled with Phil for the preceding years of what might be called marital limbo. It was hard to know the extent of the difficulty, but he thought he should flag this with them first.

'Thank you,' said Imelda – quite sincerely.

He paused.

He opened the will and read it.

The sisters, hunched on the other side of the table, looked at the papers in his hand and thought about their mother sitting in this room, not so long ago – in her nice oatmeal-coloured suit, perhaps, her official, cream handbag and shoes. She would have known the cancer was back. She must have been alone.

It was hard to hear anything he said.

She left the house to Imelda. To Carmel, she had bequeathed a portfolio of shares and savings bonds; blue chip investments, which would bring more than two thousand a year. Sadly, Mr Ledwidge said, the debts would have to be paid before the estate could be settled, here meanwhile were some papers for them to sign. The girls thanked him and then did nothing he had asked them to do for quite a while.

It became apparent – really quite slowly – that Carmel's shares would be used to pay the outstanding debt. Because the debt was money and the shares were *like* money, but the house was incontrovertibly the house. And Carmel couldn't figure out what was going on exactly, because other people – their Auntie Deirdre for example – seemed to expect this too. It was assumed that Carmel would hand everything to her sister, because Imelda had been so dedicated to their mother, and because that would be a nice thing to do. Besides, Carmel was earning now. Imelda was still finishing her endlessly unfinished PhD, so she *needed* the house, which happened to be a four-bedroomed early Victorian, not too far from the sea.

It wasn't about the money, they were all agreed on that.

The important thing was to honour their mother's wish that Imelda continue to live undisturbed in the home they had shared to the end, and out of which Carmel had walked, of her own free will.

Carmel ended up ringing the solicitor about some other matter, and when his expensive voice came on the line, said, 'Is that supposed to be fair?'

There was a silence.

Carmel said that something was happening, she thought something wrong was going on. The solicitor, who had known Terry since college, said it was his impression their mother was devoted to both her children. This seemed a bit familiar. Carmel had not expected him to be kind.

'Is it possible she did not always open her post?' he said.

Carmel was shaking as she drove around to the house. She had no idea how she parked, whether she closed the car door behind her, as she fumbled in her bag for her key and went inside. And she would have no memory of what she said to Imelda, who was sitting in her expected place in the dining room, now opposite an empty chair. It was a terrible row. Just terrible.

According to Imelda, Carmel put hands on her sister, but this was not Carmel's version – not by a long way. As she remembered it, Carmel stood beside Imelda and slid her horrible dinner off the table and on to the floor. It was a gesture, not an assault. But Imelda lunged up at Carmel, the chair overbalancing behind her and a sound like a stuck seagull coming out of her throat. Carmel shoved Imelda back into the upturned chair legs, and pushed again while her sister was dancing her way out of them. And again with both hands, when she was upright, back and back further. A little *hugff* of air came out of Imelda as she hit the wall and Carmel shifted into a brighter place. It was hard to tell the shape of the room, or the order in which things happened. It was as though her skull was filled with light. Despite which, both the women's movements remained unheroic, comical, utterly silent.

Imelda came off the wall flailing. This obliged Carmel to reverse through the double doors into the living room, past the twin armchairs with their floral covers, up against the curtain which she grabbed and twisted between them, and someone – probably in fact Imelda – trod on the hem so a few hooks popped off the plastic rail. Carmel shoved at the shape behind the cloth and caught Imelda on the chest, a lucky push which landed her sister on the floral carpet, squarely on her bottom. The stupid look on her face made Carmel smile and she was on top of Imelda with slapping hands, then more effectively with a few solid kicks to her crawling-away backside. Halfway to the hall, Imelda spun around on her hands and knees, her face a contorted mask of purple and spit. And still she was silent and Carmel was silent as she scrambled to her feet and Carmel renewed her advance, jabbing her fingers into the space under her sister's collarbone until Imelda was backed up against the banister. Imelda's knees lifted in a series of failed kicks, her hand clawed at the side of Carmel's head, and she managed to duck out and run down to the kitchen, where there was the sound of the cutlery drawer yanked out. Carmel arrived before she could find a knife and Imelda grabbed the sugar bowl instead, spinning around to hit her sister with a swirl of white. This was such a surprising weapon, it gave them pause. Carmel put her hand to her face and felt the coarse grains sticking there. She shook out the collar of her shirt and heard a fizzle of sugar hit the floor.

The bowl was still in Imelda's hand: a heavy glass, three-legged thing, that Phil had once stolen from a coffee shop in town, it was now empty and scabbed with white. Imelda had not thrown it at Carmel, who glanced down to check, and then up at her sister's face.

All of this had happened in silence even though there was no need for them to be silent – they both remembered this at the same time. Their mother was not upstairs.

She was dead.

'How dare you,' Imelda said, her voice rising to a shriek. 'How dare you come into my house like that.'

And Carmel bellowed right back at her: 'She loved me just as much as she ever loved you.'

Though that was not, strictly speaking, accurate. It was their father who had loved Carmel best. The wren poem was written for her. Her name was right there on the page. 'For Carmel'.

And, oh, / my life, my daughter.

Carmel did not stay for the empty aftermath. She had no interest. She drove home with sugar in her hair, her hands sticky on the steering wheel. Impossible to get rid of it all; the granules crackled underfoot in the kitchen of her own flat afterwards, for days.

In the ensuing silence, there was nothing for Carmel to do but wait for her share of the inheritance to come through. Actually quite a lump sum, if she wanted to work it that way, which she did, and got herself a mortgage for a place – much smaller of course, and too close to a busy intersection, but her own.

It was a year where the sisters did not speak except through the costly and forbearing Mr Ledwidge who said later he had never seen anything like it, and he had seen them all.

Migrations

It is October. White-fronted geese
are back in The North Slob,
pink footed, greylag, Whooper swan,
beating the air over Donegal to
Carlingford Lough. All over Ireland,
the birds are wintering down.

In the family grave at Killiskea,
my cold mother and her cold sister
disagree in death, as they like to do.
I am the last of them, servant of the line,
bird keeper. I pick a fallen quill
from the strand at Omey
look to the sea for ink.

MOST OF THE time, when Carmel slept with someone, it was because her period was due. She woke up one morning with a man in the bed and, when she went out to the bathroom, the blood was right there – as though he had poked it out of her. For which she was often grateful.

So that's what was going on.

'Good morning!'

An odd bunch, over the years, her former lovers. You wouldn't exactly invite them to the same party – or to any party, some of them – though she was a bit of an outlier herself, Carmel realised. She looked at the girls from school who found one or another man to marry, 'Oh, he's lovely!' and could not help but find it all a bit high-pitched.

Shortly after college, Aedemar Grant announced her engagement – that is actually what she called it – and Carmel was glad not to be asked for bridesmaid. Orla Hughes did the honours, and her puffy apricot dress was the only bit of comic relief in an otherwise relentless day. The groom was not the bed-creaker from Capel Street, but another version of the same thing: solid, back-slapping, sound: good man, right you are, careful now, there you go.

'In all fairness,' he said in his speech. Six times. Carmel could not imagine what it would be like to live with such a person. Aedemar would, *in all fairness*, be a long time hanging his washing out on the line.

'I'll give it six months,' she said to Orla Hughes, but two years later, Aedemar was still very much married, with a baby on the way. And that was another hoo-ha, from the coy refusals of alcohol to the coy announcement, to the considerable amounts of self-obsession. Aedemar did not seem to realise that this thing would happen to her body whether she was stupid, or clever, or in a coma. She thought it was in some way about her.

The baby quickly made it known that it was, in fact, massively about the baby, from the last-minute epidural, to the grade 4 tear, to the six weeks of colic, not to mention all the love required, often of a hysterical kind. The same mixture of cooing and shrieking around the cot that happened around the wedding; the sweetness of it set Carmel's teeth on edge. It was the sound women make, she thought, when they are offering their lives up for slow destruction. And *loving* it. And doing it *for love*. And feeling *sorry* for people who did not have this *love* in their lives, because my goodness, it was the winning ticket. It was success itself. It was the only game in town.

Brian, her gay friend, asked Carmel to have his baby one evening when they were all very drunk. Or to have his baby goo mixed with his partner's baby goo and the partner said, 'He doesn't want a baby, he can't even manage a dog.'

'I do want a dog.'

'Seriously?'

'I have always wanted a dog.'

'No you don't.'

'I am great with dogs,' said Brian.

And Carmel wanted to wind the conversation back to where it started; to the joke that wasn't exactly funny and could not be mentioned again.

Because it was already known, somehow, that Carmel would not have a man in her life. How did that happen? She was only twenty-seven. People knew what kind of a person she was, and what were her prospects and limitations, most of which they had set themselves. 'You are so independent!' they said, or, 'I don't know how you do it!' The worst was, 'Oh, you wouldn't like it.' This was something Aedemar took to saying about some ordinary human event; a child's birthday, a trip up the mountains. And it was true, Carmel would not like it.

Even so.

The evening of the gay goo conversation, Carmel went into her new house and she took off her clothes in front of the long mirror in the hall. Up close, it was not hard to understand why people wanted to stay away. The pearl of her breast was grained with something that would become droop, the nipple was bobbled with superfluous pink bumps. Carmel passed her hands over her lower belly and looked up into the mirror with a sad expression on her face. But it was no use – her image had no interest in how she felt, or tried to feel. It was indifferent to the drama of the glass.

And then, from six feet back, she looked fine. She looked, at this distance – standing in the shadow and lit from one side – painterly and human, a woman hopeful and alone. At exactly this many inches and feet away from someone else she could conduct a great romance.

But really, Carmel had no patience for these postures. Her body was not her enemy, it was a practical thing. And her new house, when she walked in it, opened out from room to room.

*

Orla Hughes announced she was giving up pubs, she had found herself a wine bar.

'Why didn't you ask me?' said Carmel.

'Oh,' said Orla. 'I didn't think you would like it.'

She was right. What Carmel liked – what Carmel missed since her college pals grew up and grew away – were three or four pubs in the centre of Dublin, a table full of pints, around which stupid, large opinions might be aired. Now, Orla wanted to hook her heels on to the crossbar of a high stool in a short skirt, and she wanted Carmel to sit beside her in a silk camisole and clumped mascara, trying to attract attention she did not wish to receive.

This pathetic wine-bar phase lasted about three months, after which Orla disappeared into an affair with her boss – one that had actually been going on all along. In a fit of irritation, Carmel took a guy home from the office Christmas party, and did not enjoy it one bit. The next day, she lay beside the space he had left, traced a hairline crack in the ceiling plaster and thought, Maybe I'll do the house instead. Maybe that.

It was a neat house in a Victorian terrace, with granite steps up to the hall door. The neighbours put the kitchen downstairs, but Carmel decided to have the bedrooms on the garden level so you could walk out in the morning in your bare feet on to grass. One day she would knock through on the top floor, so it was all one long room, with a big south-facing window at the kitchen end. She could put an upholstered bench under the sash window overlooking the street, so you could sit and watch the world go by. Everywhere her eye fell, she saw something to improve.

After Carmel stopped sleeping with men, they seemed to like her much better. They got along really quite well. She was such a terrific colleague, Carmel was promoted and then promoted again. At the age of thirty she was running a

rival language school to the one where she had started out –
they could eat her dust – and she was beating her former
employers into the ground. She had not slept with anyone
in three years, and that was absolutely fine. There were
days when it seemed as though the world spoke about
nothing but sex, when she heard people be publicly horny
and weirdly self-exposing, forty, fifty times a day.

'The less you do it,' she wanted to say, 'no really, believe
me – the less you will care.'

One day a student came to her office with a cramp in his
stomach that bent him right over. Carmel put him in her
own car and drove to A&E but, once within sight of the
parked ambulances, the guy declared the pain was gone.

'No hospital,' he said. 'No hospital!' like a man with a
visa problem, though Carmel knew his papers were fine.

'Seriously. You should go in.'

'No.'

And he indicated, with large and irritable authority, that
she turn around. Then he told her to drive him home, which
she did. She brought him inside his, quite expensive, flat
and, when she stopped at the door to say goodbye, his face
fell to her shoulder, followed by the rest of him. He col-
lapsed down around her and took a shuddering breath
which may have been the beginning of tears. Carmel patted
his large back and, after staying a moment too long, lifted
her face as his hand pressed into the curve of her spine.

'Thank you,' he said. And this was such a broken,
vulnerable word, Carmel allowed the kiss, and she continued to pet him as he moved her across the carpet and
through the open bedroom door. He seemed very experienced. Edgardo, he was called. An older student, maybe
twenty-one.

After the first rush of it – the push of his thigh, the slip of his tongue – Carmel started to notice his hand as he placed it here or there. Her skin going wrong. Her body souring at his touch. It was always so unpleasant, the moment when desire turned into the opposite of desire. She wished she'd had a few drinks, to get her over the hump.

He came almost immediately – which was a relief of the wrong kind, for Carmel – but instead of withdrawing, he rummaged softly around a moment, he just kept going. And this new tempo caught her off-guard. Carmel was briefly exhilarated by it. She found herself willing him on and, when his rhythm caught, she blanked into a different state. It was as though a switch had been thrown. Afterwards, she wondered if this was what everyone talked about when they talked so incessantly about sex. She did not think it was. This was not perversion or pleasure, it was huge and empty and, at the bright, distant edge of it, a feeling of agony, almost. She thought if it happened again, she might not survive it. And, for the four remaining weeks of Edgardo's stay in Dublin, she had sex with him five more times. Each time was different, and all were slightly annoying. There was the insistent fact of Edgardo, an arrogant young man who would grow up to be, one day, a powerful fool. There was more or less ordinary intercourse; arousal, aversion, soreness; sometimes a sense of completion, more often a sense of loss. Only on the last night, with his packing scattered around the place, did she absent herself again, or realise, after the fact, that she had been gone. It was not flying, it was stepping through a trapdoor and waiting for the smash. Which duly arrived. And when she came back to herself, there was his warmth and size beside her. Edgardo, who did not pause to stroke her face or whisper, 'Thank you', before pulling the sheet away from himself; some kind of anger lifting off his nakedness into the dark air of the room. In the morning, he would be gone.

'At home, I have a woman,' he said.

'I am sure you do.'

It was unconscionable. It was completely unprofessional. And it made her pregnant – a fact she decided not to discover until some weeks after she had mislaid his file.

Carmel was an unusual person. Everyone said so. 'God you're great,' they said. 'I don't know how you do it.' When her bump began to show, at around four months, they stopped saying anything, and Carmel was happy to find that she had started to hate them all.

The Bird of Lagan Lough
(translated from 'Int én bec',
anonymous, ninth century)

the wee bird,
yellow-beaked,
blurting sweet
melody over
grey water
is a blackbird
hidden in gorse
(yellow, of course)

HER EARLY CRIES were so thin and pathetic, Carmel woke up to them dreaming of the moon. It was summer and they were both often naked, more or less. The baby lay on the loose skin of Carmel's deflated stomach and she was such a damp little thing; she sweated and wriggled, as though surprised by the emptiness of so much air.

They did not leave the house for a week and then they really had to leave the house to get more milk formula – even though Carmel had three more days of formula left in the cupboard. Hunger was different now. When Carmel was hungry for her child, it felt like murder, or religion, it was a fearsome thing.

It took two hours to get the baby ready and into the lethal, incomprehensible sling (this button? this clasp?) before Carmel could walk out into the loud world, with a creak in her ass and her breasts rock solid on either side of its lolling head. This happened despite the fact that the baby was bottle-fed. Carmel's body could not be stopped. It kept trying to feed the skinned little animal she carried mewling on her front. Because birth was not the end of pregnancy, she thought, it was just pregnancy externalised.

Her shoes did not fit, so she was wearing slippers on the street, she had no choice. Walking was also difficult. Pain had been hard to locate, recently, there had been too much of it – such an explosion of agonies that, afterwards, Carmel could not gather it all back in.

But her thoughts were sweet-minded and abstract, and this also amused her. The blue of the sky on that August day was unforgettable.

'Look, Nell! The sky!'

Cerulean blue. The colour solid, and blank, and fathomless. Carmel stood under it, with her baby on her front, two bare souls.

For some reason to do with her pelvis the midwife had set her on her side and someone – maybe even Carmel herself – had to hold up the top leg high to allow the baby through. This leg was heavy as well as numb, and the midwife was a bitch who seemed to think Carmel deserved all that she had coming to her.

'Good woman,' she said, in a prissy voice that made Carmel want to kick her with the powerfully weighty top leg that was hooked, foot dangling, mid-air. At which point Aedemar Grant walked through the door with a toddler in her arms and they both looked (you could not do otherwise) between Carmel's legs.

'Oh well done,' she said, brightly. And, as though dragged unwillingly away, kept repeating through the closing door, 'You're doing great, Carmel! You're doing really well!'

Carmel did not need to be told how she was doing. She had survived worse. That is the thought that stuck in her head and would not leave. The chaos and the pain made sense to her because she was also, and quietly, somewhere else in the room. She was flat in the light that came from the window, she was tucked in the swish of the midwife's uniform.

She was not, however, in this large body they rolled on its back while, through a distant ring of fire, the baby came.

It was a storm. And the eyes that looked at her from the centre of it were exactly right. Carmel had been alone all her life. *Did I mention that?* She had been alone since she was twelve years old. The baby knew all this. The baby carried the whole black universe with her, in the pupil of her eye. She brought it through a gap that life itself had punched through Carmel's body. They looked at each other, and all of time was there. The baby knew how vast her mother's loneliness had been.

Aedemar drove them home from the hospital. In the boot of the car was a box of barely used baby clothes, washed, folded, organised by size. Also a second box marked 'Year 1–2' and another labelled 'toys'. And this junk was paraded into the house and down to the garden room at the back while Carmel sat on the sofa upstairs and lay the swaddled baba on the wooden floor. She did this because, if it was on the floor, it had nowhere further to fall.

'What is she doing on the floor, Carmel?'

When Aedemar laughed, Carmel considered what else might be done with a baby. And her friend picked her up and set her in Carmel's arms.

'Hello Nell. Hello you.'

Three days later, out of food, Carmel stood in the shop and looked at a packet of porridge oats, a tin of beans. She reached for a jar of peanut butter and reared back so fast, she nearly fell over and killed the baby that way. Could you catch an allergy, just by looking at the jar? They ended up with three cans of milk formula, a tub of cream cheese, and some bad sliced pan. It was all white, she noticed, as the conveyor jolted towards the till. Carmel put the stuff in her bag, after which, she could not think what else to do, except return to the safety of home.

Look Nell, the world! They walked past a fruit stall outside the vegetable shop: pyramids of oranges, pineapples stiffly reclining, a tumbling slope of yellowed grapes. The vendor called Carmel Missus.

'Can I get you anything Missus?'

'I'm grand, thanks.'

'Ah, would you look.'

Carmel had forgotten, in this first taste of the outdoors, that the house they had left was full of flowers, many of them pink. Pale pink, neon pink, blushing pink: dahlia, gerbera, lily, rose. The biggest bouquets came from people who had eyed her bump in silence, months before (because a pregnant woman is a shameful thing, but a baby is always a wonder). Even Imelda brought some. She arrived in Carmel's hospital room the day after the birth and slapped a bunch of chrysanthemums on the bed, probably from the shop downstairs. They were dyed vivid magenta and a chemical blue.

'Lovely!' said Carmel, whose body was warm with pain and with new, liquid impulses towards this creature in the cot. When Imelda asked, 'How are you?' she did not know what to say.

I am a tide.

'Good,' she said.

Imelda had a big story about parking and how it had made her late. Carmel had no idea what time it was, or why her sister was not looking at the baby. She opened her mouth to say as much but complained about something else instead.

'The night nurse was a bit mad, I thought she might be on the gin. She called the baby a whore.'

'A whore?'

'She came in and said, "Will she not stop crying for you? The little hoo-er."'

'She didn't say that.'

'She did, actually.'

'She wouldn't.'

Imelda was unconvinced. She walked to the window, which gave on to a small yard, wrapped her cardigan across herself and looked down.

'Have you got a name?'

'Nell.'

'Nell?'

Carmel held her silence. There were things in her life, she thought, that were beyond the reach of her sister's *opinion*.

Imelda had finally finished her doctorate. She had a small foothold in the university, teaching medieval French and she lived on in the house in Dun Laoghaire, like some kind of remnant. She could get nothing fixed or done. She painted one wall, but not the whole room. She kept the curtains of horrible velour.

'What do you think?'

She still asked permission of Carmel to change a house that Carmel manifestly did not own.

'Whatever. Go for it.'

Her skinny sister redid the cardigan, paced from the window to the cot and back again. Her glance sliding across the baby until something caught.

She paused, intent.

'Look at *you*,' she said.

Imelda's lurid blooms now took pride of place in the riot of pink in the front room, which was all starting to turn in the summer heat. When she came back from that first trip outside, Carmel set Nell down among the floral madness and took a roll of photographs because she thought she should.

It was a solid five months before she could get to the chemist to get the prints developed, and another unknowable length of time before she escaped to pick them up again. Carmel flipped the photos quickly from the front of the stack. Nell, lying asleep among the wilting flowers, looked like a bundled little corpse in a funeral home, somewhere hot and tragic.

You can't throw out a picture of your own baby, that would be like throwing out a whole person, because your baby changes so fast, you will never see that version again. Carmel picked the photos up. Set them down. Walked away.

Twenty minutes later, she snatched them from the table, ripped the images into small, and then smaller, pieces. She brushed the flakes of paper into the bin and turned to look at her fat, sturdy daughter, who was sitting up in a mesh playpen. Her smiling girl. Who was always transforming herself. Who was always new.

In the long months since she was born, they had burned through three au pairs and two office assistants, one of whom said that Carmel was a complete thug. Or, actually:

'A complete fucking thug.'

And Carmel thought, *I am not a thug, I am a woman in love.*

It was like running a war: steamers, sterilisers, power naps, lists, telephone numbers, backup numbers, other mothers, a great GP, and then, one frantic day while grabbing stuff in the local shop, an ad on the noticeboard for a minder three streets away, a woman called Debbie who had the gift of calm and was happy to do 'whatever'. Carmel wanted to slide down her door frame and sleep on the stoop. She wanted Debbie to mind *her*, she said, jokingly, and Debbie said, Hahaha.

There were weeks when she was on autopilot, months she could not recall. Carmel let her hair grow because there was no time to get it cut, and one evening ended up in casualty with an untended ear infection that spiked in agony at the exact pitch of the baby's cry.

'This is no place for a baby,' a nurse said, when Carmel finally tried to skip the queue, so she could get Nell home and fed.

She was right. Three of the patients were drunk. Others were infectious, or disfigured by injury. How could she have brought a fresh and fragile human being into this place of broken bones and botched lives?

'I'm sorry,' Carmel said. 'I'm really sorry, I blacked out in the kitchen,' and the nurse rolled her eyes. Ten minutes later her name was called but she did not hear it, because that side of her head was so loud with pain.

The doctor was also affronted by the presence of the baby, who had to be held on Carmel's lap. He took tweezers, dipped a long piece of gauze into ointment and packed it delicately into Carmel's ear. She could hear him with the other side of her head, hissing with disbelief as Nell filled a nappy, while looking intently up at her mother.

'Well done!' Carmel mouthed.

Outside, when she found her car, she considered the idea that she was not herself anymore, she had gone mad. She also found her car had been clamped.

The baby went quiet. Which was new.

When the unclamper arrived, Carmel said, 'The car park was full.' She did not call him a fucker, she thought that might be against the law.

'You pick your place,' he said.

'It's a hospital. The car park was full.'

'Nothing to do with me,' he said.

'Stay classy. No really. Shame. Shame on you.'

On the road home, she bashed the steering wheel and shouted, 'Try the morgue, you cunt. Lots of bad parking outside the morgue,' while the baby slept, unwakeable, until they stopped outside the house. Carmel cut the engine. In the back seat, Nell opened her mouth to inhale.

In the middle of all the chaos she caused, the baby glowed. Sometimes, even at the end of the worst, sleepless night, the blissful Nell-ness of Nell took Carmel by surprise. She was, through all her different versions, so fully herself. Her wryness and humour, her heedless, slapdash zeal: there it was at two months, at five months, at a year. When Nell later asked what her first words were, Carmel wanted to say, 'Ah sure, fuck it,' because they might as well have been. And it went without saying that she never did a single thing she was told.

'Did she like my present?' Imelda might say, not knowing the indifference of this child – perhaps of any child – to all her pieties. Nell slithered out of thank you cards and dutiful phone calls every birthday and Christmas. She was a miracle of distraction. Carmel could be standing over her, could be literally on top of the child saying, 'Here is the fucking crayon. Draw your auntie a nice picture. Just. Whatever. A bird. A flower.' And a year later the same thing. No further on.

By Mary's Holy Well

A ribcage on the dune at Carna
yields to the sky, a sprung clasp
grown through by marram,
harebell, scented purple clover.
Pink arrowhead of orchid
trembles in the absent heart,
the lungs, wind-ruffled campion.
No difference between breeze
and breath in this emptied fox,
or sea-sucked lamb, a newborn
dead, its hunger eaten by grass.

NELL

I AM CURRENTLY obsessed by light. It is hard to turn this into cash. An obsession with light does not commodify.

At the beginning of February, my period app turns up a grey date on the calendar: this means I am not ovulating, not bleeding, not going about my business. Just grey. Should be the first day of my period but really isn't.

The app asks about my mood: *happy, frisky?* I select *mood swings.*

I skip the sex-drive questions, I always do: *no sex today?* a sad heart with a line through it. Fancy a go of yourself? Don't forget to tap the cuddlesome *masturbation* heart when you are done.

Yeah, maybe.

I am so premenstrual it's not true.

A message tells me I haven't had unprotected sex in this current cycle. Thanks, period app! The last time I had unprotected sex, about two years ago, I took the morning-after pill and went to the doctor to test for STIs, I actually went twice, I had six different itches down there, my anxiety levels were through the roof.

These days, I have condoms for chlamydia, and also a secret coil. My mother dragged me down to the clinic to get it installed, she waited outside in the car.

And, yes. Sometimes, when I think I am sexually insane, I remember all this.

I am fine. It is two weeks since I had sex, which was on the fourteenth of January – a little red heart below it, surrounded by a red shield. Protected.

As I swipe back through my life, I find seven little red hearts dotted through the calendar days, sweetly precise. We have had sex seven times in the last four months, always midweek.

I think, That doesn't look like a relationship to me.

And yet, there they are.

Hearts.

Day 34: still grey. I tap symptoms, *acne*, *cramps* and *tender breasts*. I am having a ghost period. I log vaginal discharge *eggwhite* as opposed to *creamy*. I don't know what *eggwhite* means. I press three times, switching it on and off.

eggwhite

eggwhite

eggwhite

And then the mood icon

angry

angry

angry

angry

The app sends a message telling me that it *cares about my well-being*.

Down in the crappy, MDF kitchen, I put a pan of water on to boil and crack an egg to poach. I think about picking some of the gloop up between thumb and forefinger and don't.

The egg slops into a silicone cup, one of a poaching set, in blue and green, which was a present from my mother. She also gifted me orange cooking tongs, a mauve spiral cutter for making courgette pasta and four differently coloured chopping boards. These tasteful objects sit in my smelly, rented kitchen like bits of broken middle-class aspiration. As Lily says, How come I can afford a designer dress and not the house to hang it in? What happened there?

We are the redundant generation, I think. We are fodder.

A pipe knocks inside the wall. Beatriz, my silent housemate, has turned off the cold tap upstairs. She spends hours in the bathroom but you never hear her flush, it is a great mystery. Beatriz works in elder care and her lady is 'very difficult, *very* difficult'.

I think the smell is coming from the washing machine. Stuart, my other housemate, leaves his washing in the drum so long that, sometimes, you have to wash the machine before you wash your clothes. Stuart is a floor supervisor in a hotel dining room where he earns piss nothing, which is a lot more than he is worth, if you ask me. The hotel belongs to some guys from school and Stuart calls them 'the guys' like they didn't own a complete hotel. All I can hear when he talks about them is a man talking about money.

The money, the money has a really nice mother. The money, the money doesn't believe in fancy watches, he says you could pay someone that much to follow you around and tell you the time. The money, the money lost half a stone on a zero carb but it was all water weight. The money, the money gave him one of these great sleeve bracelets for Christmas, you know those elasticated things newspaper men used to wear, the ones with the green visors.

Oh yeah, cool.

At the weekend, Stuart goes out for the best night ever, he crashes on someone's amazing sofa, he comes home rancid, goes into work hanging, stays out again for a few creamers with the money, the money, or people who just know them actually because they are in Lisbon buying a building. All this while the clothes rot in the machine. Stuart is worried he can't afford the big wedding in Italy and then he 'finds' the cash. He comes back in wrecked. There was no room on the private plane, he says (as if). I tell him his clothes are in that black plastic bag outside the back door, and he says, I don't believe this. Seriously?

I think I should have slept with Stuart, then I could work for the money, the money on their social media. All I need are salon eyebrows, a very light, fake tan. But Stuart doesn't sleep with women like me. He has tried it on with girls I knew at school, but not with me, because I am not the money, whatever that is. Also, I will not do his laundry for him, and he seems to think I might.

Which is very frustrating for him.

What is it about eggs? You float them in water or you sink them in water, and that means they are good or bad eggs, I can never remember which.

Once when I was cooking with Carmel, I got twin yolks. This was the best thing ever. Carmel said, It's your lucky day.

I wonder will I ever get another. Because a double yolk is like a fairy tale – where you are asked to choose between things and get both.

I hold the cool egg in my palm and I wish, I wish.

Outside the kitchen window, there is a breeze-block wall, and at the top of it, a small, slanting oblong of blue sky.

I wish I could be pregnant or not pregnant.

I wish I had a boyfriend or no boyfriend.

I wish I had a relationship that existed and then ended.

Not this wrangle, where I don't have him and he still doesn't leave.

Egg in hand, I wish for possession.

I crack it on the edge of the counter and empty the contents into the green poacher.

Not a double.

I put on some toast, check the app to see have I got my period yet.

Seriously. I think my phone will know this before I do. I set it down on the counter like, *I just did that.*

I grab it back up, tap the *stress* icon and also the one for *alcohol.* I swipe back three weeks and add *stress* and *alcohol* to every second day: *stress stress stress alcohol alcohol.* Give me a break, period app bitch. I will tell you everything! just let the damn thing flow.

no sex

no sex

no sex

I tap the *masturbation* heart and then untap it. Jesus. Who cares?

In the boiling water, the poaching eggs cloud and stiffen to white.

The app pings back, *drink more water, ping! take more exercise, ping! wait till tomorrow.*

I lift the pan and turn the cooker off by its big, cheapass plastic knob. A pair of yellow, breasty eyes, looking up at me from two coloured cups.

I walk over to the kitchen table and bang my uterus against the edge of it, quite hard. I try to do it again, but I have lost the element of surprise and my body is too wary. I jump up and down a bit. Nothing feels as stuck as a stuck period. I am a cloud refusing to rain.

ping!

The app has offered me *a secret chat.*

124

The toast pops.

And, Fuckit! I say out loud yanking open the fridge, Give me some fucking butter!

I look up the brother, Fiach, who lives in Baldoyle. He is slimmer, more wiry than Felim. He has a LinkedIn with the word 'executive' in it and his profiler does not crack a smile. Felim sometimes has a hurt look to him, but this lad is saying, Don't even fucking bother.

If I was pregnant with Felim's child, it might look like that. Long face, small ears, handsome enough. One day he'd turn around to me and say, Mama, you are just pathetic.

And when he grows up, he does what he does.

I have a ghost baby inside me all day. It aches and turns.

In the evening I work up a post about sperm, the way it is *icky but not exactly cruel. Jizz doesn't want to hurt you, it just wants you to clean up after it. You can't be raped by a tadpole.*

I consider writing a story about a world where this stuff is considered sacred: the sons of the world coming downstairs to say, Mum, Dad, I've had my first ejaculation, the sheets hung out the window and everyone invited to the party, lots of champagne corks (of course) followed by much frothing champagne.

Or maybe that happens already.

No, I am not talking bar mitzvah, I am talking zinc tablets, annual check-ups, locker-room conversations about motility, consistency (Hey bro, eggwhite or creamy?), men crying on documentaries because of medical gaslighting, the doctors who say they are imagining the pain from the surgical device inside their penises that is there to help with shooting speed, lots of language about all this, because we need to understand that this is a real problem and not just a product of the foolish, prideful male mind.

In the evening, my tadpole line goes viral. Kind of. I click and look and click and count and that feels very damn fine to me.

In the middle of a dream about a tropical storm, bent palm trees, gulls tossed through the wet air, Carmel – in the form of her sister Imelda – is shouting at me to keep bailing the boat, keep bailing, and I wake to find my sleeping crotch slippery with fast-coming blood. Pyjamas, sheets. The full disaster.

The app suggests ibuprofen.

– *please log your menstrual flow.*

I shower and sort myself. I go downstairs, pull Stuart's wet clothes out on to the kitchen floor and put the sheets on a cold wash, the way my mother taught me to do. I dress the bed in new sheets, crisp and white, then I lie there, feeling rage and self-hatred peak, turn to self-pity, ebb away.

It feels like losing love.

I turn and hit my pillow into a state of plumpness, like a girl in a rom-com.

New month, I say, new man.

Six days later, Felim arrives straight from work. It is a cold day in February, the world feels dead, and there he is, impossibly, at the door. He has had a few drinks but not too many; he is in good form. He is wearing a vest under his office shirt and I want to laugh about that or make a comment – it is such a *vesty* vest. On the outside, he looks great, but the inner layer is vintage, it is from 1973.

Vest! I say, because I can't help it.

He pauses, gropes behind to find his phone, and swings it around as I scrabble under the duvet, naked.

Gotcha!

Go way!

Come on, Shyboots.

No.

Really?

Really.

You're gorgeous.

We had both moved so fast, I don't know what he caught and what he missed.

Come on!

No!

He tries to grab the duvet off me and there's a gawpy, adolescent look on his face, nothing erotic about it.

No! I say. Fuck the fuck off!

What's your problem?

Really?

Deep in the wall downstairs, the water pipe thumps to a stop and shudders in the reverb. Beatriz is in the bathroom on the other side of my bedroom wall and she has turned off the cold tap. There is a cough, followed, remarkably, by a toilet flush. You never hear Beatriz flush. I think she waits until no one is home.

I put my finger to my lips.

Cute, he says.

Felim snaps this gesture, meshes his fingers in the back of my hair.

Turn it off, I say.

What's wrong?

Put it down. I look terrible.

This is not fully true. In the seven months since I saw him in the newsagents, thumbing through the magazines, I have lost nine and a half pounds. Some days I do not make it down to the shops for food. I have never looked better.

So send me a good one.

Thank you. Yes. Yes I will.

He taps about a moment and then holds the screen towards me. A swipe of the index finger and twenty, thirty pictures swirl past – the body parts, the smiles, the different filters, bathrooms, bedrooms, the angles and poses, the girls.

The girls he has on his phone.

Do, he says. I'd love that.

The phone pictures are flickering through my head as I start the blowjob. I wonder who they are and if he knew them personally, and it's like I am not on my knees I am a photograph of a woman on my knees, with a real dick sliding into my face and that's so everything, it's like *this*, and *that*, and *yeah!*

Nasssty!

After a while, I remember that there is no camera, there is just me, bored in the mouth and working hard. I reach up to place a hand on his chest and encounter the stupid unsexy vest, so I focus on the spicy frizz of hair instead, the flatness of his torso, the stale taste of his penis at the end of a working day. I speed up, start to gag, give in to the clutch of his fist in my hair. I am a mechanism between his hand and his pleasure. I am nothing and, as he pulses to the finish, I have an image of him smashing my face against the cheap bedside locker, the make-up scattering across the rug, the paperback book, the foolish feathered lampshade, a series of Polaroids shot like it's the seventies, blood, bruises, runny mascara, me. Click click click.

Good girl, he says.

And he does push me away. Not very hard.

When he has hauled his trousers back up, he sits in my little chair, with his shirt unbuttoned and his fly waiting to be done. I listen to the silence from the still-occupied bath-room, snatches of speech from two local women meeting in the street, occasional traffic moving over the speed bump two doors down. He takes out his phone and considers me in the lens, sitting back on my haunches, naked, in the small space between the bed and the door. He clicks.

That wasn't so hard, he says. Was it?

I don't know how long we stay like this in the ebbing light. I get up and sit on the edge of the bed. In the chair by the window, he seems to sleep. His phone lights up and he looks at it. Lets it fall back into his lap.

Nothing has moved. The book is on the bedside locker, the lampshade lifts and drops a feathery filament, the number on the digital clock loses a segment and 8 becomes 9.

Felim sits forward and puts his hand on his head, briefly. He says, What are we doing?

Sorry?

I just think it's. What are we doing here? This isn't.

Isn't what?

You know, Babe.

He trails off. I say nothing. *Babe.* This is an amazing word coming from this man. Where does he think he is?

If I had a house, if I had a proper place to live, if I had what used to be called 'a job', would it have been a proper relation-ship? That is one question, I ask myself. I was a throwaway thing, not only for him, but for the people who paid me and, you know yourself, the infosphere, the nation state, the com-panies that brewed all my fun alcohol. For Meg-the-influencer, with her six, differently coloured chairs.

And even saying that about her makes me feel sad, because Meg-the-influencer got pregnant and lost the baby famously – which is one way to two and a half million views. I had to write some of that for her, and it was pure heartbreak. But then Meg said I had the wrong voice for it, I was all wrong, she actually said I was toxic, she needed someone new.

These days I am obsessed by light, it is so hard to commodify. I am not talking about a beautiful dawn, or holidays in the sun, or the light that makes a photograph look good. I am talking about brightness itself, the air lit up. The gleam on the surfaces of my typing hands.

I love the gift of its arrival.

The light you see is always eight and a half minutes old. Always and again. And you think it is shared by everyone but it is not shared, exactly – our eyes are hit by our own, personal photons.

Am I wrong?

I look it up and find that our eyes eat photons, absorb them. Our eyes make images by destroying light. Like black holes. Jesus, I think. There's nothing to say to that.

For a long time after he left, I saw him, large in my small chair, unbuttoned, saying, What are we doing here? Calling me Babe.

And it was like the early days, when I knew that we were destined and aligned, we were as one. He called me Babe, and that word was a slit in the room through which some other reality shone fiercely in.

I was, by then, trying to get a routine going.

Brush teeth – add a splash of water to face!

Leave shoes by bed at night – wear shoes in the morning!

Exit house to buy oat milk – keep going and do your emails in the coffee place, watch some people, smile at a small child, walk home.

Write list of birds you see on your walk.

Watch the birds who come for your scattered seeds on the kitchen windowsill. Do not ask to be lucky.

As I tried for one small thing and added another small thing, I was stopped short by the thought of the photograph he stole, squatting on his phone, my nakedness filling the cool slab in his hand.

He would never call me again.

I had to make him call me.

I angled my phone one way and another way, ran around to fix the lighting, turned my face away from the lens with some body part in the foreground. I loved the way I looked, I had never looked better. And I could not send. I thought about the wet cave of his mouth, tried to photograph the line of my neck, the under-hook of my knee. I wanted to show him the feeling of having my eyes closed.

I remember once I asked him what he was thinking. He said he was thinking about the football. I said, What do you mean when you say that? What do you see in your head? Do you organise the team? Replay the moves? Argue with the ref? And he said, I just think about checking the results.

I remember the time he talked about his brother Cathal who did not get a honeymoon, he was so tied to working the herd, their father always on his case. You have no idea, he said, the shit-shovelling and the bills for the vet, the endless forms to fill. How hard it is even to get away on a date, even for an evening. He said the land was a hard thing to love and it never let you go.

I remember him sitting in my little chair, buttoning his shirt, after he called me Babe. He said, I don't think I can keep going with this. It is like drinking, to be honest. You do it even though it affects your game, and the despair I have seen, I am not kidding you, in some of the lads. Did I tell you the time we were in Prague and a fella tried to off himself in his hotel room, and we brought him back, more drink on the plane, and no one knew. I always felt bad about that. I feel bad sitting here. Sure lookit – it is what it is. But I don't want to be this person forever, do you know what I am saying?

I remember all the times he gave me the look. The sad-boy crystalline. How it made his eye-colour more intense and his black pupils shine.

Save me. Love me. Fuck me. Only you.

The soul-piercer.

I woke in the middle of the night knowing that he had put the photos online: not just the sad one of me sitting back on the carpet, but also me diving under the duvet, my fat arm and my probably hairy leg and my gleaming horrible snatch maybe, and there is no way out of this, I am going to have to block him, change handles, go off grid. New name, new passport, new country, different planet.

I am going to have to die.

I must die.

That would solve it. That would be nice.

In the morning, I think, Maybe the pictures aren't that bad. Certainly, I shaved my legs that day. Certainly, he thought I looked good. And who cares, it's just whatever. A billion of them online, who ever clicks? More porn than people to look at it. And it's not even porn. Happens all the time.

These thoughts cycled uselessly in my head, many times a day, and they always ended in a pleading little voice that reached out for him, tugged at him.

Delete!

Chiddik!

If I could make him like me, I could stop this.

Delete!

If he knew I was unhappy, he might do what I asked.
Chiddik, chiddik!

I thought I could fix the problem by talking to the guy who caused the problem and that seemed more and more urgently true to me until, finally, I sent a text.

– *let's see! piccy please*

And received an instant reply.

– *send a nice one!*

After which creep-out, he texted me for two days straight.

– *where now?*

– *what doing?*

– *show me*

And then, nothing.

I stand in the shower till the hot water runs out. I stay till my fingertips wrinkle, while polar bears swing their sad heads from side to side, looking for all the lost snow.

On Sunday, I text Carmel to say I won't make it over for lunch, I think I am coming down with something.

This is a mistake.

– *Come lie on the sofa and I make you spaghetti.*

– *Will drop by and pick you up?*

– *You need paracetamol?*

– *There in 20*

I send a voice message, because that sometimes works.

Hi Mum, I'm just curling up with a book I am not actually hungry, I think it's some kind of bug.

Ten seconds later, the phone rings for a live, in-person conversation. Carmel is using her beige, slightly happy voice. There is no problem. She is not worried about me in the slightest. By the time we are done, I have promised to be home by 3.

I drag myself over to the station and take the train out by the bay. The tide is very distant – acres and acres of flat sand all the way to the horizon where a massive tanker sits on a thin sliver of sea.

I have this idea like a shining thread that I will split him. I will make him suffer in a way so cold, he will thank me for it. This thought makes me close my eyes. When I open them again, I see the bay from a different angle, a little further down the track: the massive blank incinerator, big as a steel castle, the Pigeon House chimneys, Howth Head, peaceful and stern, the outsized tanker squatting on a ribbon of water.

It's like all the pieces are too big for the board.

The thing I always forget about my mother is that she doesn't do reassurance. Her friend Aedemar actually said this to me once, she said, Your mother doesn't tell people that everything is going to be alright.

And I said, Will it though? And Aedemar, said, Yes of course it will, sweetie. Of course it will be alright.

Carmel says things like, I think you may be overstating the problem. Or, I don't see any sign of infection, but we'll keep an eye on it. She also says (and this is terrifying), Sometimes, the bad thing happens, and what do you do then?

But the first and really annoying thing she does is look for a different problem altogether. Are you eating? Have you eaten? Do you need to rehydrate? Have you done your poo today? All of these questions are posed between arrival, hanging up my coat, using the bathroom, and going into the kitchen to help set the table.

I say, I am twenty-three.

So?

I am twenty-three.

I worry about you.

You don't have to.

I do though. You look pale.

The sight of her hands does something to me as she picks out the bowls from the cupboard. They are working hands, very simple and strong. She has so little vanity, my mother. She has never had a great romance.

What? she says.

Napkins?

The usual place.

The food is, as she promised, a simple spaghetti, with a tomato sauce so dense it is nearly black – her special pasta that exists in an orb of its own garlic, you can almost see the halo hum. Green salad. Walnut oil. Worth it.

We start in silence. I go, Oh. This is nice.

Is it?

Carmel can never taste her own cooking. It's like she imagined she was making something better.

So how are you?

Good.

I twist the fork until the skein of spaghetti is neat enough to put in my mouth, lose some, twist again. Carmel likes to see me eat, but her eyes are so greedy I never manage much. She needs information, she needs news. She gets what I call a babba-look on her face, a bit roundy and stupid.

Any news?

(What can I say? I conjured myself a stalker who has now deserted me, I have fallen into the howling abyss.)

Nothing much.

How's Maya?

I never hear from Maya, I have almost no interest in Maya, but we follow each other online and this makes Carmel think we are friends for life.

Yeah good.

What's she up to?

She's in Galway, doing improv, or learning improv.

Improv? My god. That girl.

Mum.

I never met a child who didn't like ice cream.

Well it's not something you can control, Mum.

Clearly.

I find it hard to agree with my mother, because every time you agree with her, it's like you lose and she wins. But sometimes we do agree. And what do you do then?

I haven't seen her in ages, actually, I say.

No?

She's such a flake.

I tell Carmel how she'd send seventeen messages telling you she might make it and then can't, or she was on her way but something mad happened, and then another mad thing, she got the time wrong or the venue wrong, or even that she is nearly there, hang on, and still she doesn't arrive.

What's the point of saying a time, if you don't mean it? says Carmel. I arrive.

Me too, I say. I also arrive.

It's a great mystery.

Carmel dabs the wooden salad servers into the bowl. There is some early sprouting broccoli in there from the garden, and it is delicious. There will be a bag of it waiting in the fridge that I will take away with me and, for some reason, fail to eat.

You don't get men doing that, Carmel says. You don't get men saying, Oh, sorry, I was just out the door and then a seagull flew into my neighbour's glasses and I had to stop to help him because he is old and nearly blind and you *have* to believe me because we *both know* this story is not true. Men just get on with it, she said.

Get on with what, though.

Whatever. The thing.

You mean like the rapey thing, the violence thing?

God you're obsessed, she said. I am not talking about sex I am talking about punctuality. Men turn up on time, because it's not that complicated.

Like fascism and trains.

All I am saying is, that fuss – whatever it is – happens strictly between women.

Or he doesn't text and then he doesn't show?

Oh sweetheart.

Honestly sometimes I think you are actually trying to do this.

Do what? Carmel says.

I just hate it. I hate the way you say, everyone is stupid and they only have themselves to blame. Especially women.

When did I say that?

Especially women. You're always saying it.

There is no such thing as always, Carmel says.

And there's more to life than being sensible, I say, in a sensible voice, because Carmel has gone cold on me, and I feel it like a slap across the face, an actual blow. It is like we are in a different room, the colour of the walls has shifted a tone, the place is larger and more blue.

I go back to the salad, and stab at it.

What do you think of the broccoli?

Yeah, good.

Carmel has a high-elbow cutlery style. She wings those arms right out, cuts, folds, skewers, lifts, chews. I do the same on the other side of the table, and the phrase that pops into my miserable head is:

Eat your heart out, Ma.

Eat your heart out.

When we are finished, I clear and stack and wonder why we cannot save each other – two people who surely need saving and whose love for the other is absolute. Because I do love my mother. I love her so much it appals me, what I am about to do now.

I say, Mum, I think I need some money.

Right.

I think I need to go away.

OK. Right.

Just for a couple of months, maybe three? I need to.

What?

I'm going to do this travel thing.

Thing?

You know. Yeah.

On the train back into town, the line of silver sea has unloosed an easy flood that moves over itself in long, shallow waves towards the railway line.

I got the tattoo three days later – fully sober, by appointment, on a Wednesday afternoon. I asked for the words *love is a tide* below my collarbone.

Not in a wavy line, that would be wrong, and not with a bird flying above it, that would also be corny. The font was minimal, handwritten-naive, with lots of skin in between.

Love is a tide.

The quote was a message to my future self, the kind of truth I wanted to prove over time. When it was done, I was so pleased and so nicely sore, I blew a kiss at myself in the bathroom mirror, where it read backwards.

Wait is a oval.

This was also how it looks on Snapchat, though not in photographs taken by other people. I don't know why people don't talk about this more. I can't actually read my own logo here, guys, unless I twist and squint, and even then I only 'catch' the 'tide'.

I love it, though.

I run my finger along it quietly below the bone and believe in better things to come.

There were a few coos and compliments, but no one asked where the quote was from, and I did not say. It is from a poem written by my grandfather, Phil McDaragh. So my skin feels like it owns this already. It will be something from home, I can carry with me, when I am away.

Or that is what I said to my mother who spotted the ink under my collar, the evening we moved my stuff out of Ballybough and into the back of her car.

What's that?

It's a tatt, I said.

Right.

Do you want to see?

She shut the boot.

Time enough, she said. I'll be looking at it for the rest of my life.

We sat into the car in silence as we considered her statement – how true, or untrue, it might turn out to be.

Later, when I was storing stuff in my old wardrobe, and putting some of it into my suitcase, she came in with a cup of tea.

Let's see it, so, she said and I pulled my shirt across.

Very discreet, she said.

I think so.

That's enough now, you've done it.

You don't recognise the line?

She looked again and her eyes narrowed like, Oh right.

Don't you think it's romantic?

Well if you like it, she said in her beige voice. Then I do too.

The Calendar of Birds
(translated from the Book of Leinster,
anonymous, twelfth century)

From the ninth of January
all birds welcome the dawn
into their dim underwood,
whatever the hour of its rising

On the eighth of April
the flickering swallows meet us
so we can ask, where
have they been since October

On the happy feast of Ruadan
every beak is opened, and from this,
the seventeenth of May, the cuckoo
calls non-stop in her thicket

In Tallaght, birds pause their songs
on the ninth of July for Mael Ruain,
undefeated by the carrion crow,
the bird of war. We pray for her protection

Across cold seas the barnacle geese arrive
on the day of Ciaran the joiner's son.
On the feast of wise St Cyprian,
the brown stag bellows on the red plain

Six thousand white years
the world has had good weather,
but seas will break in everywhere
as night ends and birds scream

Sweet as yet is their song of praise
to the Lord God in heaven,
the shining King of the clouds –
be glad and listen to their call.

CARMEL

WHEN NELL WAS nine, and Carmel desperately trying to get back into the world, she met a man in a queue for tickets at the Abbey Theatre. He took her by the elbow and said, 'Oh sorry, I thought you were someone else,' after which he said, 'You're Phil McDaragh's daughter.' He was so softly surprised, Carmel wanted to tell him that, *really*, he had no idea who she was. She also, in the backwash, wanted his forgiveness for all her silent cruelties.

'Yes. Yes, I am.'

'I love his little poem about the wren.'

In the interval, he came up and drank with her and Orla Hughes and talked about the play. He was on his own, he said. And indeed, he looked like the kind of person who came to plays on his own. Orla recognised him from their schooldays. It was Ronan Bresnihan from Emor Road.

'Where have you been?'

'London,' he said.

He asked Carmel did she write poetry and she told him to fuck off.

'I do not.'

He wished he could, he said.

Later, he asked for her number. He looked alright.

They dated in a normal way. At least they dated in a slightly fictional way – Carmel had never been asked for her number before, that wasn't how it happened. But Ronan invited her out once a week and, after three weeks of this, they went to bed together, very quietly, after a long session on his sofa. The sex was more of a murmur than a shout, but she liked his narrow body under the duvet. His chest was glazed with fine blond hair and the skin underneath was the colour of honey, which was unexpected. He was not a man you would ever imagine undressed.

Ronan played the clarinet. He was part of a small ensemble that accompanied an amateur choir every Thursday night, and he also did weddings and funerals, for which he got paid, sometimes quite well. He had a friend who was a priest and was happy to recommend him to couples or to the bereaved.

'Right,' said Carmel, who supposed that priests must have friends too, though maybe of a slightly generic kind. They met up and did things together, apparently, walks and cups of tea.

'What do you talk about?'

'I don't know,' said Ronan. 'The rugby?'

Carmel was surprised he followed the rugby, he was so gentle and prone to abstraction. Also he did not drink alcohol, though he hopped up to go to the bar, whenever her glass was getting empty, he was happy to do it. And though Carmel might have liked someone more exciting, she also thought they might fit. Ronan was nice. And there they were, the pair of them, having a fizzy water in the interval of a concert by an overly modern string quartet.

'You follow the rugby?'

'My father,' he said – and there was an amount of complication held in the word – 'was a big Leinster man.'

Maybe that was it. A bastard of a father. That might be enough to do whatever had been done to this unclaimed man of thirty-five, who spoke of this or that ex-girlfriend without rancour. He dressed like a stockbroker on holiday and was constantly, regretfully intelligent. Ronan did nothing but muse aloud and apologise.

'Sorry, I just think . . .'

'When you think about it. Sorry, but. I really think.'

'It's not exactly Rembrandt is it? Sorry.'

He was always bursting your bubble, or some bubble, but the things he did allow were sometimes sweet. He found a dishwasher in his apartment six months after moving in. He thought it was a dud cupboard door until, one day, a bag caught on the handle as he was putting away the shopping and, when he tugged at it, the thing opened downwards instead of across. A cube of brushed steel, secretly shining to itself under the counter. It didn't even smell.

Carmel had never been in a modern apartment block in Dublin. Ronan's place had a big picture window in the living room, with a view of the River Dodder, and in front of the glass was a music stand with his clarinet standing upright beside it, as though growing out of the carpet. Carmel tried to figure this out, and saw a tripod at the base.

'Oh,' she said, 'it's stuck on a stick,' and he giggled behind her, as though she had said something rude.

His bed was firm and clean. Carmel was not sure she had ever slept with a man whose sheets were so pristine. The third time they did it, she thought perhaps he had not climaxed, but he was using a condom so there was no real way to tell. He sorted himself in the bathroom before coming back to bed where he fell happily asleep beside her. Carmel slipped out from under the duvet and got dressed quietly in the darkness. When she turned back at the door, she saw that he was awake again and she took this image as something she could remember. The big window, the night-green of trees outside, the white pillow where his head made a dent, the feeling of Ronan's eyes looking at her, in a moonlit room.

She started to check her phone during the day for messages, though he always called on Wednesday at lunchtime in order to organise something for Saturday night. It took a couple of months to see the pattern.

'Yes. That's when I call.'

'Very reliable,' she said.

'I try to be,' he said, without any attempt at charm. They went to dinner and he asked about Nell, as he always did, with the right amount of interest and the right amount of distance. And he never suggested they go back to her place, as though he understood what all that might entail.

Coming up to Christmas, Carmel decided to make a move. She asked if she could bring Nell to the carol service his choir held in town.

'Oh,' he said.

'Or, don't worry.'

'No, I just. Sorry, it's not exactly King's College,' whatever that meant. Carmel took his hand as they walked along and set it against her cheek.

'Cold,' she said.

He had lovely, fine hands.

Ronan warned her to arrive early but even so, the church was almost full and they had to clamber for a seat and then wait while nothing happened for about twenty minutes. Nell was half-bonkers by the time the musicians filed out of the sacristy and started to tune up and there was another delay before the choir came out, looking giddy and momentous. They were dressed in various styles of black and some wore Santa hats or reindeer headbands which bobbed about as they sang. They wove and ducked. They smiled and turned the page. The women were all different shapes and ages, and Carmel briefly imagined herself standing among them, working her lips over the bright and surprising syllables of 'Good King Wenceslas'. When Ronan played, she felt such a pang.

Afterwards she brought Nell up to say Hi, and though the child had not met him before, and did not know, on any conscious level, who he might be, Nell did a surprising thing. Ronan asked what her favourite Christmas carol was and she said, 'Santa Baby', a song Carmel thought long out of vogue. As she did so, Nell swung her hips and belly around in a shy, childish circle. She reached for Ronan's hand and touched it, as though checking out its warmth and weight.

'Do you like "Santa Baby"?' she said, with her head to one side.

The child was flirting – if that was the right word, at nine. She was doing it badly, or else outrageously well, because Ronan shifted and her mother rose an inch or so taller, saying, 'Time to go, Nell.'

'You said we would get an ice cream.'

'Ice cream? I certainly did not.'

So they fought about that instead.

Carmel was left, after all this, with a new and more challenging daughter. She mentioned it to Bronagh, another single mother from school, and Bronagh, who was a bit more working class than Carmel, roared laughing. She said about her own daughter, Maya, 'She loves men. Oh my God, she absolutely fucking adores them. Just show her a man. A traffic warden, or a doctor, or anyone tall, actually. If he's over six foot she goes all,' and she put her hands under her chin like a pair of geisha fans.

They stood together at the side of the hall, watching their children blitz the Christmas fair in a gang. The girls wore skirts over leggings and UGG boots at the end of spindly legs and they surged from stall to stall. Nell ran happily from Bric-a-Brac to the goldfish, pointing, grabbing, holding something up to enquire the price. And each time Maya made it to the front of the busy little cluster, the group moved on.

Maya was being excluded by the other girls and Bronagh, who knew all about it, was white with concern. She couldn't exactly go up and confront them – the little *bitches*, she said – and the teachers were no help, they treated her like a fallen woman because Maya's father wasn't around. Carmel thought she might be right. There was a chill there, it was a convent school. Even the couples who were separated pretended they were still together, and the children pretended not to care.

Carmel, who knew Maya from parties and sleepovers, saw the girl try to figure out what she was doing wrong, and fail at that too. She trailed after the group, her face pinched and increasingly mad, Carmel thought. If she were an adult, those blank, burning eyes would look properly insane. It was a savage business, being nine or ten. Maya was starting puberty, which surely did not help. The last time she slept over, Carmel had to sort the girl's sanitary needs before bending to tie the laces on her new sneakers, because she did not know how.

'Rabbit ears, rabbit ears, jumped into the hole.'

Nell, as usual, didn't give a damn. When the children ran out into the yard, she walked the tippy edge of kerb, her arms wide and windmilling, as though this was a feat for which she needed complete and fearless solitude.

The week after Christmas, Ronan stayed over for the first time.

'I have a friend staying over on Tuesday, Nell.'

'What?'

'I have a sleepover.'

Carmel spoke in her 'neutral' voice, which worked most of the time. This was the tone she used when Nell, aged four, called a stranger in the playground 'Daddy' because she thought that's what little girls called big men. It was the voice that Carmel used for all questions of origin, 'No darling, not everyone has a father,' and for Nell's various sweet misapprehensions – for years she thought the phrase 'single mother' meant 'mother of a single child'. Nell was still gloriously the centre of her own life – though she was beginning to have her suspicions. She usually had a neutral reaction to the neutral voice but, recently, you didn't know where it might go.

'My friend, Ronan.'

'OK,' Nell said.

'He's nice.'

And then he was there. Two days after Christmas, Ronan wandered upstairs fully dressed, a late arrival to their breakfast table, where he twitched his chinos at the knee as he sat down saying, 'Absolutely, porridge. Lovely. Sorry yes that would be fine.'

'You remember Ronan, Nell.'

After a couple of bolted spoonfuls, Nell pushed away from the table and ran out of the room.

'Alright?'

She was gone so long Carmel began to hold her breath. The child thumped back up the stairs and arrived through the door festooned with a string of paper swans. This, she untangled and unwound and set along the table as though Ronan were not sitting in the way. As she tipped and nudged each swan into place, she shifted sideways towards him. You might say she sidled.

'I did them,' she said.

Ronan was, in his response, almost elegant.

'Are they all the same?'

'This one isn't.'

'Maybe it's a goose?'

There was silence from Nell who considered this suggestion both stupid and intriguing.

'Have you ever seen a mongoose?' Ronan said.

'A mongoose?'

'Sorry.'

'That's not *even* a goose,' she said.

'I know. Sorry.'

Carmel mopped the counters and pretended not to watch. Nell had regressed in the most amazing way. She was acting like a five-year-old, but it was not the five-year-old that her mother remembered. She was starting a fresh version of herself, a new line.

In a flash of uncertainty, she hissed to her mother.

'What's his name?'

'Ronan,' Carmel said.

She turned to face him.

'Ronan,' she said in a formal voice. 'Do you like them?'

When she was small, Nell would not let Carmel speak to any other human being: not to a shop assistant, not to a teacher, nor to a neighbour in the street. Just the fact of her mother's lost attention made her tug and whine.

'Mum.'

'Mu-um.'

'Mu-uh-um!'

Carmel had expected possessiveness when Ronan arrived, it never occurred to her that he would be the one she would want to possess.

Nor had she expected this *fawning*.

'Leave Ronan alone, Nell.'

'I am just showing him my origami, Mummy.'

So she was 'Mummy' now. The child had shifted into a

different social class, already. Carmel tried to think what her daughter sounded like. And actually, she sounded like the kind of girl who ganged up on other girls, at school.

'Can you clear your bowl, Nell?'

No response.

Carmel stacked the breakfast dishes with some vigour, she pulled the lip of the bin bag and tied it in a hard knot. She could not believe it. The endless amount of time she had spent on this human being. Nine years of her own existence that she could not clearly recall – a kind of siren going off in her life for nine years straight. It swept over her in a fury, the sense that she had been so utterly trapped and was now being cast aside.

'OK, you. Enough is enough.'

Nell turned to her with a haughty look.

'In. A. Minute.'

Ronan, who was still discussing the paper swans, looked down.

'Unless it's ducks,' he said, quietly.

He was right. None of it was serious, and it was all lovely. Nell was innocent in her attentions – if not entirely benign – and he made himself simple for her. It was something to see.

They were in the empty days after Christmas, when there was nothing to do except eat leftovers while, all over the country, families stayed home. In the afternoon, they walked along by Seapoint, Nell in the new coat she got from Santa, which had a sweet Victorian look slightly at odds with her sheepskin boots. She prattled engagingly to Ronan while they dodged children on new scooters and Christmas bikes. When they turned up the west pier, she flinched from a dog – Carmel did not think Nell was afraid of dogs – and Ronan told her he had the gift of animal pacification. Did she know what that was?

'What?'

Ronan looked out over the bay, as though the story he had to tell was written on the water. He was named for a saint, he said, long, long ago, who sailed away from Ireland on a boat made of stone. When he landed in France, the place was full of wolves and St Ronan went into the forest that covered all of Europe at that time. And the wolves came right up and sniffed the hem of his garment. They sat down and whined and lay down and rolled over to show their hairy-baldy wolf tummies, because he was an Irish saint and that was his gift, would you believe. As well as the stone boat, which did not sink.

They both considered the oily-smooth sea and a drama of purple, evening cloud above it.

'Would you rather be killed by a leopard or a wolf?' he asked, and Nell, who had forgotten to be coy, said, 'Yeah, dunno. Maybe a leopard?'

'Trick question, Nell. Wolves only hunt in packs. I'm sorry, but if you meet just one wolf, you are not about to die.'

They arrived home heartened, flung themselves down in the living-room chairs, and there were no arguments with Nell over screens or stupidity, she was busy the whole time, she suggested boardgames and carried books to read, she plonked them on Ronan's lap and he did not resist her demands, not once.

After dinner, the pair of them sat on the sofa turning the pages of a book about marsupials. Nell said that duck-billed platypuses have poisonous thorns on their elbows.

'Or whatjecallit,' she said, rubbing her own elbow and Ronan was genuinely taken by this piece of information.

'Honestly,' he said. 'Australia.'

'I know,' she said.

Carmel kept a lid on the clamour she felt, watching them together. Impossible to tell if this new configuration was real, or if it was some kind of game that Nell was inventing while the adults played along. They were a family. It was overwhelming, and possibly fake, and it gave Carmel too much pleasure.

At half past midnight, Nell was still up and when Carmel had finally physically hauled her down to her bedroom, there was more distraction and delay about her story and what story, until Ronan came to the other side of the door and suggested he could read to her, if she liked.

'Absolutely not,' said Carmel.

'I want it,' said Nell.

'No.'

'I want it,' she hissed. And there was a brief, mute meltdown; Nell a stretching, breath-holding fiend under the duvet as, from the other side of the door, he dutifully retired.

Full of apologies and regret, Ronan left before lunch and when he was gone, Carmel turned to Nell.

'So?'

'What?'

'What did you think?'

'Yeah alright,' she said.

Half an hour later the house was too quiet and, when she checked, Carmel found her daughter in the downstairs bathroom staring at a catastrophe of blood that spattered the toilet bowl. This turned out to be nail varnish, a bottle of which Nell had poured down the ceramic, very carefully, in the interests of some forgotten game.

'It just happened,' she shouted. 'It just happened.'

They shrieked and flailed in the small space of the room, the pair of them in a state of chaos and bewilderment.

'What did you do? What were you *doing*?'

'It just happened.'

'What were you thinking?'

'I don't know! It just happened. It just happened.'

Until Nell found the exit and, like a wasp from the jam jar, was gone.

Ronan spent New Year with his mother and aunt, who lived together in a cottage in the Wicklow hills. In January, the Wednesday phone calls resumed, followed by their weekend excursion for culture or food. In a way, it was as though the day with Nell had not happened. Ronan continued his pondering; the sad business of correcting the world's many misconceptions, and he still requested sex as though asking for directions from a stranger on the road.

A nice stranger. But even so.

His talent with children – or his talent in forgetting them – made Carmel wonder about his life. There might be a child of his own somewhere, and she would not know it. He had spent a decade in London, returned to Dublin when his father was dying and stayed on. This man was a big hospital consultant; very well known. He was the reason Ronan had to leave in the first instance, he had to get away. But there was a lot of love there, despite everything.

'Of course there was,' said Carmel.

'Yeah. Sorry. I don't know.'

His father was not an easy person – Ronan had dropped out of his doctorate, many years before, because he could not live up to the man's expectations.

'You have no idea.' His face emptied out at the thought of it.

He had worked so hard.

Carmel did not know what to say to this.

'I had all my research done,' he said. 'Too much research.'

'Oh well,' she said.

'Sorry?'

He looked at her, and blinked.

Ronan was so fortunate, Carmel thought. He had an apartment he could clearly afford, a job that took up six hours a week. This man had more free time than anyone she knew. He had a wall of hardbacked books, inherited paintings on the walls, some of his day was spent in meditation. Now and then, he tried his hand at poetry, but nothing he did was any good, he said. One evening, he showed Carmel a folder of large-format photographs taken around his mother's cottage, and these clearly meant something to him, though she could not see why. The colours were ordinary and the mountains looked very solid and close. But here or there you saw the distant glow of a rape field, a tiny stir of wind in a field of green barley; some intimation of movement caught your attention; a wrinkle running across still water, a scud of shadow along an ordinary stretch of bog. Carmel could not decide if this effect was accidental or exquisite.

'Lovely,' she said. 'Is that up by Bohernabreena?'

'Actually sorry, that one's Kippure.'

They had known each other five months. She felt, as she looked at the pictures, that she was no further on with Ronan. It was like she still hadn't found the dishwasher, even though she knew there must be one there.

Over the years, Carmel began to think there was something she did not understand about other people. *Carmel you have no imagination.* Some days, it was as if she did not get the flavour of things – until she saw Nell, of course, when the movie always turned back to Technicolor. But, some days, her life without Nell was like sitting in an empty room. On the first day of February, her snowdrops appeared, trembling in the shady part of the garden. It was the kind of thing Ronan might photograph, she thought, and terrified herself with the feeling of something new.

The next Saturday, she got Nell a sleepover, and stayed at

his place. When he woke up and saw her in the bed, Ronan sort of sprang away.

'Coffee?' he said.

After breakfast he wanted to walk along the Dodder. It was nine o'clock in the morning after a night of heavy rain and Ronan was discoursing about the rivers of Dublin, a subject on which people were often sadly misled. Take the Liffey, for example – he was sorry, but that was not the name of the river, it was what they called the alluvial plain. The river itself was 'the runner' and this made a lot more sense, because when does a bog become a stream? When does the ordinary movement of water turn into a blue line on a map?

Carmel had not seen him so expansive.

Her father had a poem about it, he said.

'About the Liffey?'

'No, of course not.' (How could she get her own father so wrong?) It was a little ditty of a thing, a tum-tee-tum that he started humming and reconstructing.

'Will you come and dance the polka / Said the Dodder to the Tolka.'

He swung an imaginary, carousing baton.

'Will you tum-tee tum-tee tum-tee.'

He turned to her. He was very happy.

'How does it go?'

'I have no idea,' she said. 'Seriously, I think you're making it up.'

'Said the Poddle to the Slang!'

The poem was 'River Talk', she must remember it. But she really did not. They were approaching the arches of the Milltown viaduct, which stretched across the narrow valley. Ronan stopped and pointed to the other bank.

'And there it is. Seriously. The very Slang.'

No one knew about this stream, he said, which came

down from the mountains and through Dundrum, all underground, in a big concrete pipe. It ran beneath the housing estates and the roundabouts, it was under the hair-dresser's and the school. And you know, 'slang' was a word for a strip of field alongside a river. As well as being the name for this particular river. As well as a word for a type of word, as in 'slang'.

And though Ronan was by now completely irritating, Carmel was stilled as she watched the confluence of the two streams, black water into black water. It had been happening for so long. They came on old pathways, bearing different traces. It was a secret way of telling the land. She felt her father's feet root in her shoes, and something else settle in her shoulders: the restless lope of him, the way he looked about, missed nothing, ate the scene.

They had reached the shelter of the grey stone arch and Ronan turned to Carmel.

'It's nice, isn't it?'

He did not mean the poem. He meant everything was nice.

It was starting to rain again, but there was a brightness in the air. The river ran full and fast, and all the colours were stronger for being wet.

'Yes, it is,' she said.

He kissed her.

'Hey!'

The stone rang as he lifted his face and shouted.

'Hey!'

Carmel took him by the lapels and shoved him towards the river.

'Please shut up,' she said.

It was because he liked her. That was why he was talking so much. Because she had spent the night at his place and woken up in his bed and was now walking beside him in the rain.

The feeling ran through Carmel swiftly, and it left her mortified.

He liked her.

Ronan was still talking about Phil, who had walked the length of the Dodder back up into the mountains. It was in a piece in *The Bell*, maybe.

'Who wrote it?' Carmel said.

'I forget actually.' It was a mock-heroic thing. When he walked past Austin Clarke's house – which was on the bridge in Templeogue – he threw a discus of dried cow manure at the front window, because of a review Clarke had given him in the *Irish Times*.

'You do know it.'

'Yeah, maybe,' she said, stuck on the word 'discus'. It sounded like Phil, alright.

He spun around in the road and hurled it, old-style, 'like Odysseus at the Phaeacian Games'. And Carmel was back in the house on a Saturday morning when she was a child: the whole terrible business of the newspaper, of hiding the paper, or delaying the paper, because their father would get up cranky and late, and if he had his breakfast before he got to the paper there was a chance he would not lose his temper over Austin Clarke at the top of the books page, handing down judgement on the poets of Ireland. On bad days the thing was bundled up into the bin, practically unread, on worse days you would get a clatter upside the head, and he would be gone roaring about the house trying to find his other shoes. It would have been on such a Saturday that he lobbed cow shit at Austin Clarke's window and bragged about it afterwards in every pub.

Like Odysseus at the Phaeacian Games.

They were terribly ashamed of his talk – the way it might come back at you.

As, indeed, it had just done. How many decades later?

But they were not exactly ashamed, Carmel thought, of the shouting and the hitting, which seemed a kind of internal event. This man was twice her size and he was her father, so the back of his hand was like the weather, you just kept out of the way. If you couldn't do that much, you only had yourself to blame.

There was no badness in him, that is what their mother said. He was a big child.

Ronan was discussing the brick chimney they had passed on the riverbank, which belonged to the mill after which the area of Milltown was named, and Carmel interrupted him to say, 'I think I'll head home.'

He did not falter. As they headed back up the path he pointed out some moorhens swimming in the rain.

'Nice weather for the ducks,' he said.

A few weeks later, there was an event in the local library to mark a bequest of Phil's archive and Carmel didn't know whether to invite Ronan or not. It was already very fraught. The material came from the American wife, a woman they were now obliged to call 'Connie'. She had offered to donate Phil's last notebooks and Imelda was convinced this was some kind of move on her part. There had been phone calls and correspondence to clarify who owned what, and Carmel was fed up with all the fuss.

'She is not *taking* anything,' she said, 'she is giving something away.'

To which Imelda replied, 'Yeah, right.'

The previous year, Connie had arrived in Dublin and invited the two of them to tea in the Shelbourne where they sat on low sofas, looking at the cake-stand and discussing airports.

'Did you come from JFK?'

'I actually flew in from O'Hare.'

There were scones on the bottom tier, tiny sandwiches in the middle, fancy pastries at the top – all of which remained untouched. It was a little competition. A cake-off.

'So, what brings you to Ireland, Connie?'

Fifteen years since their father's funeral, and here she was – a ghost in crêpe pants and a good blazer. Her hands were precise on the lifted cup and saucer, her voice was light and even. It was important to put things in the right place, and the right place for Phil's last notebooks was in Ireland.

'You think?' Imelda said.

Connie was looking to 'rebalance her life' she said. She made their father's legacy sound like a spa treatment, or some kind of lifestyle choice. She did not mention the fact that she had fucked him, married him, stolen him, hauled him off the toilet floor when he was dead. Nor did she say that she was their stepmother – that would have been absurd. She was about two years older than Imelda. And twenty pounds lighter than Carmel, at a rough guess.

'I think he would be happy to see them come home.'

The woman paused, stilled by some memory in her mind's eye. They all caught it; the flash and after-burn of Phil.

Carmel lurched forward and took a tiny eclair from the top tier.

'I think that's a lovely idea,' she said.

'I'm so glad.'

Connie set the cup and saucer down, and there was a considered silence.

'It has been lovely meeting you,' she said. Carmel thought the American was sad about her first marriage, that she wanted to be done with it now.

Perhaps that went for all of them. It was time to let the old fucker go.

'What did you think?' she asked Imelda as they walked

back to Dawson Street, and her older sister said, 'The nerve of that woman. The utter and absolute nerve.'

The bequest was marked by a small gathering in a local library with a few lesser poets and a table of middling wine. Ronan arrived in a tweed jacket and mustard-coloured cords. He fit right in. When he was introduced to Imelda, he said, 'I always loved his translations from the Irish, they are so unpretentious.' And she said, 'Yes. Yes.'

Speeches were made, glasses raised. Imelda, as chief daughter and designated mourner, unfolded many sheets of paper, dipped her face towards the microphone and spoke of the great love between her father and her mother which would, in Phil's poetry, never fade.

Connie stood to one side for all this and kept smiling. She was wearing a dove-grey pantsuit over a black satin blouse and Carmel wondered briefly what she had seen in Phil, who was so barely presentable, even by the standards of the day. Also, whether she'd had some work done since they'd met her in the Shelbourne because she now looked years younger than Imelda, who was intoning in her widow's weeds up on the podium.

'And grateful too, that we had such a man to call "Daddo".'

Nell watched it all with solemn eyes and afterwards went slowly around the photographs on display. There was her grandfather in a knitted tank top on a forest road, there he was with a stalk of hay in his mouth. Some of the images were familiar to Carmel, others showed a life his daughters never knew. Phil in the same hand-knitted top, but with skyscrapers at his back. Phil in a university gown receiving a scroll onstage. A couple of black-and-white snaps were taken in grey-toned, over-lit Greece, perhaps by a journalist. A mighty low angle showed a man at a table outdoors, bare-chested and tanned, and it was Phil, writing a poem. At the same table, an after-dinner scene: Phil's arm is slung around a woman who leans away from him to pose with an elderly man. The woman is dark-haired and beautiful in a way you can only be when young – but even Phil looks unbearably young. Three years after he left them in Dublin, he looked just great.

And moody, in a poetical kind of way. The girl was the one he turned out into the street in her nightie – at least that was how the rumour went. In the photograph, they are clearly in the middle of an argument. In the poem, she is bleeding from the wrist.

> Persephone leaves her throne
> nine seeds of bright blood
> braceleted about the bone

There was nothing Carmel could do with these stories except ignore them over the years.

She was the stranger at the gate, holding on to the bars with red woollen gloves. She was a woman weeping at his funeral, who had no right to weep. She was a girl in love with death, who slept with Carmel's father because that felt like dying to her.

Connie was standing beside her, in a waft of light perfume, and this caused Carmel to startle. It was as though the American moved around on rollers. She said: 'Thank you for being so reasonable and generous in all this. It was something I needed to finish. I am so happy we got the chance to be together for this evening, it has been very special for me. Oh, and is this Nell?'

'Yes it is. Say hello, Nell.'

'Hi Granny.'

Connie laughed, and she was like a different person, all opened up.

'By marriage, yes. I suppose I am.'

Ronan was peering at the photograph of the table scene. He held one hand behind his back and bent to read the label.

'Is she the poet?' he said, straightening up.

He was speaking to Connie.

'Do you know her?'

'Oh no,' he said. 'Oh my goodness, sorry. No.'

It had to be said that Ronan was getting a bit annoying – except in bed, where he was less and less shy. Carmel was beginning to look forward to the end of their Saturday evenings, though there was an amount of chat to get through first. He was really very talkative. Ronan had a habit of asking things that other men would not ask. Did she know how to change a pin on a bank card? What was the difference between tungsten and fluorescent bulbs? Could she drive a van? Do you have to do a special test to drive a van? Should he use whitening toothpaste or toothpaste for sensitive teeth? Did the government have her bank details, or everyone's bank details, and how did she personally pay the Revenue? Should he switch from clarinet to guitar?

He enjoyed long walks and, after that first stroll along the Dodder, it became a Sunday proposition. They went up Bray Head one week and the next they did the piers. Nell came willingly, that was the shocker, she put down the Nintendo and went to find her shoes. In the car park in Killiney she ran over to Ronan and they started up the hill together as if that was what they had both come here to do.

Carmel followed behind them and was a little sad. The gorse was out and the air just as aromatic as Phil had described it, on his first date with her mother. She thought about Terry walking this path in her bluebell skirt that she never threw out, after. It hung in the wardrobe in Dun Laoghaire for years. The waist was tiny, it must have been about eighteen inches. They used to sneak in to try it on, but Terry was neater and more beautiful than either of her daughters. Cotton with a sheen, whatever that fabric was called.

Near the top of the hill, Ronan and Nell stood to look down the coastline towards Bray.

'They're all Protestants,' he said, indicating the fancy real estate below. 'Apart from the archbishop, you see that tower, in the distance by the trees?'

He was talking, not of the celebrities and solicitors who lived in the area now, but of the families who built here more than a century ago. He pointed out a house that once belonged to a tea planter with estates in Ceylon. The one beside it had twin sons, born in 1900, on the cusp of modern times.

'I've done my research,' he said.

One of the twins was a doctor who joined the Allies during the war, or just *after* the war. He went to Bergen Belsen and brought five orphans back with him to Ireland and this man was called Collis.

He corrected himself.

'They were both called Collis.'

And, then, as though irritated by some implication, 'They were twins.'

'You said that already,' said Nell and Carmel realised he was talking about his thesis, the great work he had abandoned many years ago.

The other twin volunteered for the land army, and went digging for victory in the English countryside and then he wrote about that. He wrote about the countryside and the changing seasons and how to harness a horse. His book was called *The Worm Forgives the Plough*. So that is what they each wrote about. Genocide and farming.

'Right,' said Carmel, wondering how to distract Nell from his blather.

These twins – Ronan was insisting now – wrote books about two completely different, two very important things. They were a fork in the road for humanity. They were the cleft. Also their mother preferred the elder brother from the day they were born. She was quite clear on that point. Minutes between them and she preferred the first.

'They were *identical*.'

'Yes,' said Nell.

They stood in silence for a moment and looked at the view. The sun's setting rays slid, low and horizontal, along a fold in the landscape filling it with yellow haze which ended at the seafront of Bray. Behind that, the Sugarloaf and the Little Sugarloaf – he began to name them for Nell – Katty Gallagher, Djouce, Kippure.

Nell said, 'I think it's time we went back to the car.'

'I think you're right. What about that one?' he said, indicating Carmel. 'Will we bring her with us?'

Nell laughed at his joke. She took Ronan's hand and Carmel's hand, like a child in a Hollywood musical at the end of the story, when everything has been fixed.

The next Sunday they went along the cliff side between Bray and Greystones, and doubled back to the car park. When Carmel pulled her seat belt across, he asked her for a favour.

'I need a lift on Wednesday. Just a thing in Vincents that I need twilight sedation for, and they won't sign off on it unless you have a lift home.'

'A thing?'

'Just, you know.'

Carmel was busy on Wednesday – she knew this because there wasn't a day when she was not busy. Also, the way he was talking, this wasn't a root canal, it was some kind of event below the waist.

'What thing? What kind of thing?' said Nell from the back seat.

'What time?'

'I don't know,' he said. 'Sometime in the morning.'

Carmel wondered what it would be like to live your life in vague tranches, like 'morning' and 'afternoon'. She put the car in reverse, checked back over her shoulder.

'Yes of course.'

He was silent on the trip home and, when they got to his place, turned to Nell with a tragic air.

'You see that river?' he said. 'That is called the Dodder, and there is a kingfisher who lives somewhere along the water, I don't know where, but if you are very quiet, you will see them, because there are two, and one is as bright as the other. They are a pair. Do you know how to spot a kingfisher?'

'Yes.'

'You have to pretend you are not looking, and if you are lucky, they come.'

'Right.'

'Don't forget that now.'

'I won't.'

'Good luck, Nell!'

It was, of course, a colonoscopy. And the nurse, of course, knew his father when she was a student, she 'adored that man'. And the consultant, unbelievably, asked Ronan about his father's death before he pushed the camera in. Ronan was bewildered on the way home. Carmel had to haul him up to the apartment and wait for the sedation to wear off, she lost half a day to it.

Polyps. Ronan's annoying medical connection magicked up a phone call from the consultant the next morning to say he had snipped them out 'on the way past', and sent everything off to the lab. A week later the polyps were benign apart from the one that wasn't, which would require another small procedure and a loss of some colon tissue – not much – as soon as they could schedule it. Ronan was distraught. A Saturday trip to the theatre was disturbed by his wriggling in the seat beside her. He could not eat. He rang her up to tell her about his toilet habits. After one slightly anguished performance – in which he said her name repeatedly – sexually, he ceased to perform at all.

On the day of the operation, she drove him to hospital, walked him in to theatre with her hand on the gurney and his eyes fixed on hers. This time it was a full anaesthetic and he had not come out of recovery when Carmel arrived back from the office some hours later. She stood there, sixteen tasks left hanging, no idea what was going on.

The nurse said, 'He'll be discharged maybe even tomorrow, we can't say when.'

'Right.'

'Could be anytime, just to give you the heads up. It all depends.'

'Tomorrow?'

'Or the day after.'

'Right.'

Her name must be on the form. Carmel did not know what was written beside her name – partner, girlfriend – but it seemed that she was in charge of Ronan, now.

Was it because they'd slept together? Was that enough? This did not seem like something she could ask the nurse, who was leafing, with efficient mournfulness, through a thick file.

'You have my number?'

'It's right here.'

'Great,' she said.

Did the nurse think she loved Ronan? And did love mean all that?

Carmel couldn't figure it out. How had she ended up with this job, for which she had never applied? Was it the sex – which got good for about two minutes and then wasn't? Or staying over? Maybe that was where the spell got cast. Maybe, if you were a woman, the act of sleeping was enough. It could happen on a bus, you could do it on a plane. You could nod off, wake up beside some strange man who was now yours to mind for life. Carmel wanted to laugh, but actually there was an inner shrieking in her head going, I have a daughter. I have a daughter. I have a daughter, you bitch, she is only nine.

The nurse checked her face, reached for Carmel's forearm. 'He is doing really well.'

Ronan did not do well. There was an infection, a small crisis, a setback, a stay of three weeks. His beard grew in, slightly blond at the tips, and his gentleness continued to break Carmel's heart. Or she wished it would break her heart. She wished that she could lie down – just once, just for a tiny while – and recuperate from her life. And she also wished that she had people to look after her, as Ronan had, without question, women who wanted to look after him. Lovely nurses and a great phlebotomist, a smiling, sad person he may have dated once. She met them beside his bed, women from the choir with cards and chocolates, a sister – never previously mentioned – his aged mother, glimpsed from a distance, as she was helped into the lift. Also one male, his

friend the priest, who sat quietly and read through the newspaper he had brought as a gift, before leaving it on the bed.

'Hello, Father,'

'Ah, Carmel. I've heard so much about you.'

After Ronan was discharged, she took him to the cinema
and for a stroll in Herbert Park. One day she went to his flat
and found him sitting there, staring out over the river. The
place was neat, but the books and the fusty oil paintings
made it look somehow borrowed. Ronan said maybe they
should go away so he could rest up in the sunshine, he
thought Italy might be nice, somewhere with a pool for Nell.

'That would be lovely,' she said.

When he was in hospital, he said, he thought about her
all the time.

'All the time,' he repeated and he looked right at her. This,
Carmel realised, was her cue to walk towards him and kiss
his mouth, that looked redder now because of the beard.

Later, he asked her to bring the rubbish downstairs with
her when she left, and she obliged, wondering as she went
why she was doing all this for a sexual relationship that had no
sex in it, trying to put a shape on a man who was in love with
his own disappointment, who nursed it and sought it out.

She did not call again. He did not call.

It was maybe then that Nell stopped climbing into her bed
on a weekend morning for a chat and a cuddle, and when
Carmel asked about a new skirt she had bought, Nell said,
'Jesus, Mum, *whatever.*'

'What do you think?' She twirled like a fool in front of
her daughter.

'What am I supposed to think?'

'Do you like it?'

'Why would I like it? You're like a hundred years old.
It's a *skirt.*'

River Talk

Said the Dodder to the Tolka
Will you come and dance the polka,
Will you join us for the quadrille
Said the Poddle to the Slang

It is the gurgle of the Dargle
When he's giving up the gargle
It's a dance of happy water,
From the Santry to the Swan.

And my blood runs quick,
My pulse begins to talk
I am flowing to the side
Where you decide to walk
As the storm comes in.

Love is a tide, it is mist
Becoming cloud, it is rain
On the river, water into water
Heart into heart. It is all
Downhill from here.

Will you come and dance the polka,
Said the Dodder to the Tolka
Will you join us for the quadrille
Said the Poddle to the Slang.

ONE OF THE kitchen lights started to fritz and go out and Carmel really did not need the hassle. The bulbs had a big, industrial filament; they were sourced through an expensive shop in town and she had been absurdly pleased to get them. Carmel had ripped the old units out after Ronan, and the more she looked at the new island she put in, the more she saw how massive and ugly the thing was. After a few despairing weeks flicking through interiors magazines, she found these lampshades in a vintage orange, which were like cheery tin hats. Carmel set a bowl of oranges on the island to distract from the depressing gick of the surface stone and the fix worked, more or less. Your eye travelled between the bright colour above and the bright colour below, so the counter dropped out of vision and the bowl, which was a lovely shade of blue, seemed to float in the centre of the room. Cerulean blue. Carmel bought cool, rough-skinned Jaffa oranges to put in the bowl and Nell liked to take one after school. You could hear the slap slap as she walked around the kitchen, chucking it idly from palm to palm.

One trip to the lighting shop later, the dead bulb was

replaced and all was well, until that also went, not long after. Carmel could not figure it out. The row of lamps was wired from the same light fitting, the fuse was not blown. Carmel stocked up on bulbs on her next trip into town and ten days later, it happened again. Or it didn't happen. She flicked the switch and the one between the island and the sink did not go on, again.

When she finally managed to get an electrician into the house, he checked the fitting and swopped it out for a new fitting, though there was nothing wrong with it that he could find. The next time, she persuaded him – against his better judgement – to rewire all the way back to the light switch, and the new bulb fizzled out before she could get a plasterer to seal the ripped line running down the wall.

Carmel thought she would go mad. Every time she thought she had it sorted, she heard that same faint, *ding ding* that preceded the death of the light, and when she came into the kitchen and flicked the switch, on the now ruined wall, she got the same result. Nell, peeling her orange over by the bin, said nothing. Or she looked up and said, 'Huh.'

And Carmel knew.

'Did you do that?' she said.

'What?'

'Did you do that to the light?'

'What?'

'Did you break the light?'

'No.'

'Did you throw the orange up at the light?'

'Did I throw it?'

This repetition, in Nell's parlance, was the word for 'yes'.

'Yes throw it. Yes, throw.'

'The fucking orange,' Carmel said.

'The fucking orange,' she repeated.

'Did you fucking orange?' Carmel's grammar dissolved

as she took the child by her spindly upper arm, slapping at her legs as she circled around – swiping at them and missing, for the most part. So Carmel reached into the bowl and threw one after the other orange at Nell's legs, and that seemed to work, after which they were gone and Carmel threw the empty bowl which bounced off Nell's back and hit the floor, smashing there, so that Nell was stepping and dancing in the shards, which certainly did not bother her mother, who had been through a lot worse, a hell of a lot worse, than a stupid broken bowl.

'You think that's bad?' she said. 'You think that's bad?'

She dealt Nell a crack across the temple with her knuckled fist and, when she fell on the ground, stooped to deliver an open-handed whack on the girl's narrow, bare thigh, which lifted an immediate echo of itself in a flush of red, while liquid blood came from somewhere else, blood that was outside Nell's skin streaked across the floor.

Nell was in her school uniform which was also the colour of dark blood, and she was not screaming. That little leg. And also her head. Carmel had hit Nell a concussive blow. Nell, who had been howling as the oranges flew, was now silent and panting, twisted away from her on the floor, her limbs at an angle, her cheek to the smeared parquet, her knickers – at ten years old – on show, and the five-fingered ruin of Carmel's hand curled up, held high. The hand that hit Nell.

Outside, a pedestrian passed, oblivious.

'Where are you bleeding, where is the blood? I have to see the blood, Nell.'

'No.'

'Nell, I have to see. Nell.'

Nell looked up at her mother and did the Expression. The distorted, eye-bursting rage-face, like a shape being pulled two wrong ways.

Carmel felt empty and a bit silly, then. She may even have laughed. She reached towards her daughter but Nell gave her mother a big *look*, which slowly became a hurt stare. Some satisfaction rising up through it.

You lost.

You lost your temper.

Carmel sat on a chair with her back straight and her hands balanced on either leg. The hand she had used to thump her child was still clenched and she pressed the heel of it down into her thigh. She was like a statue. Some little figurine, or she was huge and stony, a sitting pharaoh in the desert. At the edge of her eye was the open line of the ripped wiring, with daggles of plaster along the edges. On the ground, Nell made herself smaller. A little scrape of broken pot shard as she curled inwards in silence, and tried to cry.

Carmel remembered how she had checked the window. She remembered the flick of her glance, the passing stranger who may have heard, and a slash of shame unzipped her. This was the break that she had asked for. She was not a person anymore, she was not something else either.

She was just not. The feeling was worse than horror, because she could not gather the horror in. She was a painting by a man whose name she could not remember, a thing with the head of a cat. And her father, her father. He was. Her father was. Right there. Her father was bigger than the world and a lot less wonderful. He was vast, like a wall.

Nell was crying properly now, and Carmel willed herself back into the room. She felt the blood pulse in her feet, and she asked the blood in her feet to go all the way up to her hands, her head.

She moved.

She got down on her knees beside her daughter on the floor and Nell had changed again. Something about her mother's brief absence from the world, whatever it was – her absence from her self. Nell lunged upwards into her arms. Poor thing. Beautiful girl. She was asking to forgive, to be forgiven.

'Oh I am sorry.'

'I'm sorry.'

'I am so sorry.'

They crooned to each other.

'I didn't mean it' (even though she must have meant).

'I didn't mean to' (even though).

No one meant it. No one ever meant anything.

'I am so sorry.'

The blood on the parquet had come from a cut on Nell's foot – more of a scrape, it had already stopped when Carmel turned her about to find and assess the damage. Nell did not seem concussed, not in the slightest. There were no bruises, and that was very hard to believe. The oranges had hit or missed, and left no trace. The red mark on the perfect skin of her thigh blanched out – it faded up and away. All the drama had been in the shattering of the stupid bowl, it seemed.

What would you have to do, Carmel wondered, to actually land a child in hospital? Her wonderful daughter, her heart's delight and only joy.

Nell.

It did not seem possible: they had broken the entire world and there was nothing to show for the crime. Or she had broken it – she had to correct herself – it was Carmel alone who had done this thing.

A few days later, she did see a darkness in Nell's hairline, a yellowing bruise in the curve of her back, where the bowl had hit and bounced. Carmel went to ask her about it, and then did not. They were both too confused. They were busy forgetting.

The Penny Drops

I am Brock,
four-square, low to the ground
under which I truffle out orange shell cases,
scraps of rotten cloth, the bonescape
of another animal, the thing you dropped
the day it happened.
Brock knew
by the whisper of its fall
above his head.

Brock can tell
the weight of a body,
the measure of a man's tread.
Brock whickers and waits for the wind
to make good, grass to spring up, earth to silt over
the thing you lost: an acorn, a pebble,
a coin with a hen on the front.

My father had handsome stripes,
my mother was a ghost badger, very beautiful.
The thing to do with dogs, she told me,
is clamp down on the snout, crossways.
Let the dog do the work
of getting away.
I am Brock, I swim in earth
I go through.

These days, I snuffle about my root cathedral,
setting snail shells in a row.
Above me, the wind blackens
a dropped penny and dogs make hulloo.

PHIL

THERE WERE TWO fields in the smallholding where I grew up, a few miles outside Tullamore, and each was, to my boyhood, a universe. The near field was a patch of grass and ragwort, trodden over and back by our few cows. The far meadow was a buzzing, sighing world of high hay and drowsy bees. A third place lay between them, like a pea inside the pod of the hedgerow. This was a small rock quarry, long disused, and I thought of it as a fairy place. In the evening, I left saucers of milk there, in secret patterns, and found them the next day, limned with dew. A raggy thorn bush on the rim was all I needed by way of verification. It was a fairy tree. Our family was watched and ignored by the people of the Shee; other-worldly beings who spoiled the butter and left changelings in the cradle. These fairy folk were the great replacers: they saw what you wanted and gave you something else.

Our household comprised seven children and two adults in a stone cabin, which was lime-washed white and slowly streaked red again on the north-facing gable wall. At night, Old Brock chirruped in the yard, the fox fought and screamed and the green, lacy creatures that lived in thatch turned eyes, in fiery pinpoints, on your sleeping. Dawn was preceded by the run and rustle of hunting birds, and it was not a house to me so much as a creaking ship, a groaning night creature, ploughing the dark waves.

On the midsummer eve when I was nine, I claimed a turn on the edge of the bed and, when all were asleep, swung free of the blanket, hefted my clothes and sprung the latch on the front door. Outside, I stepped into my trousers in air that held, as yet, some murky light. I prepared the trews by pulling them inside-out, as a protection against the Foidín Mara. This is the strange, lost feeling that can come upon a man in a familiar place, a sign he has entered the fairy side of things, and the cure is to turn your clothes the wrong way – back to front will also do.

The gutted trousers pulled high in my fist (for I had forgotten a belt), my practised feet found the path to the old quarry over rough dirt and through cool grass. I reached the edge of the place, walked around to the thorn bush that grew on the lip and sat myself slightly apart, waiting to catch sight of them, or even to catch one in my fist. When I had the fairy man to rights, I would make my wish.

This wish was very simple: that Hanorah Casey would let me walk beside her as we came home from school. That she might take my proffered flower and hold it in her young hand until she reached home. That she would press this flower, and keep the papery ghost of it in her missal forever. Dimly also, in the recesses of my wanting, was a desire to touch her black hair, which was longer than any other girl's and brushed nightly one hundred times. Hanorah Casey was her father's only child. Her mother had died in childbirth and her grandmother doted on Hanorah. She brushed the hair with a china-backed, hog-bristled brush, bought for the price of a pink pig on a fair day in Tullamore. In the summer evenings they could be seen outside the house,

Hanorah in a kitchen chair and her grandmother behind her, singing as the sun set, and it was thought all this tending gave the girl airs.

When lessons were done and we ran about the road playing, she kept to one side. At the crossroads, she walked off without a backward glance. So that was, very precisely, what I wished for. With all my heart and with my eyes squeezed shut, I wished that Hanorah Casey might turn one day after she had bent for home. After she shook out her school-day plait, while I stood admiring the otter gleam of her black hair, I wished she would check over her shoulder to see me looking yet.

The midsummer night sky was swimming with stars. The last light of yesterday and the coming light of tomorrow ringed the pale horizon. I sat and stared into the dark roots of the fairy thorn bush. I stared until the air in front of me became particulate. And in that soot I saw . . . something: a stirring in the grass, a quick lozenge of light that flickered away. It was a shining, shivering blackness. And there was a laugh. Clear as anything I have heard, before or since, I heard laughter.

The laugh came out of deep, velvety silence. It was released so close to my ear, he might have been sitting inside it. Knowing, delicious, spiteful: the moment I heard the sound, I realised some part of God's creation was jealous of Hanorah Casey's black hair.

I don't recall how I made it back to the cottage door, though the ruckus I caused when I got there went down in lore as the night I went off with the fairies.

'And sometimes I think,' my mother used to add, 'that we never got him back again.'

I had always been a dreamy child. After this night, I began to think I might be a cruel one, as though the fairy laughter had implicated me in all that was sinister in this world. I wandered down to confession, which was not in those days an organised thing, and I told the priest I had stolen one of the long matches from the cardboard box on the beam over the hearth. Indeed, I had the match in my pocket, still. I told him I had a mind to burn the house down, and when he asked what had gotten in to me at all, I said it was the tiny red eyes that glowed in the thatch at night.

The priest, who was a bookish man called Father Madden, considered the problem. He said I should bring to mind tears of the Virgin Mary, that quenched all sparks of wickedness, and the miracle of these tears was that they were shed for me alone.

I told him in addition I had kicked my brother Francis in the bed, because he would not let me be and Father Madden said that a brother can be a burden as well as a blessing, you only have to look at the story of Esau and Jacob, and a wriggler in the bed can be a very great trial.

'He makes me sick,' I said.

'Does he put his hand on you?'

There was no answer to that.

'He pinches me, Father.'

Father Madden said if he touched me again I should whisper the Hail Mary at him, and if that didn't work, get out and sleep on the floor.

Such was the power of priests in the close spaces of Ireland, that after this time, my middle brother was permanently rotated to lie by the wall, with the eldest stretched between us. And though, to this day, I sleep better with my nose dipped over the edge of a mattress, I found it hard to find gratitude for the priest, who had slipped some knowledge he had of me deep into my dreams.

In this way, sin was piled on sin and I thought there would be no end to it. Before the month's end I was back kneeling in the box, telling Father Madden I had sinned against the love of God, due to the obduracy of my despair, and that this was a grave matter which put me in fear for my mortal soul.

The whole business of sinning, once you were in it, could only get worse, I said. There was always a bigger one behind the little one, if you had a mind to look.

'What age are you?'

'I am ten and two months, Father.'

And in that moment, I believe, Father Madden decided he would make a priest of me.

Every Friday, I was to call to the parish house, go to his study, take a book from his desk and lay the book from the previous week down. If the room was empty, which it rarely was, it meant a parishioner was dying and he had been called to administer the last rites. So to my many other sins was now added the hope that some poor soul would make an exit on a Friday afternoon, because the price of each book was the report I gave to Father Madden, while the next volume, burning with possibility, was tucked under my arm.

The parochial house was an echoing place. The first carpet I ever felt under my bare feet was in the hall, even the wooden knob on his study door seemed fancy. The housekeeper looked on as I tugged, and Father Madden's tired voice came from the other side of the door.

'Twist it. Twist.'

Inside, there was a fire in winter, a bright window of many panes, shelves of books and sometimes a biscuit left on a plate, from his afternoon tea.

'So what did you think of it?'

This ritual continued for more than one hundred books. We moved from devotional pamphlets to the lives of the saints, especially the Irish saints, and then to *Songs of the Gaels*. This was my favourite: the contents page alone might kindle old sorrows and new longings in a boy's heart: 'The Palatine's Daughter', 'The Song of the Black Potatoes', 'The Foam White Sea City', 'I Am Asleep and Don't Waken Me'.

I think Father Madden enjoyed my precocity. I stood in front of the desk, my toes pawing Turkey carpet and a biscuit in my hand, singing my responses. Each visit lasted ten minutes and no more. As the months went by, this felt like too little time for all I had saved up to say to him.

My close association with the church brought other blessings, and it seemed the fortunes of our small household were finally on the turn. A place was found for my mother doing substitute teaching in a schoolroom in town, and this later became a secured post. She was soon cycling off to work, her cheeks rosy and her arms grown lean in the beating of children that were not her own. There was money that Christmas for a flitch of bacon, a cake thick with raisins. The next summer, we would move to a healthy, slate-roofed house on a street in Tullamore, a house that had the additional excitement of stairs leading to separate bedrooms on the first floor.

That last Christmas in the little cabin was a time of endings. My sister Deirdre left for a nursing course in England and this was the occasion of much weeping and many farewells. In the midst of all her goings-on, the eldest boy slipped away. It just happened. He was in Dublin for some small reason, and then gone to America. This was my brother Barry, and he had always been kind to me.

My father stood at the door with Barry's letter in his hand, and he looked out at the two poor fields, the single cow with a blind teat, a few bullocks. There was no grand estate for a son to inherit, and yet the departure of his firstborn was so deep a blow, his name would not be spoken in the house again.

To the envy of all, my middle brother Francis was then

taken out of school in order to tend the farm, so he was always about the place now, and free to torment me at any time. My afternoons were spent out of his sight, roaming the byways, where I was king of the hedges. I watched the nests of birds, stuck twigs into cowpats; I saw mayflies split to let a better mayfly out. You could find me on the railway bridge saluting the bargemen as they slid under it with their loads of turf or porter. Another small bridge carried the canal itself over the Tullamore River, and this intersection was mysterious to me, the way slow water crossed quick water and each travelling a different way. A ruined castle stood close by that place, with a patch of woodland where I touched the scars of its ancient trees, pulled rainwater from their long buds. In a patch of sally scrub that no one cared about, I wove the rods about my head and into this little den I carried the priest's books to read, with the sounds of the countryside visiting and leaving as the mood and wind took them.

The blackbird says: – Have it yourself, or be without it
The corncrake says: – Very late, very late
The finch says: – Pink, pink
The lark says: – Pee-pee-pee. No shoemaker on earth can make a shoe for me

As spring came in, I was grown desperate for acknowledgement from sweet Hanorah Casey, and this was also the case for the other boys at school. In all our games, she was the prize. In my dripping hut of sally rods, I wrote poems of love unrequited. (To this day, I am not sure there is any other kind of poem.) Some instinct told me it wasn't fighting or football impressed her, so I took to reading soulfully and in public, using the priest's books as a lure.

One morning, my luck turned. I had a guide to Irish wildflowers from Father Madden which I flicked through as I walked, telling the difference between speedwell and forget-me-not, and as in a dream, she was at my shoulder, looking in the ditch and checking the page.

'We need something for the May altar,' she said.

And so she picked and I named; a bog-bound Eve and her loving Adam. We found cranesbill and sweet violet, a scraggy handful of bitter vetch. Hanorah stripped the leaves and made a posy for the table at the top of the schoolroom with its statue of Our Lady and two bud vases, one on either side. We glanced at the altar from time to time, and once or twice we glanced at each other, and I was never as happy after, as I was that first day in May.

The evening before, which was May Eve, my father went about the land sprinkling holy water in the corners of the two fields and came back in, as from a funeral.

'That will be the last of it,' he said.

In truth, he hated the work of farming and would thrive in town, where he took up, full-time, his occupation of blaggard-at-large. My father, Damien McDaragh, was a small, fiercely beautiful man, a great dancer in his youth. Sometime before I was born, the socket of his right eye had been caught on the horn of a strawberry cow and, though he kept the eye, he could not keep it from drifting towards the wall. This cast gave him an untrustworthy air, and he did his best to live up to it.

He had a great hunger for gambling. Sunday evenings would find him in a tight cluster, tossing red pennies at the crossroads, and he paced the land now at dusk, eyeing the badger's sett on the boundary. There was something about Old Brock that was an insult to my father: he could not leave the place until he had drawn him out from his earth. At the big fair in Tullamore, he found the man who had the dogs to settle the score for good.

He ducked in through the door that evening, half cut on porter, slapping his cap on his thigh. The dogs were the mightiest dogs in County Offaly. One of them was a mixed terrier, the other was a Kerry Blue. The word was already out, the earth would be dug on Saturday, and the match would take place a day later, in the evening after the May procession.

The sett was at the end of the far meadow in a rumpled piece of earth that gave way, on the other side of a bit of wire, to a few trees. These belonged to Jackie Mike, an oddity of a man who bothered no one. Spread under those trees, in the spring of my eleventh year, was a coming wealth of bluebells.

Saturday marked the arrival of the dogs. The men of the house went down to the place with shovels, and a barrel, and an old winnowing sheet. As the smallest, I was dispatched under the wire to Jackie Mike's, where I stuffed three holes with rushes and tallow fat and lit the straw with a long match. When these had been smoking a while, the stranger took his smaller dog and slung him along the tunnel which was Brock's front door. After a long silence, a scream came from inside the ground on which we stood: the depth of it, muffled by clay, was very stirring. The dog backed out, dragging a cub by the scruff, which it shook out vigorously, as soon as he got the little badger clear.

By some miracle, the cub latched on to the dog's shoulder, mid shake, and the two were locked together in a circle of suddenly bucking, bloody fur. At great effort, the dog whipped the badger loose, but he lost a chunk of his own hide with it, leaving a whirl of bright blood on the grass. His handler was on him instantly, pushing his snout down to the ground and fixing the young badger with his boot. After a feint of reluctance, the dog was obliged to yield his prize.

The stranger gestured for a shovel which he lifted high and brought down fast on the badger's narrow, elegant head. There was a clanging sound, the noise of metal hitting bone. The cub twitched and stared, his skull intact. As the shovel was lifted again, I looked into the animal's eyes and he into mine and we understood each other completely. Brock knew me as well as he knew his own death. We were, in that moment, as intimate as living creatures ever could be. The shovel came down again, even as I looked away.

My father and Francis were digging out the entrance, meanwhile, where smoke now curled through the collapsing clay. Out through this burst Old Brock, magnificent and large. The crying dogs pounced forward and away, the stranger called, 'Stay back.' He hurried up with the winnowing sheet but misjudged the breeze and it landed wide. The dogs kept the badger at bay and it was thrown again. This time, Brock found the edge and slipped out from under it, moving towards open ground. A third, swift attempt landed true. The animal moved blind under the hemp, a shifting mound that stopped, moved again, stopped entirely. The stranger knelt and wrapped the cloth skilfully under the animal. He twisted it into a bag and lifted the thing high. This jerking, screaming object was then dropped into the barrel and the lid set down.

I was the only one of the group who saw her go: a ghost badger, not entirely white, her stripes two fawn shadows on a fair, wise face, her pelt a rufous shimmer in the dappled woodland. At her side was a black and white cub and dangling from her mouth, was the one we had tried to kill. It had skittered out from under the stranger's boot as Old Brock burst out to face his attackers, and to save his child.

I did not tell.

*

That evening, my heart on fire, I went back to the ruined sett and snatched bluebells up from under Jackie Mike's trees. These, I carried to the house of Hanorah Casey, where I knocked and stood trembling. The door opened enough to let her slip round the edge of it. She stood and I stood. Neither of us moved. I thrust the posy at her and she looked at it, then took the flowers carefully in her hand. Hanorah walked with me to the wall, then further out on to the road, and with no formal invitation, we found ourselves strolling together in the May evening, talking about fine things and small things and whatever took our fancy.

On the Sunday morning, in a state of love exalted, I hung around the church gate with the other boys, waiting for the May procession. First the curate with his book, next the head altar boy with a crucifix on a long staff. On either side of him were two lesser altar boys with gold candlesticks and surly expressions. They were followed by a hundred small girls in white dresses, herded by a couple of wind-blown nuns. After these came taller girls, their ghostly long veils sent sideways across their faces, a brigade of girls in blue capes, more little ones with baskets of flowers, a few holding long ribbons attached to the bier on which a wooden statue of the Virgin was solemnly carried. At the end of all, as though wading through sheep, came the priests in surplices and birettas, Father Madden among them, walking in the rain.

I was watching out for Hanorah, whose face was shadowed by lace netting. I would know her by the queenly way she held herself apart, I would not mistake her for any other girl. But it was raining hard and I could not, in this soggy mass of white, recognise her after all.

That same afternoon, the meet was held in the quarry where the rocky ground would hamper the badger from digging down. The watching men stood in a doomy circle on the rim. Most of the money went to the stranger, my father complained after, even though he had supplied Brock, who was both hero and victim, and the perfect Colosseum to kill him in. As for himself, he lost all judgement and gambled his profit away.

I had a big round penny I put on the Kerry Blue, and I lost it just as fast when the dog came out yowling. The red terrier, his shoulder still black with yesterday's blood, was sent down the pipe into the barrel and he backed out slowly to mighty cheers. These faded when we saw, attached to his snout, the clamped teeth of the badger. The dog was not pulling Brock out so much as trying to pull himself away from it, and when he succeeded, he left half his muzzle behind.

'Let him finish,' the stranger said, for the dog was useless to anyone now. Maddened with pain, he savaged the badger's back leg, but there was blood in his eyes and it was not long before the terrier miscalculated. In a lightning strike, his throat was ripped out clean and Brock turned hissing for the next contender. This was the Kerry Blue, who would be nobly retired on a ripped ear, but not before the badger was fully crippled behind and dragging himself along on his belly.

A number of younger dogs were thrown in then to give them a taste, first in pairs and then all together. It was a good time before mighty Brock was still and even then, we did not approach, in case he had another bite in him.

The men dispersed in twos and threes. They went quietly in fear of the guards, but also in reverence for what they had seen. Among them was Hanorah's father, who did not speak to me that afternoon, nor I to him. Why would we? He was a silent man, I was a boy of eleven. But I did feel his eyes resting on me, once or twice. When all were gone and my father counting money into the stranger's hand, Francis, my brother and tormentor, slipped by to me to say, 'You heard what happened to your lady love?'

I was dealing with the badger, his lips snarled back, in death, from tiny teeth, his eyes staring. I turned in rage and fumbled this heavy, bloodied thing against my brother's chest. That was the only time I bested him, when he stumbled back and I fell on top of him, and the dishonoured corpse of Old Brock was cooling between us.

The next morning, which was a Monday, Hanorah came to school and her black hair was gone. It had been cut to a raggedy short length at the base of her skull.

Her father had taken her plait. He had walked down to a neighbour's to ask for a lend of their good shears, so the whole countryside would know what he was doing. She had been seen out walking with a boy, he said.

'Sure what harm?' said the neighbour.

The story was, he hung the severed thing on the front gate, so anyone could touch it, if that is what they so desired.

After lessons that day, we watched her as she walked apart. Hanorah was a skinny lath of a girl. The hem of her skirt was uneven, one sock held good and the other sock sagged as the children jeered her bald neck. She tried to keep herself upright, and bent in the effort. Her arms would not stay freely by her sides, but must wrap around her skinny chest instead. Such was the fierceness of my feelings, that I jeered her too. This creature. I threw a clod of grass that hit her narrow, bare calf. The girl I had once loved, I now deplored. My eyes burning with unshed tears, it was then I discovered the true meaning of that fairy laughter.

> Oh Mary we crown Thee with blossoms today
> Queen of the Angels and Queen of the May

The next year, I was that surly altar-boy followed by the little girls of five parishes, all in white. The McDaragh family had, by that time, moved in to Tullamore proper and I missed my former country life. The town was, to me, a place of buying and selling, not of faith. I remembered how ramshackle and disappointing this day always turned out to be: the blustery singing, the absence of wonder. It was poverty wrapped as innocence, in virgin white. I was on the cusp of adulthood. The Catholic Church, with all its attempted pomp, seemed to me a cheap postcard from the eternal.

Sometime later that year, I told Father Madden as much. I told him that he had not made a priest of me after all, but a poet.

I thought, at twelve years old, that I would never forget the look on the old priest's face, that I would set my course by it. Now, I know the indelible thing was the glance I exchanged with the badger pup, as he waited for the fatal blow to fall. Nothing in my life, before or since, has matched that connection. It was a peak of understanding from which my whole existence, with its loves and false joys and tedious losses, has slowly fallen away.

Facit

In a grotto outside Tullamore,
I saw the Virgin weep for me.
It was dark and I was drunk
and begging hard. Her tears

were white, her cheek beige,
her eyes uplifted to implore.
I scrambled up to her, traced
the melt of clay to flesh

along the cleft of her softening
mouth, felt with grubby fingertip
the wetness there, heard the rustle
of cloth, her opening words.

I make a monument
of my heart I make

NELL

I DON'T KNOW what I thought would happen in London, but what actually happened was an accommodation crisis, because Lily has a life and a relationship and a room in King's Cross that is exactly fifteen feet square. We weren't students anymore, she told me, and by the way the sink was not a self-cleaning mechanism, could I take the gunk out of the plug when I was done. I went online to look for house-sits, but they needed references and agency fees, and it was all very difficult. What I wanted, more than anything, was some uninterrupted crying time. I had a screaming need to be alone. I did not say this to Lily, I told her I needed to write a book. Which, when you think about it, is probably code for the same thing.

Then her girlfriend got on board and found me some pet-sitting in the middle of nowhere. A train, and then a bus to a village in Norfolk, where two hearty women picked me up in their Volvo and issued instructions, one louder than the other. It was like a double Carmel, I had to repeat everything back to them, many times. The cottage was heritage chintz, with low black beams and terrible Wi-Fi. The dog was mostly made of hair, in the middle of which was a pair of friendly, oddly indifferent eyes.

In the morning I woke to flat countryside and no signal on my phone. The fridge was full, there was a tiny butcher's shop in the village a mile down the road, also a place to buy milk and bread. This shop had teenaged boys sitting on a pedestrian rail which guarded a deserted traffic light outside the entrance. They had their shirts off in the sunshine and I tried not to look at their skinny, pale torsos as I went inside. I could not remember why I ever wanted to sleep with a man, it did not seem medically possible. Not that I wanted a woman either, though in the three weeks that followed, I caught a flicker now and then – a mother calling to her children in the fens, a girl fixing her eyelash in a car mirror – someone I might love or might want to be, in a different life.

Twice a day the dog dragged me down the designated laneway and lost herself in a stretch of marsh and rushes, then came lolloping back when I rattled her tin of treats. Twice a day I snapped a photograph for the ladies, and walked to the gate to find a signal to send it. Occasionally I got a picture back 'for the dog'. Here we are in the blue city of Jaipur, here we are in front of the Taj Mahal. At night I read their English novels and watched their English TV, I slept to the low conversational hum of the BBC World Service, dreaming about 1960s It Girls or the history of Persian poetry, waking to the dog sleeping illegally across my feet on the bed.

Every day, we opened the door to new weather and walked to the marsh, where I tracked her rustle through dry grasses, or I let her drag me further across field and fenland. Every day I wanted to be alone, but there was the dog, who scratched at doors between us, who could not be from my side. The dog was such a mood machine. When I cried, she licked the salty inside of my limp hand. When we roamed out under that huge sky, it felt like I was looking for the edge of my own fear, and each return gathered something back in.

The world was very beautiful. It was far too beautiful to abandon. Or was it too beautiful to live in? These questions were very hard to answer. I took suicidal notice of the tiny changes in the hedgerows, the differences underfoot, all the things that were hard to leave. One afternoon, I turned to the *tseep tseeep* of a canary on a strand of wire that turned out to be a yellow wagtail – so rare! – his olive-coloured back, his turmeric-stained belly and head. With a little hop of joy, I thought, I can kill myself now I have seen this wagtail, and then I thought, But what about the dog? Three times a day, I ate cheese on toast with her heavy chin laid on my thigh, her dog-eyes beseeching.

When the ladies came back I opened my mouth to speak for the first time in a week or more. The sound of my voice floated out of me, and hung there.

I'll miss her so much, I said.

I kissed the dog before I went (the fact was, I had been kissing her for some time) and wore my doggiest jumper on the train. I had that landscape feeling on the journey down to Folkestone. The line through the countryside was a closing zip and I was moving on.

In Paris I met an Irish guy.

Do I recognise the accent? he said.

I suppose you do.

We hung out into the evening, drank, ate, drank again, made out. I brought him back to my tiny hotel room to have holiday sex and this is fine, because we are in Paris and there are net curtains drifting into the room on a warm updraught there is a lot of funky old wallpaper lit by the street lamp outside, and I lift my phone to record this. I hold it above us and take the picture: his thigh, my thigh, some sheet, belly, the shadowed swell of breast. I link and send to Felim's number like I just did nothing at all.

ping!

– nice

Felim is awake and ready for this. He is a nanosecond away. He is right there.

The fuck, says the guy beside me. Did you just do that?

No.

Seriously?

He is out of the bed and he's grabbed my phone, he is looking at the picture, which does not include his face. I could have told him that. He slings it back down.

Jesus, he says.

It's fine.

Yeah. Wow.

Don't you like it? I say, but my voice comes out kind of twisted.

That's a really funny thing to do.

You don't like it?

I am wheedling – that is the word for the sound I am making.

That's insane.

I twitch away from him. He looks at me and makes some decision, clambers back on to the creaky narrow bed.

Come here.

Surrounding me with chest, arms, his upper leg, he strokes my hair, says, I didn't mean to scare you, alright?

I am with a stranger who is comforting me and also naked. And I am thinking, What the fuck, nice guy? Who gave you all that nice? I can't wait for him to leave, so I can get back out into the streets of Paris where I will swing my hair back and place my hands on either side of my face, and walk on, refusing to weep.

On the next train, I spend my time looking at pictures of the dog: enlarging, scoping, checking. She is a Goldendoodle called Sookie and she loves me as I love her. I have forty-seven pictures of this dog. I look at her button eyes, her muddy paws, her pink dab of tongue.

I go to Mal in Utrecht, where he is doing a masters and smoking too much weed. He lives overlooking a canal, or maybe it's a river. He has a bicycle, though you can also walk anywhere here. So we walk. Dutch people leave their curtains open and you can see into their living rooms as you pass on the street, and in the centre of Utrecht, those rooms are perfect, every window frames a still life. Mal says Dutch children play outside on their own, and go wherever they want so long as they are home for dinner. Also, one night, we drink late and the barman won't serve Mal's friend Adnan because he is not white.

Happened.

The first night, we rolled up and settled in to Mal's fourth-floor apartment, which is one huge room with rafters running up to a point, like an upturned boat. Mal says it is cheap because of the noise from the cafes along the water, but I sneak around online and think it really isn't cheap, and that Mal is being totally funded by his property-speculating dad. The wall over his desk is pinned with pictures of those futuristic buildings with hanging gardens and trees on balconies, and I ask how come they never get built.

Well yeah, he says.

It's just trees. Not exactly high-tech.

Say that in a Dutch accent, he says. Go on.

When I saw him at the train station, we hugged and I

remembered how he was so skinny and long. He has a fresh ink of a bee above his thumb and an open safety pin tattooed on his forearm. I show him my *love is a tide* and he pulls down his collar so I can see the letter 'A' in cursive on the base of his neck.

Who's A? I said.

Annie.

This is a guy who puts his little sister's initial above his collarbone. He is the sweetest person and I love him like he never faded out on me, never wandered off and erased all our good times.

How's Lily? Who are you working for now?

Still freelancing.

Great.

For some reason, I feel disbelieved.

Later, I tell him I've been involved with someone. Hard to say if we're even a thing. But anyway. He's called Felim and, I don't know. He's a bit, maybe coercive?

Mal looks away from me and says, Oh you.

We are smoking some mild, sweet-natured Kush, which he passes over.

He's just very indifferent, I say. And kind of mean.

My kind of guy, says Mal.

Yeah, well.

The sounds of cafes and bars below. There are people in kayaks on the water, even though it is dark, and everyone out there is having a fun time.

We talk about people from home. Mal doesn't see anyone much, he rarely checks his phone. He is a funny boy, Mal. He takes what is in front of him and leaves the rest behind.

I tell him Lily is in a relationship with an older woman in London, and I think she's a bit of a bully. Shona went into IT and fell in love with a guy in IT which seems impossible when you say it all in one go, but she is really keen, dieting for the dress, scouting 'island venues' quote unquote for the big day. Romance is clearly something she feels she can afford, or am I just jealous? Because I can't afford it, that's for sure.

The thing you don't understand, he says.

Me?

OK, women. The thing women don't understand is that love and sex are opposite things.

Oh shut up.

True.

You never had a crush?

Like you would not believe, he says.

Well then.

I'm just saying, love is a higher function, and I am all for that, please, yes, may we all get there someday. Meanwhile, sex is a beast.

This makes me laugh, even though I don't want to laugh. There is some extra hit in this stuff, and I can't stop the giggles. They well up, burst out of my face in a slow-motion, peristaltic wave. I am a broken-hearted woman, trapped in a body that finds everything hilarious. It feels a bit like vomiting.

The fuck is this?

And Mal says, Good evening, Utrecht.

An unspecified amount of time later, I remember what I want to say.

No it's not.

Mal circles the joint in the air.

Love requires (he pauses, looking for the right term) two acts of submission, and sex (he pauses again) really doesn't.

On Saturday evening Mal goes up to the big city and he comes back in the door secretly pleased – like he just killed someone and got away with it. Sunday is all comedown. He wakes late, eats three Koka Noodles in a row, then lies down for a long existential wrangle on the sofa.

Mal is studying urban spaces. Everything he does just leads him back to the thing he is trying to escape, he says. He'll end up working for some developer, getting his ugly pile of bricks past the planning authorities. But what can you do, people have to live someplace. You might as well plant them a few fucking trees.

Right.

You think you can walk away but you really can't walk away, because, guess what? There isn't anywhere else to go.

Right.

So yeah. I think. Yeah. You might as well plant a few fucking trees.

I am sitting on a slim, trendy, egg-type chair: a long scoop of orange leather on a swivel podium. An object beyond the dreams of any Irish landlord. And I see a future for Mal, because it is a bit like his past. But I do not see a future for me.

Mal tells me a story he read somewhere about a planet where everyone is the same gender, let's call it 'male'. So they are all equal and happy until one of them starts to like another one a tiny bit more than the rest. He wants this guy's company, his particular attention, he starts to miss being with him, it is possible he is even – shock horror – attracted, and this feeling spreads through his system like a blush. And this is actually a metabolic shift, his body starts to change, which is mortifying because everyone can see it happening, including the special guy, who is also completely embarrassed and maybe a bit disdainful. After a few weeks, the one with the crush is fully transitioned to a different gender, let's call it 'female', and some male shags them, maybe not even the male they wanted in the first place, and that is how the species propagates. So the trick on this planet is not to fall in love. Not ever. Because if that happens, you are literally fucked.

Huh, I said.

You are the pussy.

No I get it, thank you. I do get it.

And you might like being the pussy, because that can also be nice.

Back in college Mal used to say the golden rule was never shag someone who has more problems than you, but he spent six months with a guy who was so fucked up you couldn't be near it for too long. This guy, Paul, was lit up by damage, super-skinny, lip-chewing, the lot. And anytime you saw them together, they bickered and bitched like something out of the 1990s.

What about Paul? Was that love?

Oh Christ, says Mal. I don't know. I couldn't fix all that. I couldn't.

What?

That was really hard.

Now Mal is going to bondage clubs at the weekend and I say, that is so exciting, can I come, I'd love to see some – whatever – piss play. But I also don't mean it, and I worry about him. I worry he might get hurt by being hurt. I worry – I cannot help it – that it will make him less of a person, in the long run.

It's not like that.

Why not?

Just. You go in the door. And it is what it is. And then you leave.

In the morning Mal goes to class and I walk the streets taking pictures and making notes. I buy a ticket for the cathedral tower which is, they say, the tallest in the Netherlands and then I have a panic attack inside this tower, entombed in its stone walls, a hundred metres above the sane and lovely city of Utrecht. There are 465 steps and it happens on step number 440, or thereabouts.

My journey upwards starts in a beautiful tower room which has a narrow stairway in the corner. This turns at right angles, on stone steps worn slippy and black, up to a high space with soaring windows on each side. In the centre of this room is a massive wooden frame holding rows of bells. People duck under the beams to stand inside the biggest one, which has a clapper as long as a man. I do this too, to sense the bell's weight and balance, to feel a hum inside the metal walls. I ding with a knuckle and think of sound as a force that might knock you down.

The room on the next level contains a rotating brass drum like the guts of a giant music box, many cogs and gears, another frame of bells, worked by a slightly clumsy keyboard. This array, a sign tells me, is the carillon.

Finally then, the spiral staircase to the roof, which appears to be inside the wall – a single-file twist around a slender pole of stone, with not enough room to pass if you were to meet someone coming down. There is barely enough space to put both feet on the narrowing slice of each step. A really fat person might get wedged in here, I think, and then I feel very, increasingly fat. I turn and turn around the central axis and I don't feel I am climbing higher so much as winding tighter, wringing myself out.

I cannot breathe.

The couple behind me are Polish perhaps, and behind them are voices that sound American. I fill the staircase to bursting, I am an international impediment. The Poles stop and turn back to say, Moment please, and below them an American voice says, Mom? Below me the stairway clogs up and clogs up some more.

I am really working my lungs now. I think I might be able to stagger up sideways, with my back against the circling wall, but there is an opening to shoot arrows through, and I think I might fall out of it, down to the ground below. I worry I will hit my head on the roof, even though I know the roof will rise with me as I go, because the roof is the underside of the ascending steps on the next twist round. My body does not understand this. My body thinks the roof is getting lower. My body wants to crawl and, after a small time, I allow it to sink down, reach out with my hands, use my left leg, left leg, like a demented half-crab, one step after another, up out to the open air.

I stand up in a wire cage, stretched between decorative Gothic stone. You can see the city below and the flatness of the countryside in every direction. The American family look out on the Netherlands, the Polish couple look out. The wire cage empties and fills again, empties and fills, while I focus on the rational, Dutch horizon line. This view has been available since 1382. On a fine day you can see both Amsterdam and Rotterdam. I think of the far skyline slowly scribbled in with new buildings over the centuries. The breeze is nice.

The third or fourth time the place empties I empty out too, following a neat, probably Korean, middle-aged foursome. The wall is under my right hand, and this feels better to me, though I can still only use one foot, repeatedly. As I go down, I say the word 'carillon' to myself over and over.

Carillon

Carillon

Carillon

Down at the bottom of this awful screw the carillon is more antique and lovely than before. I am walking through a musical instrument, I am inside it.

Another level down, the big bells are splendid again. I

stand looking up at the frame on which they depend – my heart in a flurry of exaltation.

I think that maybe I should stop smoking Mal's fearsome Dutch weed. I don't know if I suffer from claustrophobia or vertigo, a fear of towers, a fear of spiral staircases (why is anxiety always described as a spiral?). I have body dysmorphia, I have panic, I have issues. But I also think that beauty is to blame, because without beauty there can be no fear.

How do I phrase this? The machine of the tower has tipped me into another place. The fear I have is the fear of angels. It is not terror, but awe.

I wait until there is no one on the narrow, slippy-stoned staircase, which I negotiate on my bum, not because I am afraid of falling, or of the people behind me, but because I couldn't give a damn anymore. I have discovered the angelic. I reach the big room. I go down the broad stairs and saunter out of there, breathing light and air.

Back in Mal's flat and I say, I love you but I have to go. And when he looks up from his desk, I think Mal is a bit of an angel too.

Not yet, he says.

Soon.

That evening I try a post about phobias, gleaned from the list on Wikipedia which is not exactly original, I know.

Fear of yellow

Fear of eyes

Fear of buttons

Fear of love

It does not list a fear of staircases, even though they are in every horror movie ever made.

Do you remember that drawing thing when we were kids called Spirograph?

Mal says, I really do.

He finds a video, offers a joint which I decline, and we watch a pair of anonymous hands turn geometric shapes and flowers, by way of a pen stuck through a plastic cog. The cog turns inside a ring in an oddly lopsided way, giving one further petal each time.

You don't have to worry about the math of this, says the video geek, as he switches a green marker for a red.

And you think it might go spiralling further and forever but the shape completes itself, each time, the line joins up to finish a last petal, so it is not a spiral so much as a complicated, twisted circle, and this is very satisfying. Mal turns the video to quarter-speed, mutes it, lets it play.

I look up fear of angels and land in Christian Internet. This is a very scary place which tells me that the first words out of every angel's mouth are, Do not be afraid.

Every angel that ever appeared.

Fear not, fear not.

From the train south, Mal and I continue our conversation about love. I know what I want to say now.

– *Love is not a higher function. It is the first function, it is the first thing we know.*

He sends a meme. A quote from some Japanese writer set against a pretty sunset (for some reason). It says:

– *The masochist is always in control.*

I am writing a guide for anxious travellers, maybe on WordPress. Or a real book, even. A little piece of auto-fiction. I will call it, I don't know.

It is for people who think they might kill themselves if they see a yellow wagtail.

For people who assume they are the problem.

For those of us with bossy mothers, which is all of us.

It is for people who look at the patterns their clock makes switching numbers, instead of recognising those numbers, instead of thinking, It is time to get up now.

It is for me. Because my life fell apart and I called that Felim. Or I called it, Be mean to me.

The name of the book is, The Beautiful Father And All The Father's Beautiful Things.

The name of the book is, Do not be afraid.

NELL'S BELLS, *a blog for the anxious traveller*
Week 3: Florence

The pictures in the Uffizi are too famous to see properly. You will hear yourself gasp with recognition when you wander into one of these rooms and find Botticelli's *The Birth of Venus* on the wall. It is there, and you are in front of it. The physical object brings you into the presence, not just of the painting, but of the painter's intentions. You can see the brushstrokes. You think, This is genius. You do not touch. No one touches, though lots of people want to touch. They smooth and caress the air an inch or two away from the canvas and the alarm goes off. The attendants don't startle. The place is rammed.

No one in the crowd looks at anyone else, they only look at the walls. Or maybe the lovers glance at each other. *Yes, here we are. We have seen this together.* Mostly, the onlookers behave as though they are alone, communing with greatness in the midst of rabble. *Get out of my way!*

On the day I was in the Botticelli room, I saw a girl with tears running down her face. I saw a young man with a copy of *The Birth of Venus* printed on his T-shirt. I saw people accept that they have seen it with a nod, and move to the next thing. A woman sat on the floor breastfeeding while looking up at the painting and, at first, I thought there was something very wrong with her breast. There was a big squishy brown mark on it about half the size of the baby's face. But of course, it was her nipple. Which was insanely large.

On the wall, Venus's nipple is pale, and neat as those annoying buttons that are too little to keep your shirt closed. All the painted women in the Uffizi are whiter than any human flesh. Many of them look like Cate Blanchett, if Cate Blanchett could not act. This is especially the case in the early rooms. Here, groups of pale, serene people gaze off in different directions doing very bad acting indeed. Oh, I am being born from the waves. Oh, I am getting pregnant talking to an angel. Oh, I am dying in agony. Oh, I am sexually attractive. Further in, and historically later, the acting improves, then it goes madly over the top, Slaughter! Mayhem! What a nice party, let us all laugh!

How many naked bodies are in the Uffizi gallery? This is a real question. There are probably more bottoms than breasts. Especially fine, I found, are the slightly squished bottoms of figures who are sitting on a rock while draped in fabric that doesn't cover their bottom. There are nursing Virgins – it is a palace of breastfeeding – and lots of little Jesus babies, each one looking solemn and tinily endowed.

In one room I counted five penises, four adult and one infant. Many of the hundreds of penises in the Uffizi are very small and also anatomically incorrect. Hard to describe, but the ballsack is somehow hung around the whole base of the shaft and not from underneath it. They have a wrong ... the word that comes to mind is 'integument'. This error was the reason I began to see them in the first place. If they had been accurately portrayed, I might have filed these many hundreds of genitals under 'Art' and gone about the place experiencing the sublime.

You never see a penis in public. In real life. If you did, you would shriek, run, call the cops. You would not find it 'sublime'. You would be 'shocked' you would be 'frightened' you might feel 'disgusted' or 'soiled'. Someone, please, tell me why.

Anyway, after all the historical, beautiful and oddly imprecise junk on the walls, you start noticing the decapitations. Judith chopping off Holofernes' head, outraged Medusa, severed at the neck, at least two Salomes, drooling over the head of John the Baptist on a platter. It is always the head (just saying) no one loses a foot or an arm.

Among the thousands of painted figures, I spotted only one person of colour, though it was some time before I thought to count. In the pictures I have on my phone, one hundred per cent of the tourists are white. Many of them are women, although, on the walls, I saw the work of just one female artist. The Uffizi is fully weird and very niche. Near the end, is a beautiful image of a woman with her chest bared to an old man. She is breastfeeding him. He is her father.

After that, a self-portrait by Rembrandt, that made me cry watery tears of salty joy.

Fully dressed, unbeautiful, a little self-defeated.

Hello, Mr Harmenszoon van Rijn.

I did not leave this gallery slowly, I ran out of it at speed. I raced down the stairs and into a wall of heat. Across the road is a colonnade, where the younger tourist can sit and chew a huge sandwich wheel from a local stall. This is what I did. Recovering from Art, watching a crumb-scavenging pigeon, with a red stub where its left foot had once been. Thinking about nothing, my brain wiped clean.

Unmissable. See this before you die. And then die.

Five stars.

The Yellow Bittern
(translated from 'An Bonnán Buí' in the Irish of Cathal
Buí Mac Giolla Gunna, 1679–1756)

Oh yellow bittern, my heart is with
your feathers in the field, your wings
scattered like great Hector's unburied bones.
You did no harm –
in damp country, it was thirst that killed you:
a key turned in the weather and the lake
was shut in ice. If you had but called me,
I would have broken it
so you could wet your beak,
great-hearted drinker, my friend.

The rest of them I do not mourn,
the cuckoo, the wren, the grey heron,
but the bittern honk across the marshes
was my own mournful boozing cry.
My wife says it will be the death of me,
and I say, Look at that poor bastard of a bird,
killed with the thirst. Put ice in your gin,
my friends, and slug it down. The afterlife
is one long Good Friday with the pubs not open.
Drink! while you have a mouth on you.

CARMEL

CARMEL WAS IN her fifties before she realised she might find
Phil's old television interview somewhere online. She
clicked about late one Friday night and there it was – a fact
that made her close her computer and trek to the fridge for
another glass of wine. She turned on the TV for the first
time in months, sat on the sofa and did not remember going
to bed. Sometime in the night, she dreamt that she opened a
door in her own house and found a room filled with clay.

When she came down in the morning, the laptop was
where she had abandoned it on the dining table. Carmel
clicked to find her father's image frozen on the screen. She
was one long night older than when she had seen him last,
he was still fifty-three.

Phil was leaning forward, his expressive brown eyes
hooded, mid-blink. Hard to tell if they were about to shut
or open. It was too much to consider in one go. Carmel
closed the laptop and looked around the room.

Everything was as it should be. The counters were clear,
the sofa cushions only slightly askew. At the street end of
the house, the window caught the morning light and the
blind seemed to blush larger than its allotted square.

She went about her breakfast, screwing the coffee pot together with a metal shriek and putting it on the stove. It was too early for the radio and the silence made her actions seem very loud. The oats sighed as they left the paper bag, the frozen berries chinked against the dish.

She wondered what she was waiting for.

Carmel sorted the cushions while the porridge circled in the microwave, she took last night's wine bottle from the floor, straightened the small pile of books on the coffee table. Nell was coming home later in the week. She had promised to phone and tell her which day. Is that why Carmel had looked her own father up online? Click, click. As though that were a casual thing to do?

She held an intact blackberry in her mouth a moment, before biting through to the pith.

At the far end of the room, the window blind dimmed and then pulsed to the clearance of a passing cloud.

Phil told them never to pick blackberries after September was out; never eat one when it has turned to mush. This solemn warning was delivered when they went brambling in the Dublin hills in their plastic rain ponchos and rubber summer sandals. Sometime Phil had a car.

According to their father, the Devil pissed on the berries at the end of September. It was just superstition – they believed it, even though they knew it was not true. Some insect bred in the fruit at the end of summer; it drooled saliva or squirted its eggs in between the bumps. Or a fungus maybe. He probably explained that to them, too. The Devil, who was actually a fungus, got into the berry to ooze and breed, and he softened the flesh from the inside.

Carmel remembered the squeak of her feet in the wet jelly sandals, the feel of cool rain on her scratched skin. She and Imelda carried their harvest in plump and bleeding white plastic bags and their fingerprints were dyed a livid purple, like nature's own criminals. And she did not know if this was a happy memory, or just a landscape – the far hill gone tawny with bracken, the two girls in bright cones of yellow under a heavy sky. Somewhere over there, their father standing with his back to them, doing something.

As she washed out the porridge bowl, Carmel had an impulse to clean the fridge. The thing beeped at her as she wiped and went, top shelf to meat drawer, working the wet cloth until it chilled in her hand. She decided, while she was at it, to defrost the freezer drawers, to root out the last of her daughter's long-abandoned bean burgers and Quorn. The boxes came out squeaking, ice against ice, and the cardboard went limp in the warm air. Carmel ran a cloth along the plastic pleat of the door seal, rolled up a used towel to catch the meltwater, binned the dead food. She looked around her, checked her pockets, and left the house.

Outside, it was a bright day in August. The sunlight washed a line of shops on the other side of the street, and the road was cruised by slow cars looking for a space to park. Carmel went to the new place and bought fresh turmeric, ripe mango, feta salad, big frozen prawns. She took some fish sauce off the shelf, put it back, considered chilli flakes. As a teenager, Nell had been mad for chilli. Not so much now.

Now she was all about quinoa and silky tofu. Nell was twenty-seven, she had an MA in Social Media and Communications, she had a diploma in Digital Marketing, she earned like mad for three months at a time and then, by some gargantuan effort that Carmel could not understand, went off and did what she pleased. And what pleased her was a slightly irritating purity, yoga breaks, surfing weekends, teaching English to refugees. Constant uploads about all this, of course, Nell's thumbs flying on her screen – as though late capitalism (as she liked to call it) could be defeated by hashtags and eating kimchi.

Phil the poet was also against capitalism, as Carmel recalled. A big fan of the working man, Phil sat down for his 'tea' at six o'clock and consumed the rest of his food standing up. A cold sausage, or a piece of ham from the fridge, folded into a piece of white sliced pan. Butter, of course. Her father was a keen carnivore. When she was a girl, Carmel was sent to the butcher's every afternoon for his lamb chop, pork chop, a piece of steak. There was also a 'side-line' chop and Carmel did not know what that was – how could you sideline a piece of meat? She looked up at the poster of a cow, and asked the butcher where the 'line' was.

'Where do you think?' he said.

His eyes were very blue.

Carmel stopped on the footpath briefly, remembering this, and she felt the heaviness of the bags in her hands.

When she got home, the open, dead fridge made the place look derelict. Carmel pulled at the inner lining of her nostrils – the remembered smell of the butcher's had caught in there. Pine dust laid over the sweetish rot of blood. Entirely real.

She blew her nose and washed her hands, plugged the fridge back in, made her second coffee and went outside to drink it in the back garden which was catching the sun.

Everything was lovely out here. The broad leaves of the courgette plant were mildewed silver and the flowers were glorious. Orange or yellow. The colour was indescribably dense and glowing – an angel's garment by Botticelli, perhaps. She took out her phone to photograph it in the sunlight; aimed blind because of the shine on the screen and clicked. You could fry the flowers in batter apparently. She might look up the recipe on her computer, if her father were not lurking on her computer, as he had been all morning, waiting for her to open him up again. Waiting to finish a blink.

My life now, she said to herself.

Her hands were clenched, her arms stiff by her sides.

My life now.

She was staring at the stupid courgette flower, which was pushing out a yellow courgette like an infinitely slow, vegetable turd. It was coming out the back of the blossom, even as she watched.

She should go back into the kitchen and close the old bastard down, she thought. Click, click, click. Nell would soon be home, she would ring to say when. Meanwhile, there was no need to discover what this long-dead, not terribly famous man was leaning forward to say.

But when she went inside, she looked up Aedemar instead, and sent her a picture of the courgette flowers, feeling nostalgic for the long chats they used to have by phone. Of course, these conversations, as she remembered, were mostly about Aedemar and the many people in her care. It was a whole other way of being self-obsessed, Carmel thought, because it was never you – you were never the one that Aedemar was worried about, when she worried about people, which was all the time. It happened whenever Carmel forgot herself so much as to be a little sad. Aedemar suddenly remembered every cancer within a radius, and the many old people who were (if only they knew it!) about to be diagnosed with Parkinson's disease.

'You know what I stumbled across on YouTube?' Carmel might say, and as soon as the story about her father was half-started, Aedemar would change the subject to some other woman's father who was on a trolley in Vincent's hospital waiting for a bed. Someone Carmel had never met.

'You are so lucky,' Aedemar said to her once – how many years ago now? 'You are so *lucky* your parents are dead.'

'Yes,' said Carmel, feeling miserably trapped in her own selfishness.

No, there was no point ringing Aedemar.

On the table, the silent computer stayed coyly closed, tight-lipped. Phil, her meaty father, was saying nothing. Lamb chop, pork chop, chop-chop: the smell of his breath must have been terrible, though she never noticed it when she clambered up into his lap to put her fingers in his mouth, and pull, and let the gum spring back.

Flup. Flup.

The interview was recorded in America, it must have been 1982 or 1983, when Phil was teaching there. A television studio, cavernously dark. In the centre of it, a pair of microphone stands, criss-crossed. At either end of this gleaming crux, two men, who looked older than they might have done, talked to each other from tan leather swivel chairs. Carmel tapped the space bar and let them go.

The men's voices were conversational and clear, but the words came from behind some faint scrim of sound and she ramped the volume up to check what it might be. There was the white hiss of electronic decay, and beyond that again, the shadows of other voices, as though some older record-ing were breaking through. Or the tape had magnetised itself on the spool, somehow, and the men's words were overlaid by their own future words, from further down the roll. This acoustic bleed was one indicator of the era, the other was the way her father smoked throughout; leaning forward to dab at a fat crystal ashtray, on a coffee table of glass and chrome. Phil's tie was not straight, his jacket was the usual disgrace. He twisted forward, jerked back, he hunched over in the chair and pushed the tweed away to scratch at a spot on his ribs. There he was, eight long years after the whipped-off sheet and the broken chair.

Daddo.

Phil spoke about bluebells, the difference of the American woods to the spongy bogs of Offaly, and how he missed the wren here, he missed the smallness of Irish birds, and the wren especially who was the king of them all. He mentioned courting his wife, who had walked with him though bluebell woods when he was a young man. She was from Dublin and unfamiliar with the countryside, and that, in a way, was what his early poetry was for. It was his gift to her. A posy. No, What was the word? A nosegay. They lived together in Dublin for some time he said, but she got sick, unfortunately, and the marriage did not survive.

Carmel pressed pause. Went back.

'tunately, and the marriage . . .' he looked sadly down. 'Did not survive.'

'*Unfortunately*,' she said.

Speaking the word aloud into the room helped break some difficulty she had, sitting at her own dining table watching her dead father online.

Perhaps it was the accent – Carmel's mind had emptied out at the sound of it, or was loud with some blank she could not get around. So taken was she by the way he said 'wran' for wren, she failed to understand a single word of what he had said next. She was back in O'Neill's pub as a student of twenty, drinking pints of bright yellow lager, saying: 'Shush, everyone.' So her posh college friends could laugh at her culchie father.

'Which one?'

'Which one do you think?'

> The wran, the wran the king of all birds,
> St Stephen's Day was caught in the furze

It was a song Phil liked, for the fact that it was a little vicious.

He used to sing it every year on St Stephen's Day, which was the slow day after Christmas. And Carmel was back further again, she was downstairs in their house in Dun Laoghaire watching her father stage his annual, kitchen-shaking riot. Phil left the house by the front door and came in at the back, with coal dust on his face and their mother's macramé shopping bag on his head; the wicker handles hooked over his ears. He banged pots, threw sheets of newspaper, climbed up on a chair and swung the sweeping brush around the ceiling light, which clanged and swung.

Up with the kettle and down with the pan
And give us a pinny to bury the wran.

At the age of five or six, Carmel had cheered and shrieked as she was supposed to do. She did not know they had killed the little wren, in the song – or the *dreoilín*, as her father called the bird in Irish.

Droolin, Droolin, where's your nest?
Tis in the bush that I love best.

It was a country tradition. The Wren Boys went about the place in costumes and masks, playing music and demanding money in their neighbours' kitchens. But there was something lewd in that line – about loving a bush – or was she just imagining that now?

One time, the stick he was waving had a dead mouse tied to it by the tail. Was that possible? That he bopped them each on the head with a dead mouse? Carmel used to think she had imagined such things. When people told her she *had no imagination* she thought, *Yes I do. I imagined all of that.*

She had missed what he was saying. Carmel went to the top of the clip and tried to listen properly, but thought instead how young he looked onscreen and also, to her child's eye, how old and worn out. The recording was made two years before he died. He did not know he was sick. The autopsy would discover cancer of the oesophagus but, up to the last, it was just a lifestyle. Phil had a drinker's stomach, a smoker's cough. He was killed by an early and catastrophic bleed to the lung.

And when he went, Carmel thought, a room in her head filled with earth.

She paused and lifted her head to listen for a ticking noise, somewhere in the room, but it was gone as soon as she tried to catch it. Perhaps it had been on the tape.

Carmel checked her phone. Fourteen messages on her choir group-chat, talking about low thyroid. A few book recommendations. A joke. Nothing from Nell. It was hard not to want the sound of her daughter's voice, though sometimes it was weirdly difficult to identify. Especially when she was small.

'Em. Mum?'

'Yes?'

A child's voice lacked that recognisable something: the grain, or texture that made it fully human.

'Yes? Are you alright?'

Sometimes it was like talking to a doll.

'Did you find the address?'

'What did the teacher say?'

'Are you coming home?'

Nell said Yes or Nell said No. When the two of them spoke in this way, Carmel did not know what they had shared – apart from the fact that they were apart.

'Are you alright?'

'I'm fine, Mum.'

'Where are you? Are you coming home?'

Now, she watched the televised black slit of her father's mouth as language slipped out of it on curls of exhaled

Lucky Strike. Phil's hands shaped the air in front of his rotting chest as he talked of the little Irish wren, and there was just a whisper of alcohol in there, softening his tongue and wetting those mischievous, fond eyes. It was so easy to hate this man – the facts spoke for themselves – but it was still hard to dislike him. And it was devastatingly easy to love him. To flock around and keen when he died, because all the words died with him.

On screen, the Irish poet Phil McDaragh was talking about the work of Robert Frost, whose voice had called him to the forests of New England in order *to record the falling leaves*. But he missed Offaly, he missed the little Irish wren. He spoke about bluebell woods, his wife, her illness.

'She got sick,' he looked down. 'Unfortunately, and the marriage did not survive.'

He glanced up with wet eyes. Why was that? He was looking for sympathy.

Our sympathy. Carmel's sympathy. Everyone's sympathy. Poor Phil.

The interviewer viewed him with angled seriousness and recrossed his legs. This man wore droopy, heavy-rimmed glasses that made him look intellectual yet modern, bookish but also a bit of a player.

'And Whitman?' he asked.

'Ah, Whitman,' said Phil, catching his tone. 'No, no. Whitman was the opposite of Irish. He was all the things an Irishman could never hope to be.'

Carmel had forgotten Phil's rueful jokes – the way he could mock the world with his fake sorrow. He was so disarming.

And slightly creepy.

But she could barely form that thought, before it was gone again. It was as if Carmel could remember the burr of his voice inside her body, humming along the bone. Listening to him now, at a distance of more than forty years, his daughter felt again – as though she held them in either hand – the two, weighed syllables he gave to her for a name: Car-Mel. He said it as though she was the centre of the sweet, she was the salt honey dripped across your ice cream.

She got up, opened the fridge and closed it again. It was too early to eat. Carmel moved to the back window and looked down at the garden, contemplating, as she sometimes did, some kind of nymph or stone sylph in the foliage on the shady side. If you could find a nymph. Garden sculpture was very difficult.

She dropped a text to Nell.

The phone pinged, but when she squinted at it, she saw a message from Aedemar instead.

– *Yes! Deep-fried courgette flowers! Only you!*

Carmel slung her mobile on the counter, considering what to say by way of reply. What about

– *Yeah, Aedemar.*

She could write that.

She hadn't seen Aedemar for months. Sometimes she didn't know what 'being friends' meant. It was just an idea they had about themselves.

– *Gourmet!* she wrote.

Perhaps she could try for an emoji. Aedemar was big into emojis, though Carmel found them hard to understand. She deleted the *Gourmet!* and sent an image of the sun wearing dark glasses. What did that mean?

Nothing bad.

It was three o'clock on a long Dublin Saturday and she had fallen out with nobody. There was no reason why she should.

I am spread wide,
St Kevin crucified

in one outstretched hand
a robin's empty clutch
of blue and in the other,
a single feather
a tuft of down.
My hatchlings gone
my heart a bare tree,
the birds hop through
for company.

In the pool of my eye, the mayfly splits
to show a mayfly more beautiful
clambering out of its own husk
and the heads of birds bob, fix,
bob, fix, in the gathering dusk.

Finished reciting, Phil dropped his head. The man with the droopy glasses blinked slowly and kept his eyes closed. Then he stirred and asked if Phil was working on an American cycle of poems.

'No, no,' said Phil. He had tried to write about other places, he really had. But he only ever wrote about Ireland.

'I never left,' he said.

Carmel slapped the space bar and looked at him. She tapped again, to let him slip back into speech: 'You can't leave a place like that,' Phil said. 'It's always with you.'

Carmel let out a bit of a laugh and heard herself do it – a snort of air coming out of her face.

'You have a great understanding of women,' the interviewer said, apropos of nothing.

'I think I do,' said Phil.

'Their sorrows.'

'Yes.'

'What goes on in their minds.'

'Well, there is nothing so necessary as the female heart. A lot of writers. A lot of people get that a little bit wrong.'

The interviewer nodded for the next poem.

'Yes. The women I have loved. So this is a kind of bouquet.'

Carmel did not know this one, she did not think it ever made it into print.

'Woodbine' was his deflowering, at seventeen; the girl in a field, her nipples like honeysuckle, her arms entwining. 'Bluebells' was Terry, their pretty mother, up on Killiney Hill in her blue sundress, that she never threw out after. 'The thorn on the English quartered rose.' Carmel startled, slapped the space bar. How had she forgotten?

This was the cause of all their trouble. The bitch itself.

This woman had been to their house – inside their house. She sort of hinged herself on the sofa, long shins going one way, cigarette arm the other. Carmel could not remember her name but she was 'a friend of Kingsley Amis' and when they heard her speak, everyone sucked in their cheeks and made their accent coo.

'Ooh yes, I think soo.'

Everyone apart from Phil, who Irished it up for her; doing a stomping, baggy slip jig on the hearthrug and ending up on the floor.

Dark, rich, full of contraception, 'The Heron' he also called her. She was the woman as self-destruction and unimaginably filthy sexual positions. Bunty, that was her name. Carmel could hardly believe it now. Their father had left them for a woman called 'Bunty'. She had also been at his funeral. She had walked up the aisle in a large brimmed black hat – who could forget it – a whore's hat, drooping at the graveside in the Irish rain.

> High-elbowed, cretaceous, she shakes and folds,
> leathered wings, old heron, love's grey
> rapacity.

He had hated The Heron more than any of the women whose bed he had left.

Last was the asphodel, the white flower that blooms in Hades. This was the mad girl in Greece, walking the streets in her nightie, bleeding from the wrist. She had turned out to be – somehow inevitably – a poet called Selma Karras, who was now considered a significant voice. Her Wikipedia page said she had survived 'an abusive relationship' on Mykonos with 'the Irish poet Phil McDonaghue' – but at least they got the name of the island right.

There was no flower for the American Wife, who met Phil when she was just twenty-one. A neat Vassar student whose family finances were so quiet, they were like the air itself; Connie from Connecticut had so much money she did not need to spend it. She loved poetry, especially Irish poetry. More than anything in the world, Connie would have liked a poem for herself.

This, she did not get.

Outside, the light wind had picked up. Carmel hacked an overgrown clematis back from the miniature pear tree espaliered against the wall. She checked the courgettes, which already seemed bigger than they had done that morning. One yellow vegetable was now completely extruded, and the finished flower wilted at the tip. They really were hilariously rude, she thought. But there was no point standing there laughing. That would be mad.

She started to sing instead; a big, sonorous alto line. There was nothing else for it. Her father was frozen upstairs about to be more stupid and painful. With his fake modesty and feigned sorrow. Her father was up there being a bastard for all time.

He had a self-important heart.

Confidence? Was that all it took? Surely there was some

extra stupidity required. Some special kind of stupid, that the world took for wise.

Carmel stomped back into the house, suddenly convinced of something. And there it was. The lost watch was on Phil's wrist. Unbelievable. It had been there all along. She spread her fingers on the trackpad to enlarge the image. The same tan-coloured leather strap, the same creamy iridescence fanned out from the centre of the dial. Carmel remembered the way he used to dangle it into her small hand in the evening. The way the milled steel held the concentrated warmth of his skin, while the glass on the other side stayed cool. When she set it against her ear, there was a tiny churning before each *tick*:

Nearly. Now.

Nearly. Now.

And. Yes.

The mechanism was delicate and relentless. It was full of anticipation and power.

Before she knew it, Carmel was on the phone, and before Imelda had time to gather herself she said, 'You remember the watch?'

'No.'

This was a bit quick, as answers go.

'Daddo's watch.'

'Do I remember it?'

Imelda was setting something down, a cup or plate, Carmel could hear the kitchen's echo and clatter.

'Did you give it to him?'

'What?'

'Did you give the watch to him?'

'How do you mean, "*Give* it to him"?'

For Imelda, information was like money. She didn't want you to have it, in case you spent it in the wrong shop.

'It was his watch,' she said.

'I am not saying he stole his own watch,' Carmel said to Imelda. 'I am asking how he got it.'

'*How* he got his watch?' Imelda said. 'What are you talking about?'

'The day he left,' Carmel said.

'What day? There wasn't "a day",' Imelda was confused now as well as cross. 'There wasn't a day when you could say. I mean. It didn't happen like that.'

If you pushed her, Imelda might say he had not left at all. But she was also right – he left on many different days. Phil took his things away piecemeal: his badger-hair shaving brush, his other suit, his good shoes. There wasn't much. You might not notice it gone, if you were busy not noticing that he himself was gone. Their mother, indeed, sometimes talked as though he had gone out for a long walk.

The day he gave her 'a peck' was the day Carmel's memory chose to call the last. It would be six long years before a letter announcing his American divorce set her mother trembling. Carmel watched Terry's disbelief from a slight remove. He had been gone – if Mammy could only admit it – he had been really *gone*, since Carmel was a child.

'Yeah, I don't know,' she said to Imelda, walking around now with the phone in her hand. 'I saw some footage. Did you know there was footage? Phil doing some interview in the States.'

'Of course I knew.'

'Well it's there. It's online.'

'Thanks,' said Imelda. 'Yes. Right. I did know that.'

Imelda was, in her remembrance of Phil's genius, increasingly alone. There was still the occasional literary function, for which she had a selection of jackets in navy and black. Sometimes, she might be asked to make a short speech, which she was always happy to do. She looked into the middle distance, ducked towards the microphone, and though you might think she was talking about Phil, she was in fact, endlessly and over again, speaking about her mother. How she found a poem on her pillow and went out to kiss the man who wrote it, right there in the street.

'You should send it to Nell.'

'The clip. No I should, yes.'

'She was always fond of Daddo.'

'Yes. Yes she was.'

Carmel felt sorry for Imelda then, who had grown old in the story of their parents' lives. It was such a greedy story and so small.

'Where is she anyway?'

'Somewhere in Bali.'

'Is that ahead or behind?'

In truth, Carmel was not sure. Nell had taken six months in New Zealand, which was exactly opposite Dublin, more or less, in terms of day and night. Now, she was coming home the long way, and Carmel – usually so efficient – could not figure out if she was travelling back through the day or forwards into morning.

'Ahead, I think. It's the middle of the night over there.'

Carmel saw, as she said this, the shadow of the child going about the empty kitchen, picking an orange out of the bowl, and throwing it up, over and again, the slow slap, slap, slap of the fruit landing in her hand.

'I thought she was in Vietnam,' said Imelda – as though her sister had been misleading in some way.

'No, it's Bali. She's on her way home.'

'Alright,' said Imelda. 'I'll let you go.'

'Yeah, bye.'

'Bye, now.'

'Bye.'

She left Imelda back into her life in the house in Dun Laoghaire with the same curtains of balding blue velour. In the winter, Imelda withdrew to the warmer rooms, which she now shared with Will Havelard, an older boyfriend of uncertain marital status. He had moved in – finally! – after a series of minor strokes left him needing quite an amount of care. The former wife thought this was a great joke, apparently.

It was half past five – one and a half hours till dinner time. Nell was in Bali snorkelling in clear blue waters, walking the beach, sitting on the back of a Vespa in flip-flops, getting her calf burnt on the exhaust. She was drunk, or she was high, she was having sex enthusiastically or against her will with a man who had many tattoos. She was sad. The burn on her inside calf was infected, she should walk it in the seawater but Nell always knew better, she could not be advised. She would not wade into the salt sea, and now, she would slip into a fever in the middle of the night, her leg swollen tight and hot as an oven, and too late to hobble to the chemist to ask for 'Cream, cream.'

And none of this was true. Carmel was just imagining things. Her daughter was fine. Downstairs, she opened the door to Nell's empty room at the front of the house and inhaled the air it contained. The decor was stuck in one or other year of the child's growing up; a feathered lampshade on the bedside locker, faded strings of paper birds garlanded across the picture frames. The wardrobe, when Carmel went over to close it properly, was a midden; you could excavate her daughter's life by working down through the pile.

She opened the valve at the base of the radiator, pulled back the duvet to check for damp. As she unclipped the stiff sash window, she saw a little pile of books on the sill, their covers fading in the light – a volume of Phil's poetry in among them. She picked it up and sat on the bed, opened the thing at random, trying to read it through her daughter's eyes.

She had not been not a good mother. Carmel knew that. All the love in the world would not make her a good mother. It was always such a wrangle. She could not hold her daughter, and she could not let her daughter go.

She wanted to tell her about the butcher with the blue eyes, about blackberries and the Devil's spit, those plastic rain ponchos that made you damp underneath them with your own sweat. Her father pissing high into the bracken, his yellow urine arcing through the silver rain. Which was the kind of detail a mother would leave out, of course, when speaking to her daughter. Carmel wanted to tell her about the wren – whatever that story was. Some kind of warning. About staying safe. About not hitting the light bulb with a broom, when you are waving a dead mouse around.

She closed the book and set it on the bedside locker. Bali was ahead. Nell would not ring today. She was lying in the future darkness, sleeping through a night that was moving slowly towards Dublin, that was yet to arrive. Nell had been overtaken by the planet's turning, and Carmel wanted to reach through time itself, to pull her daughter home.

The Scribe's Lament
(translated from 'Is scíth mo chrob', eleventh
century, said to be in the Irish of St Columba,
521–597)

I've a crick in my paw from scribbling
My pen scuttles across the page
The ink from its slender beak pouring
Black as a beetle-back gleams

From my shapely, light brown hand
God's wisdom issues in streams
Beautiful long lines ever-flowing
Ink of the green-skinned holly tree

My small pen can't stop its dribbling
Across one and the next shining leaf
For the benefit of all good reading men
I suffer cramp and spasm, ache and grief.

AT FOUR IN the morning, Carmel came upstairs and sat in the light before dawn. She played the clip again, and all she could see now was Nell. This is what she had been looking for; her daughter's face breaking through her father's face. Nell was coming through her dead grandfather, in flickers.

– Mumma if you are there I am home Wed late and Mum-Mum I have news. Of course you are there this is a text. Bing Bing.

– No one likes statues. No myph

– *Nymph*

– Coming w friend ok?

– No statues! Maybe in a garden because foliage. But imho it's always that ep where the weeping cemetery angels move if u blink. Please, please, do not get a nym for garden which is too small. Stone eyes!!! xoxo Nell.

And then:

   – *Back on wifi Denpasar. Friend sleep my room not need fuss.*

NELL

MY GRANDFATHER LOVED my grandmother so much you could not be in the same room as them, they flamed in the presence of the other. This was according to a poet called, of all things, Harvey, who wrote: 'The way they ignored each other was more alert and intricate than another couple's kissing. Theirs was a great passion, darkly ecstatic. They both knew it could not last.'

I found this remarkable description in a letter of condolence which he sent to her daughters after my grandmother died. Who talks like that about dead, old people? It seemed a strange way to mourn. Harvey said that in her 'grass widowhood', and then beyond, my grandmother accepted everything that happened, the bad along with the good, because she had known a great love. She had said this to him many times, how this knowledge was something that could never be lost or stolen from her. She was fortunate, she had been blessed. And this *knowledge* (underlined) would sustain her in her last days.

I remember my auntie reading this letter out in a trembling voice at some gathering, maybe in a library near the old house in Dun Laoghaire. I must have been eight or nine, and I wasn't mortified, because I did not yet know how to be. We were standing to one side of the small crowd, listening, and Carmel went so completely still, I reached up to take her hand.

It was like holding something inanimate. When Carmel shuts down like that, it's like grabbing on to a garden shed.

In those days, I was on my mother's side in every argument, though I was beginning to notice that there were quite a lot of them. But really, it was something to see: Imelda, up there in her velvety scarf, going off on one about love that was 'darkly ecstatic'. After, I said, Can I see the letter? and she said, Oh, I don't think those little hands are clean.

Which is why I remember all this so clearly. Imelda was hard work.

My mother – who was also always on my side – rose to her full height and said to her older sister, She is the last of the line.

And I was like, Whooaa. Don't look at me, ladies, I be gone.

It is technically true that I am the last of the McDaraghs, though there might be some second cousins in Chicago, and a few over in Hull, where Phil's older sister was a nurse. These facts did not interest me until I left Ireland, the way they don't.

But I got an Irish tattoo in Sydney, I think it was the jet lag. I considered getting *the wren the wren* written along the opposite collarbone to *love is a tide*, but changed my mind at the last minute and asked for a fineline wren, very minimal, in that space between the thumb and forefinger on my left hand. I wanted something tiny, I said. The wren has to be plump and its beak should be wide open so, when I have nothing else to do, I can wiggle my thumb and watch it sing.

Then I got fussed about twig/no twig.

No twig! I said. It's just there.

I was on my way to Auckland, where I had friends on work visas and a place to stay. I didn't know why I was in Sydney, exactly. I thought I could write something, but the place escaped me. I went to the wrong coffee shops in the wrong districts. I didn't want to go out on my own at night, even though it felt like the middle of the day.

On my third afternoon, tripping on sunlight, I sat in the Botanical Gardens, watching the birds. I was hoping to see the sacred kingfisher because I have loved kingfishers since I saw one on the Dodder when I was a girl. I don't collect them, I just like to say Hello.

The way to see the bird you want to see, is to stop looking for it, we all know this. You have to undo your gaze, let the bird happen without you. Be alert to blue. There was no shortage of action in the Botanical Gardens that afternoon. The noisy miner, fussed and aggressive, the white ibises with their curving black commas for beaks. I thought I spotted the galah cockatoo, pink against a pinkish eucalyptus, and then decided I had not. A group of small, long-tailed birds was streaked across by the blue of the breeding male and my heart fluttered (yes) at the sight of its tiny magnificence. This was a Superb fairywren. The birds in Australia are just ridiculous. The fairywrens are so beautiful their beauty is included in their English names: there is the Superb with his sky-blue cap, the Splendid fairywren of electric blue, the Lovely fairywren with chestnut wings, various other showboats, intensely hued. There is no real fairy content in the fairywren, whose name was made up a couple of hundred years ago. Its older, local name is muruduwin.

When it came to getting my new ink, it turned out that I did not want a Splendid or a Lovely or even a muruduwin, but something more drab. I wanted a little damp, secretive thing with a big, hidden voice. Turns out, I missed the birds of home.

The artist couldn't get a handle on it.

You sure that's right?

I told her it's not the same wren, they aren't even related, they just have the same name.

Birds don't care what we call them, I said.

And she said, So true.

This woman had some fabulous work: a lotus opening on her throat and foliage sneaking out from under her cuff. She was sketching quickly on paper, working from the image I showed her on my phone.

It's a rape, isn't it? she said – by which she meant what we do to nature.

Australia was not fitting into my unfinished guidebook for anxious travellers. No one I met seemed to be anxious in the way I understood the word.

It certainly is, I said.

And I thought, Carmel would love it here.

I was talking to someone a while ago, and I said that I was not born out of love, I was born out of utility. My mother just used some guy, I said – he had all his teeth and he was white, which was a value for her, and he was tall. And my friend said, That's kind of tough on you. And I said, Not really. I think it is liberating. And he said, But still. Even the way you talk about it.

So that evening, on a whim, I messaged Imelda, asking to see the letter, and she took photographs which, eventually, she figured out how to send all the way to New Zealand. Much to her surprise, this was no harder than sending them to the other side of the room.

– *Please do not share this material it is needed for archive.*

Me thinking, Well this won't work, because there was a lot of handwriting, which is not one of my core skills, ahem.

– *Wow thnx! How amazing! Much love from New Zealand, where ooooff volcano walk in the wind (pic).*

But sometime later, sitting on the grass that needled its way out through the dead, black lava on the slope of Rangitoto, I magnified, scrolled, read it through.

The way they ignored each other was more alert and intricate than another couple's kissing.

I looked out over the bay to Auckland, and back up to the summit we had just climbed – this shallow nipple of a mountain whose name in Maori means 'bloody sky' – and it was all as pleasant as could be. Scudding clouds, choppy waves, happy tourists in the sunshine.

They both knew it could not last.

I loved the slow arrival of this letter on my phone, a formal shiver of emotion spun out over three pages of faded purple ink, more than thirty years ago. Long after they are all dead, I shade Harvey's words on the screen. I read them aloud, like a documentary voiceover, moving the image over and back with finger and thumb.

The way they ignored each other was more alert and intricate than another couple's kissing.

Beside me, my friend said, Get a room.

What is it about handwriting? I said. Makes it look so truthful and private. We talked about it because we were on a (slightly boring) volcano on the other side of the world – about the way you post something these days, and bang, whoosh.

Just as you think, Did I mean that?

You get:

– *Yes true! So true!*

Consider the poet called Harvey. He is standing at the postbox, his beautiful, heartfelt letter is halfway into the slot and, he's like, Is it, maybe, a bit mad? The envelope falls and . . . too late! His words are in the gap – sent but still unseen. That chasm from which arise Terrible Uncertainty and Terrible Joy. A place so unbearable, it is where we live all the time now, checking for the likes.

My friend says, That's kind of over, though, isn't it?

Is it?

Likes?

Dang. I was just getting some.

It's more about engagement, now.

This guy likes to explain things. He likes to tell you what you are saying and why he agrees with you. This sometimes feels like he is agreeing with himself, but I find it ticklish and nice. Better than being told what you are saying and why you are wrong – I mean, similar, but better.

He is a teacher, by trade and personality. I feel taught.

I like the letter, my friend said.

Yeah, good one.

This guy's sense of humour is so bone dry, his jokes are identical to not funny at all.

He held his own phone out to me. An armoured car, blown up and blazing – it doesn't say which war. And underneath.

– *You can hear the ammo cooking off in the heat*.

And so you could. A tiny pop bang whizz, the bullets exploding like popcorn in a distant microwave.

Huh, I said.

He said, Why are they pushing this at me? Sometimes, he bottoms out with dread. Sometimes, he thinks the whole info-sphere has exploded and we're all just *cooking off in the heat*.

We were eating careful sandwiches near the ferry landing and leaving nothing behind. There are no rodents on the island of Rangitoto, which is in the bay across from Auckland. And because there are no rats – happy thought – the place is filled with birds, the way this whole country used to be. The birds have no predators, they are too laid-back to fly much and all of them are lovely: the korimako that bongs and bleeps like the bridge on *Star Trek*, and pīwakawaka, in English, the little fantail, which really does Fan that Tail.

Auckland is a sweet, suburban place built on dead volcanic fields. Up on the surface, you are surrounded by bungalows made of wood and by people with a certain kind of face (white, narrow, hearty) but sometimes you sense the lava stirring far below. And from this rocky perch, in the middle of an Irish night, I send my dream texts into sleeping screens. Eighteen thousand kilometres between us. I like the delay. It feels peaceful.

– *Hi Imelda. Remember that lovely letter a guy called Harvey wrote about your mum and Granda Phil? Is that published somewhere? I'd love to read it sometime.*

Fourteen hours later.

ping!

In the distance, the white buildings of the city, green hills and peninsulas of the Hauraki Gulf, choppy waters, darkened by wind. Behind us, black lava fields fringed by crimson-flowered trees. The mountain we are sitting on came up out of the sea 600 years ago. We are on young ground.

From where I am sitting, the past is a lonely place.

And I think I would not have noticed this, or sought out these small intersections, if we had not been in New Zealand, which makes you think of the entire planet, all the time. I am never done, when in Auckland, looking up at the sky.

I spent a lot of time after I arrived checking maps, zooming in and out on unnamed marks, faint scorings along the ocean bed, underwater mountains that do not tip the surface of the sea.

I ended up looking at Felim's family farm in County

Louth, there was something about the size of the solid planet between us that made a snoop feel safe. The image had not been updated since we drove away from the main house, more than three years ago. The same barns, the same JCB parked by the wall.

I thought about Felim, the way he called people in his life 'his lordship' or 'lady so and so', no one had a real name, not even poor, dead 'Ballsy' McKenna. I don't think he ever used my name, unless as a taunt.

I wondered if he was getting on better with his girlfriend, now that he wasn't abusing me. I doubted it. It was clear to me now that he'd never stopped seeing her, the entire time we were fucking. She was a real person, I was a mistake. I was another photo on his phone. He wanted to have children, and she might do that for him. Two boys and a girl, or the other way around. They would all troop up to Louth at Christmas, where she would stand at the sink, drying dishes with his sister Maeve. And Felim would be a nice daddy most of the time, but you wouldn't want to bother him too much, because he could get cross.

He only hurts people for their pleasure. Only ever sexually, which is completely fine, because women really want that. I certainly did. He is only horrible when people beg him to be.

Of course.

Thinking about him makes me sick to my stomach. I consider trolling him online, a few fake accounts, the single word, 'abuser', on everything he says or does.

Abuser

Abuser

Abuser

This was, for many months, an obsessive thought, but it hasn't happened in a while. My mistake, for going back to *Louth actually*.

At the bottom of the far field I see a rath, or fort, a circular bank of earth, the ring broken in a couple of places like the watermark of an old pint glass. They used to be called fairy forts, small humps and bumps in the grassland of Ireland from houses built 500 or 1,000 years ago. This was a whole new level of stalking and it sets me adrift along ley lines, over shadow settlements and ghost farms.

Before I know it, I am roaming the faint outer traces of the Nazca lines, those drawings in the Peruvian desert so huge they are unseeable by the people who made them – spider, hummingbird, a monkey with a spiralling tail – then back to the fields of home, the patches of different green, the busy warp and weft of planting or harvest, skid marks of mud through gates, the needlepoint of hay bales in rows. A farmer is captured cutting some crop in the shape of a heart, perhaps to match the slope of the hill. Farmers do all kinds of bored or sentimental things: crop circles, corn mazes, they hook up their plough in the middle of winter and write rude messages for planes. The rogue artist who drew Marree Man in Australia gave him a penis 200 metres long which is impressive, but not so monumental as the sky penis drawn by a plane over Florida, twenty-seven kilometres from ball to tip. No one on the ground knew what they were seeing, and any passengers would have been oblivious. The joke only happened on the radar, between the pilot and the guy back in traffic control. It's a good thing he was watching. How would you feel, if you drew the biggest dick in the world and no one was there to see? (If something happens online and no one clicks, can it be said to have happened at all?)

My favourite things to see from above are the calibration targets in the deserts of China and America, built for passing satellites to refocus their cameras; sand-blown, monumental grids and barcodes, most of them now obsolete.

I was talking about all this on our small hike up and then around Rangitoto (not about Felim, obviously), because my friend is the kind of guy who doesn't mind if you know lots of things, so long as he knows one more thing than you.

They're called geoglyphs, he said.

I really got him on the calibration charts, though. He stopped, put his hands on his hips, said, Huh.

He swung a bit from side to side, as though checking one and then the other part of the view. And this slightly stumped, hands-on-hip look was less than fully attractive but not a deal-breaker for me.

Later, as we packed up our leavings into boxes and bags, he said, You should put a message under a rock.

Leave no trace, I said, looking at a boulder further up the slope, feeling tempted. But what would I write?

Your initials, maybe. 'Nell was here.'

That's just graffiti. You need two names to make a story. Then it's like, I wonder what happened to them?

I slowed down, realising I had walked myself into this sentence and could not reverse out of it. He said nothing, he was looking at his phone.

Later again, we kissed. And that was a bit of a disaster. In the open air, in the middle of the day. It happened against the guard rail of the Rangitoto Ferry, we had our snouts to the wind and the weather was so fine. He put his arm around me, I leaned into him for an amiable side-hug, and he lowered his face and noodled in. This happened on the other side of the planet, some time after I read him the letter about my grandfather and less time after he showed me the end of the world on his phone.

Once we had stopped and were, casually, looking out to sea again (no celebratory dolphins jumping in our wake) I remembered all the places we might have kissed but had not – on the top of the disappointingly shallow mountain, where a wooden platform corrals you for the view, in the bristling black lava cave, on the wharf waiting for the boat. I could have kissed him anywhere.

And, now it was done – was it just a boat thing? Were all these imagined kisses just locations? Would we be able to bring it inside, get ourselves a room?

There were many reasons not to do this. One of them was that we both talked too much. It was our thing. We talked as soon as we met. We loved being interested and saying interesting things, and where does that *interest* go, if we go silent? And possibly naked? It was really hard to think about.

I found myself drawn to the open neck of his shirt. I slid my fingertips under the cloth, and there was something about the warmth and texture that I recognised. When I took my hand out again, his white neck was blotched with red.

What? he said.

Hey, I said.

I did not see how we could bring this feeling home. There was so much public transport to get through. I was out in Glenfield, he was staying across the bay, we were standing at the ferry terminal downtown. I was not sure what was happening. We were sober, it was the middle of the afternoon.

See you, I said, and I turned for Albert Street and my bus.

He sent a pic of his cheek, ear, half an eye, blurry hand wave.

He sent the selfie we took on the top of the island.

I stuffed my phone in my pocket thinking, I can't sleep with you. Honestly. I really like you, so I can't sleep with you. Get off my damn phone.

I was sitting on the bus when it pinged again. I was home before I checked it. He had sent me a poem:

> Love is a tide, it is mist
> Becoming cloud, it is rain
> On the river, water into water,
> Heart into heart. It is all
> Downhill from here.

How can sex be both super hot and not very good? Because that is what happened when he finally got over to my place and we did the deed, very fast, because if we got it out of the way, then we could get back to lingering.

Not so fast that he forgot his nice guy, You sure? as he tried for an angle, and got it slightly wrong. So I reached down to his thick, surprising penis, and found it for him.

Yes I am, I said.

Afterwards, when he was standing in the hall saying good-bye, and we were back in the uncertainty zone, he started to play with, and then undo, my top button, followed by all the rest in a row. He was very sure of himself. For a nice guy, he really knew what he wanted and this caused in me a thrill of lovely alarm. By the last button I wanted him right back, or I wanted his wanting, which rose in me too. I tried to push him on to the sofa, he pulled me down into the big chair. I had a quick flash of Felim as I fell, but when it was gone, my friend was still there, still himself, the creases on his belly showing through a cotton shirt that smelled of wind and sunshine.

What? he said.

Nothing.

Come here.

We went home to Europe the slow way. We flew up to Cairns and did the reef, then went on to Denpasar for some hotel life on the way to Nusa Penida. I chose this island because of the jalak Bali, a white mynah with an easy-going, loose white crest, and vivid blue skin around the eye, very chatty and imitative, and so endangered there are only a hundred or so mating couples left. This bird we did not see, though we did have an encounter with the passing manta rays, a creature I also failed to spot until I stopped checking from side to side and looked straight down where I saw a spread black cloak flying along the sandy floor. We swam down to the seabed, flippers going like crazy, and turned to meet another ray coming straight at us, with its weirdly open box-mouth, curved around by scooping fins. This manta sheered up and passed over my right shoulder, its white belly like the meaty underside of a low-flying plane.

After that, we stayed on Nusa Lembongan, a smaller island closer to Bali. We took a fishing boat down to the mangrove swamp and there, flickering through the high-rooted trees, was the blue bird I had waited for in Australia, the sacred kingfisher, *Todiramphus sanctus sanctus*. A little, fast flame.

Later, two kingfishers together – indistinguishable to me, although the female is described as being slightly more green.

I wrote up beaches and bays for my Natural Tourist people while sitting in a cafe on the sand. When I found Wi-Fi to send the piece, my phone pushed me a video from the early 1980s. This seemed not very hilarious in a retro sort of way, and I swiped past almost missing the name: Phil McDaragh. The interwebs had just spat my Granda out at me – many years and countries later. There the man was. A vintage clip recently uploaded to YouTube. Two comments, both friendly. Twenty-six views.

Well, howdy doody.

I clicked to make it twenty-seven.

Then I changed my mind. I got back to the bungalow as fast as the heat would allow, and I pulled out the laptop to get the benefit of the bigger screen.

My grandfather is in a low-grade studio belonging to the audio-visual department of some American college. Pinky-orange make-up, blurred shiny skin, small spits in the corner of his mouth, huge large-assed questions. Phil McDaragh is talking lyric Irish poetry to an American intellectual type who leaves three seconds of silence in the middle of every question. This is because his brain is so big, he cannot go fast.

So tell me [pause pause pause pause pause pause pause] *what made you come to America?*

The man in the other chair opens his mouth and my entire family comes out of it. Phil has a more stilted style, certainly. He is surrounded by a different time. He will get up when this interview is done and walk out into a world where Princess Diana is wearing huge frilly collars, where phones can't leave the house, the bread he eats is always white. But he is so familiar to me, I feel I have met him already. There's my aunt Imelda's wry, sour little aside. Carmel's hunchy way of sitting forward, the same emphatic finger. He has my quick twist of a smirk at the end of a sentence – like maybe we got away with saying that. The McDaraghs are all jumbled up inside him, and we sound so honeyed and warm coming out of Phil. We sound just lovely.

He makes the guy laugh.

Snarf snarf snarfle snarf. That's just ... [pause pause pause pause pause pause pause pause] *wonderful.*

It is important to be careless, he says. *I am a man walking the road – that is the meaning of the word 'poet', for me. A man walking the road.*

This is so exactly like something I might say, I pause to remember if I really did say it once, and I laugh out loud into the silence. The connection between us is more than a strand of DNA, it is a rope thrown from the past, a fat twisted rope, full of blood.

I click away for a minute, trying to remember what the baby sees in the womb, through transparent eyelids.

The colour red.

The placental tree, its veins and branches.

I am checking through images taken *in utero*, those blood astronauts with shiny black pips for eyes. I am thinking about a tree, I don't know where it was. But I remember lying on the grass under this tree with my eyes closed, knowing everything above me, the movement of leaves, the sunlight. The space was legible. I knew it with that other, unnamed sense which tells you where things are. A waterfall to my left, some distance away, and on my right, Carmel, sitting.

I look up and I am in Bali, with a view across treetops to the sea. Waiting to see a white mynah bird.

All poems, Phil says, *are of love unrequited. I am not sure there is any other kind of poem. And you know, I am not sure there is any other kind of love.*

The guy in the droopy glasses looks both amused and deeply serious.

Dante and his Beatrice?

It is not the girl, it is not one girl or another girl, it is the fact that she is not there. And when she's gone, there is none like her.

I shut the laptop, pace the polished teak floor. There is a white twitch in the corner of my eye, but when I look at the treetops, no bird.

There is none like her.

Somewhere out to sea, the man I love is surfing a barrel

wave which is so dangerous it is called 'Lacerations'. It was given this name because of the sharpness of the coral on the reef where it breaks. He said he would be home by four o'clock but he has no way to tell the time out there. Or he pretends not to know the time – there is a pontoon moored before the swell where you can buy Cokes and beer, people sit around on it with their waterproof watches, all he has to do is ask. Last night, when we walked out to dinner, I saw a guy with a scabbed, mauled torso, another with a huge gauze bandage fixed along the side of his lacerated thigh. The world has turned into the place where people get hurt, where the man I love will one day die. Everything speaks to me of his safety, his proximity – time is a mechanism to measure how long we are apart. It's not that I think about him constantly, he is my way of thinking. His mind is my compass, his eyes my only mirror. Every night we roll down bamboo shutters against the forest and he does not enter my dreams or leave them, because we dream together. My body knows he is there. When we wake, we want the same thing.

Each other. Each other.

I can't wait to show him the clip.

I hope he is not dead.

At five o'clock he still has not appeared. At half five, when London is in its mid-morning rush of email, I give in and send the link to Lily.

– *thought you might like some poetry*

She pings back.

– *who da creep?*

– *which 1?*

– *hahahaha*

I throw the phone on the bed and open the laptop, trying to save some idea I had, but it is too late.

He has changed.

Jesus, Lily, you are so competitive, I think. You grab everything, you suck the life out of all that I do and have. So now I am off on a rant about Lily, I have lost my own grandfather, and the man I love is bleeding to death, somewhere out to sea.

I let the video play, forlornly, while I move around the place, sorting clothes. I glance over at the screen and, this time, it's not like seeing myself as an old bloke, it's like seeing myself as an old bollocks. Phil is doing the Irishman – lilting, laughing and wistful. This man has my chancer's smile. And that's just wild.

What is it about him? I get back on the bed and replay, looking for the thing that Lily saw so instantly.

Ah yes, Ireland, he says. *I never left. You can't leave a place like that. It's always with you.*

Under those killer lashes, his eyes do not move.

That's the shiver. Right there.

I stroke the line of this man's poem which is written below my collarbone, and I feel Carmel's ink-curse unfold. This is the Mama-hex which says that whatever you put indelibly on your skin will turn out to be the wrong thing, over time. The wrong words, the wrong lover, the wrong place for a shooting star. The only safe thing is a heart, the only safe letters M.U.M.

I have been working on these translations, or versions more properly, taken from the Gaelic, which is the beautiful underwater language on which all Irish poetry sets sail. I think I will speak it when I am dead – which might be blessing all round, indeed. Anyway. These versions are small treasures I picked up. They are not mine.

He lifts his head, and looks at the air in front of him. There is a tweak of a side-smile, a flare of anticipation. In the upped acoustic I hear the wet inhale.

Lay your dark head upon my breast,
your honey mouth with scent of thyme

This guy is fully creepy, I think. It's not just his age, though age does bring all that nicely out. It is a kind of doubleness. The words seem lovely – but they are not lovely – and the gaze is predatory, fixed.

but I deny
them all my love, sweet love, for you.

I look away, so I do not see those dead, unmoving eye-balls, and his voice is so seductive, you might fall asleep listening to it. This is not just fake, I think. It's an actual trap.

give me your hand before we part,
oh love, sweet love of mine.

I hear the sound of flip-flops and a surfboard stacked against the wall outside. I glance across the treetops. No sign of a white bird.

Dear Nell

What an absolute joy to hear from you, many thanks for being in touch. I wish I could answer your questions, but it is such a long time ago. I was twenty-one when I married your grandfather, which sounds outrageous (It was! That was the whole point!) and I suppose you might say the relationship played out by the rules of the time. As I get older, I feel like all that happened, not just in a different world, but to a different person. There are times when I don't recognise myself there.

I still feel that the guardianship of Phil's gift was the best of the relationship for me. There is a moral pleasure to be found in the encouragement of beautiful work and it continues to be my great honour to foster talent where I can. I would love to host you here in Sag Harbor, as a member of the family at the main house. If you want to apply for artist-in-residence in the stable yard, the process is overseen by an independent board and the application form is on the website, which you have already found.

I don't know if you have heard about our new initiative: this is the Selma Karras award scheme for young female artists, which especially welcomes work on mental health, broadly interpreted. Selma lived for a while with your grandfather in Greece and, as you may know, her work is increasingly valued not only here in the States but also worldwide.

Selma is a very secluded person who, sadly, has not published in some decades. You should read her early work! I feel you would see what Phil saw when he said she was the most exciting poet he knew. You will find the turbulence of their relationship echoing through her poetry and also, in a few rare glimpses, through his. I don't know if there was, as she claims, a professional rivalry there – he was an established figure, after all, she an unpublished ingénue. With lesser mortals (I include myself in this), your grandfather was never cruel, but they had a different dynamic and he treated her very poorly, as she now says publicly, and I believe.

We who loved Phil knew, on some level, that we loved him not despite, but because of his 'badness' – in those days, that was quite the thing. It loosed something in our psyches, I think, which was not always a force for good. This is why I set up the Karras bursary scheme. I cannot absolve myself completely of Phil's poor behavior. I adored him – certainly for the first while – and this may have contributed to his slightly distorted sense of himself. I thought I had no choice but to adore him, but of course I did have a choice, that goes without saying.

I would not swap places with the young woman I once was, who loved Phil McDaragh: the changes since then, in the world, and in me as a person, have been so welcome and right. But I continue to be fond of his poems, as I hope are you. They are not quite as thrilling as the truths to be found in Karras, who confronted what Phil was at such pains to hide. Her work is an exploration of damage, his an escape from it. Even so, his attempt to go free fills me with compassion. When I read him now, I wonder if you can know too much.

But you are young! and I feel you are talented, the world is surely, for you, a better place. Dear Nell, I have thought deeply in all this over the years and am happy to stand by whatever I have to say, but this letter is for you, not for everyone. I trust your voice, it seems so honest and so resolute. I remember you as a direct, clear-eyed little girl, who missed nothing and who laughed easily. I cannot wait to meet you in person again.

Beir Bua, as Phil used to say. We make the future word by word, and line by line, and brick by small brick.

With love from your 'granny'
Connie

STANDING AT MY mother's door, I unzip my small shell suitcase, and open it out flat on the top step, hunkering down to root through my worn belongings. Under a tangle of charger cable, used underwear and sandals, I find my keys. I always do. The charm is a big, neon-yellow Tweetie Pie – one eyebrow cocked, cartoon wing-hands on either hip. This is the look that rattles out from under beds and sofa cushions, the face spotted at a distance and while drunk across dance floors, the reprimand that always comes back to my hand. Tweetie, who is a boy (I looked it up), has been with me all this time, holding the keys to a door on the other side of the world.

And behind that door, my past.

The lock turns – why wouldn't it? – and I stoop to drag my spatchcocked suitcase inside.

The hall smells like a nice hotel, orange and bergamot, exactly the way it did on the day I left. At first glance, I do not recognise the neat, white and indigo cushions on the hall bench, but of course they have been here for ever. There was like a month of her life when Carmel knew what she wanted, when the things in shops made complete sense to her and the house will be set in that month for years to come.

I send a text:

– *Hey girl*

After a moment:

– *Hey hey.*

– *?*

My messages to Carmel announce themselves to the tune of 'Oh Happy Day' by the Edwin Hawkins Singers – a tech present from yours truly. Maybe I hear it somewhere about, maybe not.

– *mn*

I attach a quick pic of my right eye, looking quizzical. Behind me, the wedge of the fanlight in the hall.

There is a thin-sounding scream, somewhere outside. My mother is in the back garden. A silence. Another cry, this time closer. Ahhgh. The sound of the back door opening, the huffing thump-thump of Carmel taking the stairs saying, Oh, oh, and then arms flung wide, Look at you! and we are in The Hug. As reunion videos go, this is the one where the grown lioness bounds up to the regular-sized human being to bat her with huge velvet paws, lick with the rug of her tongue and harmlessly gnaw. Though in my arms, my mother is smaller than she seemed on approach. She tucks in, and I graze her crown with the underside of my chin.

Why didn't you say?

I wanted to surprise you.

(I wanted to stay out of your clutches, Big Mama: take the bus take the taxi oh no not the taxi take the air coach the ordinary bus and I can pick you up along the way or hang on give me your flight number I will be there.)

Oh oh oh oh oh.

My mother stops saying oh and pulls back from me.

Look at you.

She will, in a moment, go back to being a normal lioness, she will drop me as though indifferent, and prowl about the business of her day.

Which involves, in this case, checking out the guy beside me in the hall.

Mum, this is David.

Hello, she says.

Pleased to meet you, Mrs McDaragh.

Carmel, please. You're very welcome, she says. Come in come in, you'll have a cup of tea.

God, Mother, you sound so Irish, I say.

How do you want me to sound?

This is a very good question. After that first strangeness, I step through some invisible membrane, some resistance. I am home.

CARMEL

CARMEL COULD NOT figure out what she saw in him.

The thinning blond hair swept to one side, and very fragile skin with an undertone of jet-lag grey. Huge pupils. Not much by way of a mouth. He was called Brocklehurst, which was not a Scottish name but Saxon apparently. A Durham boy, he said. He ended up going to Cambridge, which wasn't really what he wanted but he got the interview. Not that he ever fitted in, really.

Nell was sitting beside him, bolt upright. A tiny swaying to and fro as she listened to them talk. She was pink, almost abject: *please like him, Mum, please like him, please.*

Carmel did her best.

'How was your flight?' she said.

He looked younger than Nell. That was one thing. There was a freshness to him. Very willing. When he lifted the bags you saw how fit he was; not large but graceful and light on his feet.

'He's English?' she said to Nell, when he had carried them downstairs.

'You don't say.'

'Shh,' said Carmel. 'He's coming back.'

'You're the one who's doing the talking,' said Nell.

Carmel watched him over tea and the offer of a biscuit, which he declined. He was the kind of boy who knew everything. But he was well meaning, she thought. There was, in his speech, the remnants of a stammer, so he sort of ran at it. He had only two modes for the first while, enthusiasm and dismissal. He spoke fluently about some minor subject – Chinese banking, the benefits of t'ai chi, swimming in a salt pool, different lengths of surfboard, the absence of sharks around Bali – but if you interrupted him, or asked him a question, or offered him something, then, Oh no, he said. He would never think of going into finance and, Oh no, he wasn't vegan though he had been vegetarian for ever, Oh no, he didn't want coffee, not even for the jet lag, he was trying to wean himself off caffeine.

'No?'

'No.'

'Right,' said Carmel.

'Irish people don't say "no",' Nell said, finally siding with her mother.

'They don't?'

'Famously. No.'

'What do they say?'

'They say, "Oh, I don't know, I couldn't, I shouldn't, no really none for me, thanks. No really."'

'You say, "No really"?'

'And then, "Thanks". You say, "No really, thanks, really no." Only Germans and upper-class English people say "no". We find it hurtful. Or we find it disdainful.'

'I like it,' her mother said. 'Don't worry, I am good for "no".'

'Irish people all talk like old women,' said Nell. 'Even the men.'

'That is not true,' said Carmel.

266

David said Ireland was such a great place to be, even coming through the airport, it was so friendly. He looked, as he said this, utterly lonely.

He leaned across to Nell and squeezed her hand as it lay in her lap, then laid it sexlessly down again. Carmel wondered, briefly, if he might be gay, but that wasn't it either.

The boy was still talking. He had lived in Shanghai for two years, taught the International Baccalaureate, Philosophy, Mandarin and Theory of Knowledge and actually there was a limitless demand for Mandarin, he could pick and choose. Also he was qualified as a diving instructor which was useful in some parts of the world. Mostly he was teaching online, cramming the children of the point nought one per cent. They could be living anywhere, so long as there was a pool (hahaha). Some of them so wealthy it defied mathematics. But the children showed up, they were respectful. You are talking to the sons and daughters of endless money. Daddy's going to buy them a place in Yale and some of these super-rich men are very nasty people. And it just goes to show you that children are better than adults in many ways. You know when we say, That person is behaving like a child, maybe that person is being quite nice, really.

He paused.

He rushed on.

'Or maybe it's what happens with a powerful father. You do what you are told.'

'You're from Durham?' said Carmel, who had taught some rich children herself, in her day, and did not find them nice, not especially.

'No, sorry. I *went* to Durham,' he said. 'Durham School.'

He looked at her quizzically, realised she'd never heard of it, started to back-pedal.

'Kind of awful really. Dreadfully chilly. I was a boarder,'

he said. 'No, we have a place in this village called Cheswick. Near the coast?'

'Right.'

'Berwick-on-Tweed?'

'Sorry, I should know where that is,' she said.

'Don't worry,' he said. 'It's very flat and rather dull.'

'It's near Lindisfarne,' said Nell.

'Right.'

Carmel could not figure out what the problem was. Each time he boasted – and every thing he said contained a kind of boastfulness – he included himself out of it. Such an English form of self-deprecation: he insisted on being more upper class than you, then looked for your sympathy because he was such a failure at the class game. Too posh, not posh enough, there was nowhere he felt at home.

Poor little superior you, Carmel thought.

That plaintive thing English people have sometimes walking around Dublin, saying, Isn't everyone so nice? And aren't they having a good time?

'Excuse me,' he said. 'I'll just go. It's downstairs, isn't it?'

'On the left,' said Carmel.

Once he was safely out of the room, Nell hissed, 'Stop it.'

'What?'

'Just.'

'What?'

'Don't fucking start, Mum, alright? You are being such a bitch right now. And if you don't stop we will turn around and we will walk out of here. My bag is right there.'

'Your bag is wide open and scattered all over the hall.'

'David!' Nell called through the floorboards.

There was no reply from the bathroom, which was something. At least he had some manners – beat into him no doubt at his wretchedly superior boarding school. Did all that still happen? It did not seem real.

'Alright,' she said. 'I'm sorry.'

'Behave.'

'Sorry.' After a moment she said, 'I thought you were going to be gay.'

'Stop it. Now.'

'It's just an observation.'

Later, Carmel cut her finger while chopping garlic. She waved the knife, lifted her injured hand high and did a comical, wide-stepping dance from counter to sink, where she put the finger under cold running water. The blood pulsed to fill the whorls of her finger pads and flushed away. Carmel took two heaving, juddering sighs.

'Are you alright?' Nell said, coming up behind her. 'Do you want an Elastoplast?'

'Don't patronise me!'

She fled to her bedroom with her finger in her mouth, sat on her bed sucking it until she saw herself – or got a sense of herself – a middle-aged woman acting the infant, her feet not tipping the floor.

There was very little wrong with the boy.

Imelda will love him, she thought. Her sister was an unwavering snob.

Back upstairs, David the daughter-stealer, the invader and ransacker, was setting the table. He praised the food and also ate it. He smiled at Nell when she was talking and they interrupted each other constantly. On occasion, they spoke simultaneously while looking each other in the eye.

'Smart boy,' Carmel said, warmly, when he said yet another smart thing, and he took a little 'ding' of pleasure from her praise.

He slept in Nell's room of course, that was not an issue. Carmel had put two bath towels side by side at the end of the bed.

When she got up to go to the loo one last time before sleep, she heard the two of them talking in there. Nell's voice was so close and relaxed, her mother paused outside – not to eavesdrop, she did not care about the words, it was the tone that held her. She had not heard this version of Nell in many years. This was the girl who climbed into her mother's bed on a Sunday morning to have the chats, her voice full of complexity and fun. Carmel might have felt jealous of the intimacy between the two young people, but she really didn't. She felt that her daughter had come back to her true self. She was grown.

NELL

ONE DAY THE bubble burst for me, whatever the bubble is, that huge oily membrane shivering above my life, that sometimes I call love and sometimes dread.

It was a bird I saw in my mother's back garden, and for a moment failed to name. Just a little hop-about, a fat bullfinch boy with a blushing breast which was, when I tried to capture it, the colour of a lipstick called Orange Chiffon. This description came from some poem by creepy Phil, of course, but I was happy when it came to mind, it seemed right. It is actually a real lipstick, an Avon shade my grandmother might have worn. I briefly considered buying it from this vintage site before I remembered – what is lipstick made of? – animal fat or chemical fat in a twist-up stick, from way back in 1964.

There he still was, at the end of my mother's garden, such a pretty boy, perched on her urn-carrying dryad (not a nymph!) which is too grand for the house, but not the worst of the blank-eyed statuary Carmel has searched through in every garden centre, television costume drama and suburban oasis we have passed over the years. The dryad's pose is graceful and abundant, the stone nicely eroded, and her drapery is garlanded about the hip with some non-specific flowers. I thought we would need a crane to get it in, but they dragged it through the ground floor on a grocer's trolley and Carmel drove everyone mad getting it in the right place in the shade, half hidden by her magnolia tree. She ran some ivy up the base and painted the north side, as she called it, with yoghurt to attract moss. This was duly attracted and it looks very well. Carmel has a green thumb, though she says it's just a question of putting the right thing in the right place.

And now, freshly arrived and perched on the dryad's head, is this elegant boy, with his neat black cap, his coral pink chest and his dapper, white-striped wings. He looks like a butler or a retainer, some guy dressed to serve a glass of port. I am very happy thinking all this up, inventing a story for the birdy who is keeping me company on the grass while, inside the house, David flatters Carmel and Carmel flatters David, because – let us not forget – Carmel *loves* men, she finds them so sensible and relaxing to be around. So I have brought her a new man, and after she finished bristling at him, she took him into her life and under her wing, as someone to praise, organise and boss around. Now, she sits him down near the cooking action and laughs at the wisdom of his observations while stuffing her hand-turned ravioli with mushrooms of his choice because, as she says, David really *gets* food after all those dreadful meals they forced on him at school.

I, meanwhile, am out on the grass, thinking about being pregnant, which I am not. The idea comes to mind, because the sunshine is so warm on my belly, you might imagine yourself filled with it in some mythological way. I could have a sun baby, made of light. The garden dryad is mutely, sweetly convinced of this possibility, the bird is a sign that seems to agree.

But I am not pregnant – not yet, anyway – the feeling of warmth is lovely, but not indicative. So I lie on the grass and watch my lucky bullfinch, who is in no hurry to leave, hopping through the branches. The sky beyond has one of those winds of the upper air, that moves clouds at speed and leaves the lower world untouched. This movement is very fast and dramatic. In the calm of the garden, the bird flits to the pear tree by the wall and back to the dryad's head. He looks at me.

I am aware, for a dot of time, of all the swirling movement in the silence: clouds, bird, leaves, ants, atoms.

Particles, whose name I forget, hurtling through me.

The slow erosion of the stone dryad.

The bird looks me in the eye – he seems to know this is the place to look at a human being – and I look back at him. And with that smart, held connection, the story I made up for him falls away. The bird is no one's servant. He is not dapper. Words only obscure him: the lipstick, the coral, the chiffon, the glass of port, these are all impositions on his tiny, incontrovertible bullfinch self. Even the name, 'bullfinch', seems a form of littering, like a sticky label fixed to his feathers.

One sunny Sunday in my mother's garden, the bird looked at me and I saw the bird and I wanted to undo language and let him be. The bird just was. Long before any of us were here, and long after we are gone, he did and will exist. When our lipsticks, our servants, our bleached and plundered coral are all dead or buried in landfill, he will perch on top of the lot of it and sing. At least I hope so. If we are very lucky, the bird will always be the bird.

ACKNOWLEDGEMENTS

My heartfelt thanks to poets Jessica Traynor and Jane Clarke, whose light, deft interventions made Phil's fictitious lines look more like real poems. Apologies and thanks to Paul Muldoon, whom I waylaid in Dublin airport with Phil's version of 'The Yellow Bittern' (I can't believe I did that). Catherine Duggan BL was generous with her expertise about probate, Professor Margaret Kelleher fielded arcane queries without demur. Thanks to Paul Perry, poet and colleague at UCD, and to my friends in the Creative Writing Department, including the many students whose freshness and determination have buoyed my courage at the desk.

The gender-switching planet that Mal speaks about in Utrecht is taken – a little misremembered – from Lisa Tuttle's story 'The Wound', published in her 1990 collection *Memories of the Body: Tales of Desire and Transformation*. The account of a badger meet owes much to Patrick Boyle's short story '*Meles Vulgaris*'. This is a work of pure fiction: all reasonable steps have been taken to ensure there is no resemblance to real people, living or dead.

Much love and gratitude, as ever, to my agent Peter

Straus and to the team at Rogers, Coleridge & White. Thanks to Michal Shavit, David Milner and Joe Pickering at Jonathan Cape, my home for many years, and to the fine people at Norton.

Thanks to the Enrights, for holding good. To Martin, Rachel and Lorcan, for everything.

penguin.co.uk/vintage